The Other Eden

Sarah Bryant

THE OTHER EDEN

First published in 2006 by
Snowbooks Ltd.
120 Pentonville Road
London
N1 9JN
www.snowbooks.com

3

Cover design by Gilly Barnard, Snowbooks

The lines in Part Two, Chapter 7, are taken from John Webster's The Duchess of Malfi, c.1614.

13 digit ISBN: 978-1905005-11-6
A catalogue record for this book is available from the British Library.

To Pamela Alexander, my first piano instructor, and Linda Jiorle-Nagy, my last—true teachers whose gifts for inspiration reach far beyond the notes and staves.

Acknowledgements

As always, many thanks are due to Colin and Nuala for their patience and belief in me and my writing, even when the tea is late! I would also like to thank Elaine Thompson for her friendship and much-valued criticism; my mom, Suz, grandmother extraordinaire; Mara Lang, Sean Montgomery, Lucy Newman, John Caughie, Bar Purser for readings and advice, and Anastasia Karpushko Cardownie for being my willing, walking Russian dictionary. Finally, to the lovely people who make up Snowbooks: once again, I can't thank you enough.

"I am half sick of shadows," said the Lady of Shalott.

Alfred, Lord Tennyson

Part One

Prologue

Prologue

APRIL 1903, EDEN'S MEADOW PLANTATION, IBERVILLE PARISH, LOUISIANA

Night-time in a room lit by a solitary guttering candle. It is a bedroom—that is clear from the shapes of the furniture looming out of the shadows. The faint scroll of a decorative cornice, the sheen of dark wood suggest that it belongs to a person of privilege, but even in the bad light the room's trappings seem vague, impersonal, long since abandoned by their owner.

She herself reveals little more. She stands in a plain, dark dress, facing an open French door. Whether she looks out at something in the overcast night or inward at something less corporeal is impossible to tell. She is slender and small, and exudes a feeling of being almost fully developed. Her stooped shoulders and dejected arms convey a lack of confidence. Her head, piled with black hair, bends like a heavy rose on a stalk too slight.

For several minutes she stands unmoving. Then a flash of lightning sears the sky, and she turns from the doorway. The candle light reveals full lips, smooth skin, high cheekbones, black eyes with a faintly Byzantine slant. Hers is a beauty of fits and starts: the tinge of sadness in her eyes; the stray curl of hair on her blue-shadowed temple; the fear battling pride in the set of her jaw.

As she moves, the room seems to shrink and darken by contrast, her face to grow more luminous. Another flash of lightning; as the ensuing thunder subsides, a faint knocking becomes audible. The girl hears it, runs to open the door. A second girl slips into the room, wearing a white nightdress, her black hair loose down her back. There are subtle differences between them. This girl's face and posture are more assured, her eyes more artful than the other's. Nonetheless, the resemblance between them is undeniable.

"Ready, Lizzie?" the bolder one asks.

"Evie..." Elizabeth's voice falters with the candlelight.

"Too late now," Eve says. Smiling, she reaches up and pulls the pins from her sister's tightly bound hair.

"But what if he finds out?" Elizabeth asks, as Eve feels for stray pins.

"He won't find out until I want him to."

"How can you say so? We're so different; he's bound to realize."

"We've switched on Maman and Papa without their realizing."

"That's Maman and Papa. You and he will be married. What of your...your relations as such?"

Eve smiles archly. "Surely he has no knowledge of you in that way, to realize the difference!"

Elizabeth colors, but continues, "But if he does realize, you'll be all alone. What if...what if he—"

"Lizzie." Eve puts her hands on her sister's shoulders. Her

eyes are calm and certain. "It will be all right. I know that you don't like him, and you have your reasons, but he's never done anything to earn your distrust."

"He's so passionate—so moody."

"Many have said the same of me. Besides, I've watched him love you for five years, and even you must admit that his loyalty has never wavered."

"But there's a compulsion in that itself that makes me afraid."

"And the same makes me love him."

Elizabeth shakes her head almost imperceptibly, her eyes never leaving her sister's. "You should wait for someone who loves you for yourself."

Eve turns away, but she can't keep the bitterness out of her voice when she answers, "We aren't all so lucky as you, Elizabeth."

Elizabeth's mouth quivers. Eve's face is still averted; what emotion she hides is impossible to tell. Yet she does not seem surprised when Elizabeth relents. "If you have faith in him—"

"Oh, I do!" Eve cries. She smiles a smile full of hope and promise, and after a moment her sister returns it, if wanly. "You'll go through with your part," Eve continues, "and once Mother is better—" she falters as she says this, her voice losing some of its softness "—I'll find you, and we'll tell them all. And by then...well, by then he's sure to understand. Now, come here and fix my hair."

Elizabeth follows Eve to the dressing table, picks up a brush and a hank of her sister's long hair, then stands staring at it, as if seeking an answer.

"It's the best thing," Eve persists, "the only thing—" A skirl of wind extinguishes the candle.

"Eve!" Elizabeth cries. Quickly Eve relights the candle, then takes the brush from her sister's clenched hands and begins to untangle her own hair. After a moment Elizabeth takes over. The girls are silent for a time, Eve's eyes fixed on her reflection, Elizabeth's on the dark hair in her hands as she braids and binds it.

Even after Elizabeth has finished, Eve continues to stare at her reflection, as if trying to pinpoint something amiss. Finally she says, "The necklaces!" She unclasps the ruby that hangs from a gold chain around her neck, and holds it toward Elizabeth. It glints in the candlelight like a drop of blood.

Elizabeth looks at it, touches the diamond at her own throat, and says, "No. You can tell everyone we traded, to have something to remember each other by. They're...they're who we are."

Eve laughs. "You, superstitious?" Seeing the serious set of her sister's face, however, her smile dies. "All right, if you're set on it."

Elizabeth watches Eve replace the necklace. "That's it, then," she says, kneeling so that her face in the mirror is level with her sister's.

"Now no one will know," Eve answers with finality.

They watch their own faces in the mirror until Eve stands up, and pulls Elizabeth to her feet. "Come on."

"Wait." Elizabeth takes a bundle from the bed and shakes it out. It is a wedding dress, its bodice exquisitely embroidered with leaves and butterflies. She holds it toward Eve, whose hands stop her own.

"I can't take that, Lizzie." Her eyes are entreating and, for the first time, betray uncertainty.

"I want you to. If I can't be there myself, I want you to have a piece of me with you."

"No, Elizabeth," Eve repeats. "I can't wear your wedding dress. You should wear it to the wedding it was meant for."

"It was meant for my wedding to Louis," she answers, her tone sounding authoritative for the first time. "Besides, we both know you'll never make one in time." The girls look at each other for a long moment, then burst into laughter, as incongruous to the scene as daylight would be.

Eve takes the dress and lays it carefully on Elizabeth's bed. She closes the carpetbag that sits open there, and pushes the handles into her sister's hands. Eve embraces Elizabeth, then leads her to the French door. Lightning flickers again, illuminating the trees and the gardens with eerie blue light. It is followed closely by a roll of thunder.

Somewhere down the corridor, a low wailing begins. They look at each other, Elizabeth with intensified fear, Eve with steely resolve. "You've got to go now," Eve says, apprehension finally apparent in her voice. "God go with you." Eve kisses her sister on both cheeks and pushes her through the dark doorway into the night.

As Eve stands there alone, her previously calm face contorts with unfathomable emotions. Simultaneously the disembodied wail becomes a word, a name: "Eliiiiizabeth!"

Eve shivers but stands listening a moment longer, and then, drawing herself together again, she calls, "I'm coming, Maman."

She picks up Elizabeth's dressing gown from the bed and ties it over her nightgown, then opens the door onto the dim hallway. The voice becomes hysterical, shrieking strings of gibberish. But one discernible strain breaks through:

"They watch me…no peace…Elizabeth, cover them, cover them—"

Eve shuts the door behind her, and the wailing ceases.

1

I have no childhood memory of my parents' faces. My father left my mother when I was a baby; my mother died of tuberculosis three years later. I bear my father no more ill will in leaving me than I do my mother, for both served to exempt me from the poverty we had shared in the dingy mill town where she taught music and he played the church organ to earn our living.

Not long after my mother's funeral, I learned that I was not bereft of relatives, as she had led me to believe. Her body had not been a day in the ground when William Fairfax, her father, strode into my world of dirt and insufficiency, showing me my first glimpse of his own. My first memory of him is of his arms, which smelled of pipe smoke and leather, and more subtly of wealth, though at the time I was aware of it only as something foreign to all I had ever known. He lifted me to eye level and told me that my mother had died of grief, as her mother had before her. With such a lineage, he said, I would be prone to the same melancholy, and I should work to avoid their fate by living avidly. Not understanding a word he had said, I promised to do my best. His reply—a smile—was the beginning of my good fortune.

So my mother's life of poverty was never mine, but it was

years before I could accept that it need never have been hers either. At the end of the nineteenth century, William Fairfax was the wealthiest man in New England. Before his twentieth birthday he had turned a reasonable inheritance into a small fortune on the stock market. Five years later he married the sole heiress to a Louisiana plantation. If he built a wall of silence between himself and his daughter Elizabeth when she eloped with my father, the only wall that existed when she died was that of her own stubbornness and pride, and the only ill will he ever showed her memory in my presence could barely be described as such. Rather than refer to her by her Christian name, or even as "my daughter," he insisted always on referring to her as "Eleanor's mother," as though that were her only claim to any worth.

I had little cause to quibble with this. Blessed with my mother's beauty and a talent that was the culmination of an extraordinarily musical bloodline, I grew up spoiled and praised. Far from the despot our introduction had led me to expect, my grandfather proved to be a moody, kindly, eccentric man who was far more lenient with me than I deserved. Throughout most of my childhood I took his kindness for granted, earning erratic marks at the exclusive schools he paid for, constantly serving punishments, even running away once, to be coaxed out of my self-righteous indignation by his gentle words and promises. The only area in which I was irreproachable was music but, fortunately, this more than made up to him for my faults.

My childhood was the real-life fairy tale every little girl dreams of. Boston in the early days of the century was itself a scene from a picture book, a metropolis of gingerbread brownstones orbiting parks and cobbled streets as yet unmarred by motorcars, which were still a novelty. We lived in a townhouse on Beacon Street, which overlooked one corner of the Public Garden. My nursery was at the top of the house, with a picture window that looked down onto the angel statue in the northwest corner of the park through riotous tangles of ivy and roses spilling from our rooftop garden. I would sit sometimes for what seemed hours on end, studying the angel's downcast eyes and beatific expression, open arms and mighty wings. I liked to lift the diamond pendant that had been my mother's only relic of her girlhood—and was now my only relic of her—and look at the angel through its mutable lens. It gave him a semblance of life that his stone form alone could never have. As a very little girl, I had the idea that he was my guardian angel. I suppose I needed him as a tangible connection to my mother.

All told, though, I didn't find much time to miss her.

On Sundays my grandfather and I had tea at the Ritz-Carlton at four o'clock. I knew every waiter by name, and they petted and spoiled me atrociously. Every Thursday evening my British nanny, Emmeline, would button me into dresses made of the finest silk or velvet, pinch my cheeks for color, and torture me with bows like cabbage roses to hold the unruly yellow curls out of my eyes. Then my grandfather would come in a trail of tweed and pipe smoke to take me to the symphony, where the fine ladies and gentlemen always stared at me, the only child to attend regularly. It was the only place where I didn't care about the attention. I sat with my legs straight out before me on the leather seat, oblivious to all but the music.

Saturdays were the best, though. Most Saturday evenings we had engagements. My grandfather wouldn't leave me at home, despite Emmeline's protests that he was ruining me by exposing me to a Bohemian lifestyle. He laughed at her and swept me into the carriage, off to one elegant townhouse or another. There were dinners, dances, receptions of honor, all in the homes of the richest and most eccentric of Boston society. These parties were never without their share of exotic guests: foreign emissaries, European nobility, the latest names in art and music. I listened under tables and behind curtains while the adults talked of Nietzsche and Cubism and the first stirrings of unease in Europe. Later, these parties inevitably included a performance. I would sit at the piano like the child Mozart and play for the adults who watched, amazed, as I rattled off Bach fugues and Beethoven sonatas as other children poked out "Chopsticks".

That was my childhood. It ended the night of my twenty-first birthday, the twenty-first of December, 1924. My grandfather had reserved our favorite table at the Ritz and a box at Symphony Hall for the two of us and his best friend, Mary Bishop. She was a widow in her mid-fifties who had come into our lives as my first piano teacher and over the years had evolved into a kind of surrogate mother to me.

We had taken a chance on the symphony that night, as the showcase was the American premiere of a newcomer of whom I knew little and my two companions less: a Russian pianist who had only recently immigrated to America. "Alexander Trevozhov," I read to Mary, whose eyesight was poor in good light and not equal to deciphering small print in the dimness of the concert hall. He would play Chopin: the first sonata, a selection of études and nocturnes, and the G minor ballade.

"The G minor!" Mary repeated. She was wearing a variation on Chinese pajamas made of cornflower-blue silk, which matched her eyes. Her sleeves fluttered like the wings of a tropical butterfly when she moved.

"Yes..." I paused and read it again. "Yes, definitely the

first. Opus 23 in G minor." I flashed a smile in her direction, meant more for the man in the next box. "Do you like that one particularly?"

"It's exquisite! You know how I love Chopin"—she pronounced the name with the proper French accent—"but this one in particular, I believe it might be the closest any musician ever has come to perfection. I imagine you've played it, Eleanor?" Her voice and manner were serene as always, but if I had been a little older and wiser, I might have seen the depth of the emotion moving behind her watercolor eyes.

Instead I tossed the golden curls that I had refused to allow current fashion to shear, carefully noting the reaction of the man in the next box. "Oh, I played all of the ballades, long ago."

"Don't you think them beautiful?"

I shrugged. "I suppose. For the work of a feeble, dying man." And if the lights had not been lowered just then, if the musicians had not begun to tune their instruments, I might have caught the look of gentle rebuff on Mary's face or the intensity with which my grandfather was studying the program.

I fidgeted through the first two pieces: a Bach concerto and a Mozart sonata, both for violin. Then came the intermission, where I thought mostly of being seen and introduced. When we re-entered the hall, I was caught off guard by a new singing tension, twining erratically with the billows of low voices floating up to us on the close air. There was a long delay, during which the crowd's murmur grew oddly strained. I knew that I was leaning forward in my seat but could neither understand why nor make myself stop.

The moment he walked onstage the tension erupted into applause, and I began to understand. As long as I live, I will never forget that first image of him. He stood in the smoky footlights, looking hapless and embarrassed by so much attention. His face was white against his black jacket, except for two flushed patches on his cheeks. His hair and eyes were dark, his features as clean and even as a statue's.

"William," Mary asked, "what is it? What's the commotion?" She squinted at the light from the stage.

"I don't see any cause for commotion," my grandfather answered gruffly. This time I noticed the unnatural perplexity in his manner: he was generally the picture of genteel cool.

Mary rolled her eyes and turned confidingly to me. "Eleanor? Surely something's causing the excitement?"

"It's for him," I said softly. "The pianist. I've never in my life seen someone who looked so...Mary, he's more than handsome." She looked at me in surprise, unused to my complimenting anybody's looks. I ignored both her inquisitive eyes and my grandfather's perverse mood. All my attention was on the man on the stage below.

As he looked up and around the hall with an air of dislocation I was certain that, for a second, his roving eyes locked with mine. And I, who had always scorned sentimentality, was instantly smitten. I sat on the edge of my seat, entranced, as he took the bench, paused for a moment with his hands hovering over the keys, and then sank into the music.

He played the sonata first, with more skill and grace than I could ever hope to achieve. The études were so fluid that the precise mechanical workings beneath their tissue-thin veneer never once showed through. Yet none of the short pieces merited the rave reviews I had heard of his playing.

He paused before he began the ballade, clasping his hands together for a moment. When he released them, the tension in the hall seemed to mount inversely, straining the limits of oppressiveness. Inexplicable panic pushed into my throat, and I could think only of escape. I stood up, found myself fenced in by legs, skirts, handbags.

"Eleanor," Mary whispered in my ear. She was standing, too. People nearby were hissing for us to sit down. Her arm was around my shoulders, light as a bird's wing but solid, comforting. "Are you ill?" she asked, drawing me gently back to my seat. The sound of her voice, the calm of her familiar presence next to me, cleared my head a bit. I drew a deep breath and whispered to her that I would be all right, though panic still skirted the edges of my mind. I closed my eyes, trying to ignore the feeling around me. It was several moments before I realized that it had shifted, and in the space it left, music had filled in.

To say the least, Alexander Trevozhov's was an unusual interpretation of the ballade's beginning. He did not play the opening chords forte and pesante, as is written, but so softly that they were almost inaudible. In any ordinary concert they would have been, but his unexpected use of understatement, along with his formidable presence, had commanded absolute silence in his audience. I began to understand the praise of him I had heard.

I did not open my eyes, but I listened intently. It was impossible not to: the music caught and bound me, as it had caught and bound the entire house. The anxiety accrued during Mr. Trevozhov's long delay may have shifted as he began to play, but it had not abated. It seemed that the tension his presence had unfurled was slowly weaving into the music, becoming so ingrained that the familiar score sounded entirely alien.

Technically, he was perfect. But the pain emanating from every note he played was something significantly more potent than the regretful melancholy Chopin had written into the piece. Each note was askew, its emotion turned inward on itself to reverberate as something close to horror. I wanted the music to end but also to go on forever. My intense desire to run away had not dissipated, but equally strong was the ridiculous desire to run to him. I was unaware of having heard the final chords until I realized that we had been sitting for several moments in absolute silence—a sound I had never heard in that hall in my life, and which I doubt will ever be heard there again.

The hush dangled, as unresolved as the music had been. Then, all at once, it was filled with uproarious applause, a standing ovation. But I could not clap, nor stand; I could only sit staring at the light-box of the stage, for once completely unaware of myself. I did not even sense the tears streaming down my face. My grandfather looked down at me with troubled eyes. At his side, Mary looked hazily triumphant.

"Still think it's only the best that a dying man could do, love?" she asked.

Although I knew that it was only her way of telling me that I did not yet know everything there was to know, I shook my head. "No," I said softly, but with more vehemence than her mild gibe deserved. "It's not the music. He could have played scales, and it would have been the same. That's no ordinary man on that stage. His music isn't human."

Before either of them could answer, Mr. Trevozhov was playing again, this time Debussy. Again I was listening to a sound that transcended, even ridiculed the lines and notes composing the music spilling from beneath his fingers. All too soon the incredible sound had been swallowed again by applause.

When the concert ended, I insisted on meeting him, but the

crowd around his dressing room was impenetrable. Mary and my grandfather wanted to go, she complaining of weariness, he of an ache in his arms and chest; grudgingly I agreed. I turned once, though, as we retreated, to have a last look at Mr. Trevozhov. By fate or chance he turned as well. His eyes snagged for a moment on my grand-father's fragile form, then moved on to me. Recovering from what seemed a great surprise, he smiled. He gestured as though to move toward us, but at the same moment my grandfather stepped between us, blocking my view of him.

"The car's waiting, Eleanor," he said. There was no question of contradicting the steely authority in his voice; it was a tone he used with me seldom, and never without good cause. I looked at him, puzzled, but he wouldn't meet my eyes. Mary tugged gently at my hand, urging me toward the lobby, and though I tried again to catch the pianist's eye, the crowd had closed around him once more, sealing him off from me as effectively as my grandfather could have wished.

"Do you know him?" I asked, as we made our way out into the snowy night.

"No," he answered shortly, looking straight ahead.

"He seemed to know you—or to have something to say to us, anyway."

He didn't answer, nor look at me. Mary smiled sympathetically as we climbed into the car, but the truth was, I had nearly put the incident out of my mind again, turning instead to more frivolous thoughts. I had not begun to examine the intricacies of the feeling the foreign pianist's eyes had stirred in me. It seemed enough, at the time, that he had noticed me. Yet I would find myself replaying the scene many times in the months to come, sometimes with regret, sometimes with pleasure, but always with a recondite feeling of emptiness and longing.

With the lightest heart I was to have for many months, we rode through the softly falling snow, past the Public Garden, serene under its pale blanket and home to our townhouse. I saw Mary on her way home, then kissed my grandfather good night and thanked him for a wonderful birthday.

The next morning I found him dead of a heart attack, leaving me an orphan once more.

Two nights later, amidst silence still ringing with too many sympathetic voices, I finally fell into an exhausted sleep. That night I dreamed of Eve for the first time in many years. She rocked me while I cried, as she had not rocked me since the night my mother died, and spoke softly of a place called Eden.

2

Eden's Meadow was its full name. I had heard it mentioned during my childhood but had filed the name away with the memory of one briefly glimpsed, badly faded photograph of my grand-mother's ancestral home. We had never visited the plantation, and I had never had any interest in it. All I knew of the place, situated at the edge of the Atchafalaya wilderness, was that it had once been a cotton plantation.

Yet it was there that I wanted to go as soon as I learned that it was part of my inheritance. A different place, a different life: I kept repeating the words to the friends and acquaintances who asked why I would leave my past, my future, all I had always known. I could not explain to them that I could see no future in Boston, and only the broken pieces of a past. Everything seemed grey, a husk of itself. Familiarity had died with my grandfather, leaving me an uncomfortable guest in my own empty house, a stranger in my own city. Besides that, it was the dead of winter in New England. Eden's Meadow—the words themselves sounded tropical, vital.

I spent the day after the funeral wandering from room to room of the old townhouse, feeling nothing but a leaden emptiness, that gradually settled like a sea burial into the pit of my stomach. From the old nursery I looked down through the tangled web of ivy and bare rose branches to the angel in the garden. His hair and wings were covered with snow; he stared down at the frozen ground, pensive in the last of the twilight. It wasn't for guidance that I looked to that old friend, for the decision was already made. I touched the cold window pane in farewell.

At the beginning of February, I was on a train headed for Baton Rouge and a life I could not begin to imagine. It hadn't taken much to convince Mary to come with me; since her husband's death, her closest ties in Boston had been to me and my grandfather.

Despite the initial reckless sense of adventure that had made me heed Eve's dream words and seek out a new life, I was glad enough for Mary's quiet companionship when it came to the actual journey. It made the fact that we were leaving everything familiar behind us oddly comforting. Perhaps it should not have, for Eden's Meadow was the antithesis of every expectation from the very beginning.

Yankee-born and -bred, I was unprepared for the ponderous beauty of the Deep South: the superficial vibrancy, the intense, submerged energy. I could feel the roots of the grass and trees seeping their undomesticated vigor into my body the minute I set foot on its soil. My initial feeling for the place was an attraction, but one that I could not categorize as either healthy or morbid, no matter how practically I tried to look at it. With the egotism of the young, I imagined that this feeling was unique to myself, and for that reason I didn't share it with Mary. I now suspect that her feelings were much the same as mine, though her impetus in keeping them from me was far more selfless than my own. I even wonder if we might have admitted defeat then and there had we spoken to each other of our unease, gone home and spared ourselves so much grief.

Needless to say, Mary and I kept our silence, she out of concern for my well-being, myself out of pride, and I was able to live for some weeks under the delusion that it was only the newness of the surroundings that made me uneasy. Yet as the novelty of the place began to subside into familiarity, I could no longer ignore the fact that something was missing in the array of feelings it evoked in me. The more accustomed to the place I became, the more unsettled I felt, until the day I realized that what lacked was affection. I did not love Eden's Meadow as I felt I ought to; I could not, although I told myself that the reason for this was nothing but my own silly superstition. I had always been straightforward in receiving impressions, and consequently in forming opinions. Yet it didn't take me long to realize that I was afraid of Eden's Meadow in a nervous, nebulous manner completely foreign to my nature, and moreover, when I found the courage to admit it to myself, that I had been afraid from my first day there.

I remember that arrival clearly. There was little to see on the long drive from the main road to the heart of Eden's Meadow but the surreal shapes and vibrant hues of southern forest, interspersed sporadically with drowsing meadows. I was lulled by that drive. I suppose I thought that the house, when we reached it, would slip seamlessly into its dreamy surroundings.

Even as I thought it the wilderness parted, and the house stood before us in all its decrepit splendor, shattering all delusions. Over the years of disuse, the rampant foliage had nearly swallowed the house. Bougainvillea, ivy and kudzu hung in swaying curtains from the roof, tangling with honeysuckle and roses climbing from below. The walls beneath appeared to be made of whitewashed brick, pitted and cracked with time. Thick columns supported a heavy entablature, and arched French doors ran along the upper and lower galleries, a few retaining their black wooden shutters.

The driveway curved in a slow, white-pebbled circle, heavily invaded by tough crabgrass and creeping weeds. In the centre of the circle, its buds still pale green and tightly furled, an ancient magnolia spread its bare branches over the grassy island. At the far end of the lawn a grove of black cypress marked the rim of the lake, preceded by more moss-hung oaks and sycamores. The double front doors with the stained-glass seal of my grandmother's family—an apple tree ringed with water—had been opened to let in the morning breeze but were covered by screens to keep out insects.

Beautiful as the house was—or rather, would be, with some care—I felt repulsion at that first sight of it. There was something hollow and rotten about it, some abstract sadness that bordered on hostility. At that moment all I wanted was to go back to the North, to the solidity of a place I understood.

Instead, I stepped out of the car. As soon as I set foot on the soil of Eden's Meadow, I could feel its lethargy sending out creepers that tightened quickly into unease, and it became a battle of wills. I knew that it was Eden my mother had run away from, never again to see her family. I also knew that Eden was where my grandmother had fallen ill, languished for five years in a state of mental discomfiture, and then died. I could not help but compare my mother's and grandmother's unhappiness with the feelings Eden was stirring in me, and remembering that first promise I had made to my grandfather, I vowed I would not let the place defeat me.

In time the fear settled, though it did not diminish. I had long hours to spend at the piano, a particularly fine Bechstein, which had been my grandmother's. This did much to soothe

the pain of losing my grandfather. Mild winter eased into early spring, and by April we were calling it hot, to the amusement of the maids and gardeners we had employed. By May full-blooded Louisiana summer had descended, with its slack air and afternoon rainstorms. The jungle devoured it all.

Mary and I had run out of energy to talk of going home; perhaps we had accepted that we were home. We had fallen into the routine of the people who lived with us, rising early, resting through the hottest part of the day, and staying up long into the night. The days began to form a pattern, and in time the pattern became so comfortable that its collapse was as abrupt as my first sight of the house had been.

I was up that morning before dawn. This was not a symptom of tropical sleeping patterns so much as the insomnia that had plagued me since my grandfather's death. Though I was confident that the problem would take care of itself in time, Mary fretted about it constantly. So when she insisted that I see a doctor about it before we left Boston, on the basis of that peculiarly middle-aged belief that services would never be adequate anywhere except one's native town, I humored her. I suppose I humored the doctor as well, in that I accepted his prescription for chloral hydrate drops. I had even tried this cure once or twice, but I found the effects of sleepless nights more tolerable than the leaden torpor inflicted by the drug.

So I was awake to see the sunrise that morning. It stained the woods and sky the dirty copper color of old pennies. I sat on the narrow dock jutting out into the still water of the lake, watching the eastern sky absorb the color; the journal and pencil I had brought with the intention of writing forgotten. I thought of Eve. I had not dreamed of her since that first horrible night following my grandfather's death, now exactly six months past. Although I had not dreamed of her frequently since childhood—not at all, in fact, since I went away to school—I was feeling the loss as acutely as if she had been with me always. Perhaps, in a way, she had been. In childhood Eve had seemed to me a separate being from my mother, but I had come in time to attribute her comforting dream presence to my longing for the mother I had lost so early on.

I turned away from the sunrise, which had grown too bright to look at any longer, only to be blinded from the other side. I scrambled to my feet, sending the rickety dock pitching as the water rippled to life. Shading my eyes with my hands, I stared up at the western shore of the lake, where the sunlight reflected like brilliant jewels off the windows of a house at the top of the hill. I could not understand how I had lived four and a half months on the plantation and never noticed the house before, but the answer came almost immediately. As I stood staring, a cloud passed over the sun, extinguishing the brilliant windows. Without the illumination, at that precise angle, it blended into the surrounding forest. I shivered, watching the fire rekindle and then die slowly in the windows of the house on the hill as the sun re-emerged, rose higher, and paled.

A cacophony of birdsong and the drone of insects moved in waves through the dense air. Finally I sat down, opened the journal, and began a detailed description of the house on the hill. I wrote until the sun grew too hot, then closed the book and started back toward my own house, naggingly preoccupied by the discovery. I walked up through the garden on the hill, an overgrown topiary with a crumbling stone stairway winding up the centre. I knew that Colette would have breakfast on the table already, and that Mary would worry if I wasn't there. She worried so much about me that sometimes I regretted having asked her to come to Louisiana in the first place. Then again, Mary's presence was serene and solid, an anchor in the immaterial landscape of Eden.

I shook my head as I came into the shadows of the kitchen, in an effort to clear it. I dropped the journal on the counter and smiled at Colette, the cook. She was a middle-aged Creole woman with black eyes, cinnamon skin, and cheeks like apples on either side of a perpetual smile.

"Breakfast's set in the dining room, mademoiselle," she told me. "Make sure and drink all that orange juice today." I always had the feeling that she and her peers viewed Mary and me as invalids of a sort.

"Thank you, Colette. Is Mary up yet?"

"Don't know's I've heard her this morning. It's early yet."

But Mary was already seated at the dining room table when I entered. She was wearing her lavender silk kimono, and her hair hung in a long silver-blond braid to her waist. She smiled at me over her coffee cup, and all at once I was overwhelmingly glad of her presence.

"Up and out early this morning," she said.

I sat down and began to pick at the breakfast Colette had laid out for us.

"You haven't slept, have you?"

I sighed, being well weary of this line of questioning. "I slept a bit."

She lifted her eyebrows at me in mild reproach, but changed the subject. "I've almost finished going over the accounts."

"Oh?" I looked up with more interest than I felt for breakfast. After my grandfather's death I had wanted to hire a lawyer to put the estate in order, but Mary, who had always managed her husband's finances, had insisted on looking at it first. She had proven more than adequate to handle what could not have been an easy task, as my grandfather's bookkeeping had been at least as erratic as the workings of his mind.

"You'll be glad to know he didn't leave you in debt."

I sighed. "But he didn't leave me much else?"

"Around six million dollars. Not all in currency, of course. There are a number of bonds, some easily liquidated assets..."

"Six million?"

"It's not quite as much as you might have imagined—"

"Mary, I expected to be left in debt!"

She laughed. "I can see why, but you don't have to worry about that. William invested money for you regularly and kept careful track of it, though his own accounts were a shambles. Keep in mind, of course, that it's a rough estimate. And it doesn't include the value of this place or the house in Boston. I thought that you would want to keep them both."

I promptly forgot about finances at the mention of houses. "That reminds me! Did you see anything in the accounts or papers about another house on the plantation?"

"Another house?"

"Have you noticed the house up on the hill, on the left-hand side if you're on the dock facing the water? It's hard to tell—it might be as big as this one, but it looks like it was built more recently."

Mary was frowning slightly. "You know, it's funny that you mention it, because I'd meant to ask you about the place myself, and forgot about it until just now. There's no account of that house anywhere, as far as I know, but I did see it, one of the first mornings we were here. At first I thought it was my eyes acting up, but then the sun caught the windows...it was odd, the way it seemed to just appear there on the hill."

I sighed, looking through the open French doors toward the water. "Exactly. It seems strange that it isn't mentioned anywhere. According to records, the nearest plantations are Chênes and Joyous Garde, but neither of them is visible from here. I was hoping that my grandfather might have said something to you about it. He never spoke to me about Eden."

Mary shook her head. "Nor to me. All I knew about it was common knowledge: that it had been his wife's, and that ever since she died, he found it too painful to return. I asked him once why he didn't sell the plantation, your grandmother's family all being gone."

"Did he answer?"

"Not directly. It made me wonder, since your grandfather had the most direct manner of anyone I've ever known." Her forehead creased. "He was so enamored with science and agnosticism, he was the last person I would have imagined would believe a wives' tale. But he said something then that I could never quite reconcile. Something about the past being buried here, and how he didn't want to wake any ghosts."

"Here, meaning this house?"

She shrugged. "He never made any mention of there being another. For that matter, we don't know that the one on the hill has anything to do with Eden at all. Maybe it belongs to one of those other plantations."

"No. I know that our land extends at least that far."

"Unless it was sold and the records were confused or lost."

I conceded this. "What else did he tell you?"

"Nothing. He launched into a monologue about water hyacinths and how someday they would purify all the world's drinking water. Which of course led to a discussion of Shakespeare." We laughed again. "At any rate," she concluded, "I never got anything else out of him about this place."

"And not for lack of trying, I'm sure."

She laughed again, gently. "No. Not for lack of trying."

I looked away from the bright window, down into my coffee cup, where my eyes rested for a time. Part of me felt a childlike impulse to confide in Mary, to tell her about the fear I felt and ask her what it meant. Another part wanted to march up to the house and dispel the fear once and for all. Yet even as the thoughts formed, I knew that they were idle; I had plenty of ghosts to battle without searching out new ones.

"All this talk of empty houses has reminded me of a thought I've been having," Mary said, breaking my reverie. "What would you think of taking on a boarder? In one of the cottages, maybe that little Tudor one in the woods?" Before I could protest, she continued, "Oh, I know how it sounds, and I never would have thought of it myself. But Mrs. Kelly—you'll remember her—"

"We heard a string quartet at her house last year. She wouldn't stop talking about an airplane her husband had just bought."

"Yes, well, I suppose she's one of the idle rich, but with good intentions, at least. Anyhow, one of her favorite pastimes is promoting young performers, and she's become very attached to her latest find. I don't know much about him except that he's a composer from New York supporting a sickly young niece. He's looking for an inexpensive place to live in a warm climate, with lots of quiet for him to work and space for the child to play."

I smiled. "And you thought that maybe he would do me some good, too?"

Mary raised her eyebrows. "You are young, Eleanor, and young people ought to have the company of other young people."

My smile turned to a scoff. "You're not trying to marry me

off, are you? Because I'll warn you right now: I've taken an oath never to marry."

"Why would you do such a preposterous thing?"

I shrugged. "I don't want to be dependent on a man."

"Honestly, Eleanor, do you ever listen? You'll never be financially dependent on anybody again."

"That's not what I meant!" I was indignant to find myself coloring under her knowing, amused eyes. "Oh, never mind, it's a silly thing to talk about, anyway. I've never even met him. Or decided to take on a boarder at all, for that matter." I raised an eyebrow of my own—reproachfully, I hoped.

"You can agree to see him, at least. I promised Mrs. Kelly that much."

"All right, I'll see him. But warn me before you bring him here!"

"Of course," Mary replied as I left her for the music room.

3

Chopin wrote his two sets of études for the reason their name implies: they are studies, exercises meant to hone the skills of a virtuoso pianist. He wrote them if not purely, then at least predominantly for a practical purpose. At the time, the best collection of piano exercises was Czerny's. Those who have suffered through Czerny need look no further for Chopin's motives in revision.

However, as sometimes happens when the genius of the artist is great enough, Chopin's practical idea took on a life of its own and exceeded his intentions. The études are built on a mercilessly precise foundation of classical composition, covered by a fragile exterior that moves as smoothly as water, unmistakably a product of Chopin's era of early Romanticism. The results are so beautiful, and so difficult, that the public of the era viewed the pieces less as studies for improvement than as formidable tests of skill. Virtuoso pianists earned their reputations not so much for the conditioning the études provided as for the regard afforded by being able to play them.

I was wrestling with the études that summer at Eden's Meadow. I had lost ground in the past year with the unexpected shock of my grandfather's death. I planned to begin auditioning for concert appearances the next autumn, and I knew that I needed a better repertoire than I currently possessed.

I was thinking of the études as I leaned over the peeling white railing that ran along the rim of the lake beneath the topiary garden. Tossing marble chips from the path into the water, I watched the ripples circle outward, and paused every once in a while to steal a look at the house on the hill. More than a week had passed since I had first seen it, but if anything, its mystery plagued me more consistently than before. I knew that, given enough time, curiosity would get the better of me and I would have to see it. I sighed, dumping the rest of my handful of stones into the water, watching them glint for a moment before they disappeared into the tea-colored depths.

I had been working in the rose garden and was still wearing a pair of old, patched trousers, a straw hat, and sandals. Mary had told me to dress for lunch that day, and as the morning was waning, I began to climb back up through the garden toward the house with the intention of changing. I was looking down at my feet, thinking so intently about houses and ghosts and music that I never saw the man step into my path. As it was, I barely noticed his shadow in time to avoid bumping into him. I looked up, ready to protest, but when I saw who stood in front of me, I took a startled step backward instead and nearly tumbled.

He caught and steadied me, then stood looking at me, and I had the uncomfortable sensation that I was being appraised. To cover my embarrassment, I stared back. He was older than I would have guessed that night at the Symphony, probably in his mid-forties, although the pensive wisdom in his expression was that of a much older man. His hair showed a few threads of grey, and care had etched lines into his forehead and the corners of his eyes.

The thought that kept running through my mind was that I was dreaming, that he could not possibly be here in the secluded world I had made for myself, so far from the place of our first meeting—or, rather, missed meeting. I had dreamed too many idle dreams of him for this one to be true. Yet there he was, apparently waiting for me to say something.

Finally, lamely, I asked him, "Can I help you?"

He studied me for another moment, then said, "Perhaps you can. You're Miss Rose?" His accent was well controlled but unmistakably Russian.

More than slightly bewildered, and beginning to be irritated by his aloofness as well, I answered, "That's right. You must be Mary's lunch guest."

"I came to see you."

"You're the one who wants the house!" I cried, forgetting myself in my surprise at the coincidence.

"I am," he answered, half smiling.

"I'm sorry," I said, feeling all at once like an impetuous child. "I didn't expect you. I was gardening...I was just going to change when...well..."

The explanation died in light of his obvious dry amusement. He studied me for what seemed many long minutes, while I tried not to fidget.

Finally he replied, "I think it's rather becoming. You look a bit like a drawing—a Renoir. If Renoir's models had worn trousers."

I couldn't help smiling, and hesitantly his own smile bloomed, leaving me far less intimidated than I had been. He had the face of a great actor: malleable enough that whatever emotion it registered appeared essential. I reminded myself to be careful. Such a face could command trust where it was not justified.

"It seems that I've seen you somewhere before," he said, the grave look returning as his smile faded.

"Quite likely. I know that I've seen you. And heard you. At Symphony Hall in Boston, last December. You played Chopin. It was the most striking piano performance I've ever heard."

"You were at that concert." It wasn't a question, yet there was something speculative in his tone that gave me the feeling he was thinking much more than he was saying. Rather than comment further on that concert, he said, "I hear that you are no small talent yourself."

"I'll never play as well as you."

"Never say that, Miss Rose," he returned. "Such thoughts will destroy your gift. Always compare, always ask yourself how you could improve, but never let anyone undermine your talent in your own eyes."

I was surprised by the passion of this outburst, but, seeing that he was deeply sincere, I held out my hand. "Please call me Eleanor."

He took my hand and pressed it slightly but did not shake it. "I'm Alexander Trevozhov. Call me Alexander." He paused, then abruptly he said, "You've been watching that house." He pointed in the direction of the house on the hill, whose highest rooftops were just visible from where we stood.

"How did you know?" I was too startled to wonder why the fact should interest him.

"Mrs. Bishop told me I would find you here. When I came to the top of the garden, I saw that something was occupying your thoughts. You were looking up, in that same direction. I wanted to see what held your interest."

"And what did you think when you found out?"

His eyes strayed up to the hillside. His look when he turned back to me was troubled in a way that it had not been a moment before. "I didn't know what to think," he answered slowly.

The sunlight caught for a moment in his eyes, sending bright slivers into their depths. It was clear that he did not like what he was going to tell me. He sighed.

"Truthfully, I wanted to walk away before I saw your face, before whatever fascinated you could snare me as well. I know nothing of this place, but it seems to me that it courts misfortune. Am I wrong to think so?"

I shrugged, hoping that my hidden fear wouldn't betray itself. "It has its skeletons, like any old house." I willed my eyes to keep steady on his.

"Ought I to have walked away?" he asked in a softened tone.

"Probably, if you felt so strongly."

"Should I now?"

His voice was so low, it was almost lost in the murmuring trees, and there was a plaintive note in it that rebuked my pretended nonchalance. I did not know whether to be put off by his directness or to call him mad and walk away myself. I wanted to do both and could not do either, for I knew that I ought to have turned away from Eden's Meadow as well, when I had the chance.

At that moment a voice like a bell drifted out of the trees at the top of the garden, dissolving the impasse. "Dyadya!"

We both turned to look up. A little girl of six or seven stood in the doorway of the summerhouse at the top of the garden. As we watched she flew down the steps, then along the path toward us. She was dressed all in white, down to the silk band on the hat in her hand. She looked up at Alexander with adoring eyes. His own face had changed entirely at the sight of her, losing all its grim anxiety and taking on an expression of rapt gentleness.

"Dyadya," she repeated, the reproach in her voice diffused by her breathlessness and her obvious fondness for him, "Mrs. Mary and I have been looking for you everywhere! It's time for lunch." Her accent was less pronounced than Alexander's. He picked her up and smiled teasingly at her. "Who says so?" he asked.

She laughed a golden laugh. "I say so!" she cried. "And Mrs. Mary," she amended quickly. I looked up, and "Mrs. Mary" waved from the summerhouse, where she and Colette were setting a table. I deliberately ignored her, hoping that she noticed; I knew that meeting Alexander here had not been a coincidence.

The little girl looked at me. Her eyes were blue and mild. "Who are you?" she asked.

"Tasha," said Alexander, "this is Eleanor Rose. Eleanor, meet my niece, Natalya. Tasha."

"Hello, Tasha," I said, smiling. After an apparent moment of consideration, she smiled back.

"What was it she called you?" I asked him. "It sounded like 'Dada.'"

Alexander smiled. "It does, I suppose. But dyadya means 'uncle' in Russian."

Tasha and her uncle looked nothing alike. Her expression was gentle, her hair reddish brown. She was lovely, but her face was not as striking as Alexander's was, and besides that, it had the wasted look of a child who had recently been seriously ill.

"Do you live in the castle?" she asked. She pointed to the corner of the house visible from where we stood.

"It's not really a castle, I'm afraid."

"Oh, yes, it is a castle! A beautiful castle with unicorns in the stable and butterflies in silver cages hanging from the ceiling…and you must be the princess. Are your mama and papa the king and queen? Do they dance in the ballroom every night?"

"I'm afraid not. It's only Mary and me living there now, with some ladies and men who help keep the place running. And my mother and father weren't queen and king, even when they were alive."

"Oh," Tasha answered, looking mildly disappointed.

"You speak excellent English for a little girl who hasn't been in America long," I told her, hoping to distract her.

"She had an English nurse from the time she was a baby," Alexander explained. He put the child down. "Come, Tasha. It looks as though Mrs. Bishop is getting impatient. And perhaps Miss Rose as well?" He smiled again, but underneath it there was a gravity that made me uneasy. It was not unlike the feeling I'd had that night at the symphony six months earlier, when I'd first heard Alexander play.

"Are you all right?" he asked.

"Yes…yes, I'm fine," I said, not quite able to meet his eyes.

I could see that he did not believe me. "Just then you looked as though you saw a ghost. You're so pale. Are you certain you're well?"

I forced a smile. "I'm fine. Really. I just…remembered something."

He looked at me a moment longer, then shrugged slightly and turned to walk up the hill. The sight of him moving away from me drove the fear home; the subsequent realization of my own irrationality stirred the beginnings of panic. It was to prove to myself that I still had control over both that I called to him to stop. I caught up with him in a moment.

"Look," I said, "you can have it. That is, you can take your pick of the cottages, though I'll tell you now the best is the little Tudor one at the end of this path, just a short way into the woods. It's quiet, there's plenty of space for Tasha to play, and the rent will be reasonable."

Alexander turned to Tasha. "What do you think, love?"

She looked up from the wildflowers she was gathering, her head tilting delicately, like an inquisitive bird's. "Think of what?" she asked.

"Would you like to live here?"

Tasha nodded solemnly. "I think so."

Alexander looked back at me. "Natalya's happiness is my primary objective."

"Then you'll take it?" I tried to conceal my own excitement.

He paused for a long moment. Then he said, "It will be nice to have another musician nearby. Few other places could offer that."

Then he smiled an opaque smile, and we shook hands.

After lunch we all walked over to look at the cottage. It was set in a small clearing, among trees hanging with ivy, honeysuckle, and the ubiquitous Spanish moss. The style of the cottage was out of keeping with the rest of the plantation. It looked like a house from a fairy tale, with classic cream walls and dark wood trim, a steep roof and diamond-paned windows.

"It's not very old," I told them. "My grandmother had it built as a guest house. It's been shut up for years, though, along with the rest of the plantation."

"Look, Dyadya," cried Tasha. "Roses!"

And there were, everywhere. Eden's pale, pink-veined tea roses clambered over the front of the house, along the dilapidated post-and-rail fence, even over some of the trees.

"Aren't they lovely?" said Mary.

I unlocked the door. "The place comes furnished," I told Alexander. "I hope that won't be a problem. We can move out any furniture that you don't want."

He took the dust cover off the rosewood table in the front hall. It was neither ornate nor plain, and it matched the hardwood floor and cream-colored walls perfectly. "No," he said simply, "it's finer than anything we have now, and probably suits the house better."

We walked through all of the rooms, opening windows, uncovering furniture and swatting at cobwebs. There were four rooms on the first floor: a kitchen, a dining room, a living room, and, at the back of the house, a study. The kitchen was long and high-ceilinged, with white walls, bay windows, and pegs for hanging pots and pans. A few bunches of dried lavender still hung from the rafters.

The dining room was small, with silvery-white wallpaper patterned like pine needles. The living room was dark green and cream, with the same golden wood. In the study an oblong, cloth-covered object rested against one wall. Beneath the cloth was a spinet piano. Alexander turned back the cover and played an arpeggio. It was badly out of tune.

"They lose their edge quickly in this humidity," I said doubtfully.

"Still, it has a good tone," he answered. "If you don't mind, I'll have it tuned and store the one I have in New York."

"Of course. I didn't even know it was here. My tuner comes next Tuesday, and I'll ask him to work on this one, too. You're welcome to play our piano as well. It's a concert grand."

Upstairs there were three small bedrooms and a bath with all of the modern fixtures. We'd had several of the cottages fitted with them when we arrived, having had thoughts of entertaining that never materialized.

"This is my room!" Tasha called from beyond one of the doors she had opened. We followed her into a room papered in tiny roses, with a mahogany four-poster and a cushioned window seat. The room faced south, over the water.

"It's a lovely room for a little girl," Mary said to her.

"We'll have to find one of the nice bedspreads from the big house for you," I added, which won a smile.

We looked into the other two bedrooms. The one facing east was tiny, blue, and spare; the one facing west—toward the house on the hill, I could not help but think—was done in green again, with a queen-size maple four-poster.

"What do you think?" asked Mary when we returned to the garden.

"What do you think?" Alexander asked Tasha.

"I think it's the loveliest house I've ever seen," Tasha replied, and Mary and I smiled at each other.

"I couldn't have put it better," Alexander said.

"So you'll have it for certain?" Mary asked anxiously.

Alexander laughed a golden laugh, like his niece's but more resonant. "We wouldn't have anything else. Would we, Tasha?"

She shook her head. "Nothing else."

"When will you move in?" I asked.

Alexander shrugged. "As soon as I can take care of my business in New York. The end of the month, maybe? But before this goes further, I must ask about the rent."

I looked helplessly at Mary. "Having a boarder was my idea," she told Alexander. "I think Eleanor's leaving the decision up to me. Well, then, does ten dollars a month sound reasonable?"

"Mrs. Bishop," he began, "I have not been long in your country, but I can see that you could ask ten times that amount and have it easily."

Mary folded her arms stubbornly. "Perhaps, but we're not renting it for the money. We're sorely in need of good company in Eden, and I should say that it would be fairest of us to pay you for providing it."

"Honestly, Mrs. Bishop—"

"Ten dollars a month, for as long as you want to stay."

"Well," said Alexander, still looking uncomfortable, "we'll certainly be here through the summer. After that, we'll see."

Mary smiled serenely again. "Then it's settled."

"It's settled," said Alexander. To make it formal, we all shook hands. Even Tasha.

"Well? Are you pleased?" Mary asked as we sat out in the summerhouse that afternoon. She was winding wool for knitting, a ridiculous occupation, I thought, considering the climate.

I was flipping through concerto scores and shook my head without looking up. "You're a terrible meddler. Much worse than I ever thought."

"But are you pleased?" she persisted.

"All right, I'm pleased! They seem lovely. In fact, we could rent the rest of the cottages to eligible bachelors, and then you'd never lack for amusement."

"Am I that bad?"

"Yes!" I looked at her imperturbable smile, and sighed. "Mary, tell me honestly—did you know it was him?"

"Who?"

I tossed the music aside in exasperation. "Alexander Trevozhov. The one we saw last December, the night..."

"Your grandfather died."

"You must have known that I admired him. But really, asking him to live here is a bit much!"

Mary put her own work aside. "I admit, the name sounded familiar when Mrs. Kelly wrote, but we've seen so many musicians perform, I never would have singled him out. I didn't make the connection even when he appeared here, because that night at the symphony I couldn't see well enough to make out his face. I didn't put it all together until he had gone to find you."

"Then it's purely a coincidence," I said, more to myself than to Mary.

"How could it be anything else?"

The question hung in the silence between us. Mary picked up another skein and began fumbling with the knot. After a moment I took it from her, freed it, and handed it back.

"I'm sorry, Mary. I didn't mean to accuse you. It's just so strange."

She shrugged. "Maybe it was meant to be. Only time will tell."

We lapsed into silence again, and then I remembered a question that had been nagging me all day. "What was Tasha's illness?"

"Consumption. I suppose she picked it up on the boat from Europe. Apparently she wasn't expected to live."

"Do you know why they left Russia?"

"Only rumors. According to those, their family was executed for supporting the White Army. Alexander was spared as a well-known musician; he and Tasha were away from home when it happened.

She's his brother's child. It must have been terrible for Alexander, but that poor child—she's lost everything."

"She still has Alexander."

"Thank God for that." Mary stifled a yawn, then smiled self-consciously. "I think I'll lie down for a while, Eleanor, if you don't mind. My head aches a bit."

"It's your eyes. Why won't you have them checked?"

"What use is it to have them checked? They'll only tell me I'm going blind, and I already know that."

"You don't know that! If you don't know what's causing the problem, you don't know that it can't be cured."

Mary sighed. "All right, Eleanor. I'll go to a doctor. But for now I'll rest. Will you wake me an hour before dinner if I'm not up?"

I sighed. "All right. I think I'll go back over to the cottage and take off the rest of the covers. Maybe clean up a little."

Mary scrutinized me. "We pay people to do that, you know."

I met her eyes squarely. "I know."

4

The cottage was silent when I arrived, lonely compared with the earlier commotion. I found myself slipping back into my former melancholy, watching the lengthening shadows shift across the floor. I removed the remaining cloths from mirrors and paintings, tables and lamps. Soon I had finished all of the downstairs rooms but the study. There was only one frame there; a large one hanging over the piano.

As I reached for the dust cloth, a breath of air moved past me with a sound uncannily like a sigh and twitched the fabric out of my hand. My skin prickling unpleasantly, I looked around to see if one of the windows had been left open, but they were all tightly shut. For the first time I was aware of how alone I was. If I were to scream, nobody could possibly hear it. However, such thoughts offered superstition a grip on my imagination I wasn't willing to indulge. Leaning over the piano again, I took the cloth firmly in my hands, pulled it free—and then, for a moment, I forgot to breathe.

The frame held a painting. It was the only portrait in a house hung with landscapes, its size and weighty elegance suggesting that it had not originally been intended to hang in the cottage at all. It portrayed two girls in the ornate costumes of the late nineteenth century. One wore white, the other crimson. They smiled from the music room at Eden's Meadow, the crimson one archly, the white one demurely. The two faces were structurally identical: fair, soft, and rosy-cheeked, with generous mouths, straight little noses, dark eyes with a vaguely foreign tilt. Both girls had long black curls. The crimson one left them loose on her shoulders, and the white one twisted them into a coronet that would have identified her to me even if she hadn't been wearing the diamond that I had worn religiously since her death.

Her sister wore an identically cut ruby. These self-conscious monochromes struck me as tawdry, until it occurred to me that a favorite color might well be of special significance to a pair of teenage girls who are otherwise indistinguishable. The plaque on the frame read 'Eve and Elizabeth Fairfax, May 1898', but the artist was unacknowledged, and I could not make out the name from the scrawled signature in the corner.

The portrait's most basic significance was obvious. However, I could not begin to categorize the host of questions it raised. Why had Eve's existence been so fastidiously kept from me? To earn denial, she had to have done something dreadful, but what, and where was she now? Dead, possibly; and yet, even that answered nothing, least of all the question I hardly dared consider: how was it that I had been dreaming of Eve all my life, when I had not known of her existence until this day?

I sat down in a chair facing the painting, wondering who Elizabeth's sister had been. Apparently a woman with more fire than Elizabeth had ever possessed, but the mute image offered no other clues to her history. I sighed, folding the dust cover slowly. I could find nothing in the room to elaborate upon Eve's story. I walked home through the deepening twilight, deep in meditation.

Back in the big house, I found Mary already up, talking with Colette in the kitchen.

"Colette, Mary—did either of you know my mother?"

"I only came to the village when I married," Colette answered. "I never set foot in this house till you hired me."

Mary shook her head. "I'm afraid I'm no more help. I first met your grandfather a year after she died."

I drew up a chair by them at the big wooden table, and sat down. "Did he talk about her?"

"Rarely," Mary answered, shrugging. "And then only in reference to you. But Eleanor, she's been dead more than seventeen years. What's this sudden interest in her?"

"She had a twin," I told them, unable to think of a way to preface the revelation.

"What are you talking about?"

"I just found a picture of her."

"Where is this picture?"

"In the cottage. It's a portrait of them, together, with a title plaque and everything. Her name was Eve."

Mary looked at me for a moment, then said, "Would you mind if I had a look?"

So we walked back to the cottage and through its empty rooms in silence, until we reached the study. Mary looked at the painting for a long time, her face inscrutable. Somehow, the fact that she didn't exclaim, or even perceptibly react to the shocking image, comforted me. Mary raised her hand toward the painting, her fingers poised as if to touch my mother's face; then, abruptly, she dropped it again, and turned to me.

"Well," she said matter-of-factly, "this certainly explains some things."

"Does it?" I asked.

"Your grandfather's secrecy about your mother. His

reluctance to talk about this place. Of course, it raises lots of questions too...but this painting is like a missing puzzle piece. I feel I ought to be shocked—to try to erase a child is a shocking thing—and yet I somehow feel as though—"

"You've always known," I finished for her.

She looked at me, and gave me a gentle smile. "Come, Eleanor. There's nothing else to be gained here."

"There must be records," I persisted. "Birth certificates, other pictures. He can't have destroyed everything about her. Whatever happened, he must have loved her once..." I heard the entreaty in my own tone. I knew that it was childish, but I could not bring myself to believe that the man who raised me as his daughter could have denied his own.

"But not here," Mary reiterated firmly. "If there is anything like that, it'll be in the big house. We haven't gone through the library, and I don't know that we've ever looked up in the attic, either. Come, let's go home." Uneasily, I let Mary lead me back to the big house.

We started with the library's massive desk. If Mary's motive in suggesting the search had been to distract me from the more troubling aspects of the discovery, it worked. We knelt amidst the piles of paper, giggling like schoolgirls over the bits and pieces of my family's history we unearthed.

"Can you imagine," said Mary, "that William was a local swimming champion?"

"And that he graduated from Harvard? He told me he never went to college. He claimed to 'believe wholeheartedly in the concept of self-education.'"

Mary laughed. "What an old hypocrite!"

After two hours, though, when all of the drawers had been overturned and put back together again, we'd found no mention of either of the twins.

"Where would we find birth certificates?" I asked, sitting back on my heels.

"Probably in a town hall, but I don't actually know where the girls were born. Then again..." Mary tapped her lips speculatively. "William told me that your grandmother was religious."

"She was Catholic, I think."

"So she would have had a Bible."

"There's one up there." The large, leather-bound volume rested horizontally on one of the highest shelves on the far wall. "Why?"

"Well," said Mary, positioning the step stool under the shelf, "she took her daughters' names from the scriptures." She pulled the book down and came back to kneel on the rug beside me. "I'd be willing to bet she followed the old tradition of recording children's births." She flipped through the empty leaves at the beginning and end of the book. "And here it is. A birth list dating back five generations. Look, they're right here, Eve Brigitte and Elizabeth Marie Fairfax, born March thirty-first, 1882. It doesn't say anything about your mother's death, though, so I suppose that doesn't help us with Eve's story." She looked at the faded writing a moment longer, then turned to me. "Should we explore the attic?"

Shaking off the unease Mary's find had brought with it, I answered, "Why not?"

We lit candles, since the electrical wiring had not made it as far as the attic. Taking the ring of keys that had come with the house, we climbed up the steep stairs. The attic was divided into four long sections, each one leading into the next. The first was jumbled with broken furniture, and I heard the scrabbling of mice in the corners. There were no documents or books anywhere to be found. The next room held a few cartons of old medical textbooks, more decrepit furniture, and a large trunk. We set our candles down, and I went about testing keys until I found one that opened the trunk.

Inside were four evening gowns at least two decades out of fashion, all in relatively good condition. Underneath them was a wedding gown of yellowed white silk, with an intricately embroidered bodice. Mary lifted it up, studied it closely for a moment.

"Turn-of-the-century, hand-made," she said and laid it back in the trunk. I didn't answer. I didn't need to.

We shut the trunk up again, and moved on. The third room was again crammed with furniture but had no visible containers for papers or books. The fourth was nearly empty but for two good-sized cedar boxes pushed back into the eaves. None of the keys would open them.

"We'll have to break the locks," I said.

"Let's bring them downstairs first."

We enlisted the help of Jean-Pierre, Colette's husband, and in a half hour we had the trunks in the library, both locks forced open. As I had suspected, they had belonged to the twins. They appeared to be hope chests.

"How positively precious!" Mary exclaimed as we bent to examine their contents. Toward the top these were similar. There were handmade bed and table linens, along with crocheted bedspreads and doilies and table runners. The contents of one trunk were neatly made, while those of the other had obviously been rushed through.

Both held a number of recital programs, the older ones identical but for the pieces each twin played, the later ones mapping the divergence of their talents. It was Eve who had gone on to gain local recognition, in both Boston and New Orleans, while my mother apparently had stopped performing altogether by her late teenage years.

"I didn't know she ever performed," I told Mary. "I suppose it makes sense, since she taught music, but I don't ever remember her playing herself. I suppose I thought my music came from my father. And my grandmother, of course."

The rest of my mother's trunk was filled with letters, binders of watercolor sketches, and several thick volumes that appeared to be journals. Eve's trunk contained similar mementos, though there was only one journal. There was also an album of photographs.

We flipped through the letters and the journals, but both of them left off long before the period in which we were interested. I put them aside, planning to read them thoroughly later on. The watercolors were faded but not badly drawn. The photographs, I realized quickly, must have been a hobby of my aunt's. All of them were poorly developed, and most showed scenes of Eden's Meadow.

"Here's my grandmother." A small, fragile woman dressed in white sat in a lawn chair by the lake. The picture was overexposed; the hair around her face was full of light, like a halo. Her eyes were pale and troubled; I might even have said vexed, if the quality of the picture had been better.

"She's very beautiful," Mary said. "You must have inherited your blond hair from her."

"And the dark eyes from my grandfather. People always said I was a mix of the two of them."

Mary studied the picture reflectively. "She looks unhappy."

"Maybe she was already ill then. Or perhaps...well, I've heard it said that her illness wasn't all physical."

Mary looked at me carefully for a moment, then answered, "William did mention something like that to me once." Quickly she laid the picture down and picked up the next.

"Here he is."

I accepted Mary's evasion. "Holding a dead fish up to the camera, true to form."

"And here are the two girls together. I wonder who could have taken the picture, to make them smile and blush so!" Eve was looking straight into the lens with a coquettish smile. My mother was blushing deeply, her frowning face averted.

"Some spotty boy, most likely."

Mary laughed at my scornful tone. "They're not all bad, Eleanor Rose," she said, studying the picture of the girls.

"But most of them are spotty," I answered, beginning to blush myself. "Here, look at these." I flipped through the pictures, drawing her attention away from my least favorite subject.

We went through all of the trunks' contents but did not uncover so much as a hair to suggest what had happened to disrupt the lives of Eve and Elizabeth Fairfax. I went to bed well after one o'clock and lay awake for a long time, deliberately thinking of Eve. Despite my efforts, my only dreams were of a man in a house in the woods.

5

Over the following days I practiced the études as diligently as I was able, and in between I read the journals from cover to cover. They accounted for the year of 1898—the same, I noted, in which the portrait had been painted. Much of their contents was prattle, but they did contain several points of interest.

First, I learned how my parents met, a subject which my grandfather had been particularly unwilling to discuss with me. It turned out that they had been introduced at a Christmas ball in Boston thrown by the twins' music teacher, an elderly lady held in high esteem by society families as instructor to their daughters. My father was a protégé of hers, a struggling young pianist from New York. In the journal, my mother referred to him simply as "R"; I could only assume it was for Rose, as I had never known his Christian name.

They appeared to have formed an immediate attachment to each other, but my mother, knowing that her parents would never approve of a penniless suitor, had kept this a secret from everyone but her sister. She didn't mention him often in her journal, but Eve made several allusions to clandestine meetings and a steady correspondence kept up between my mother and the young musician since the meeting.

Both journals detailed a spring filled with concerts and operas, recitals at which both twins performed, and a general array of upper-class amusements. Eve described these haphazardly, referring in giddy terms to her many suitors, none of whom, apparently, made an impression on anything deeper than her vanity. My mother's entries were more precise and long-winded in their descriptions of social and cultural events, but irritatingly bereft of any personal commentary.

When the girls' school term ended, the family moved to Eden's Meadow for the summer. Here, finally, I uncovered the focus of my aunt's flirtation and my mother's discomfort in the photograph Mary and I had found. His name was Louis Ducoeur, and he was a relation to the couple who owned Joyous Garde, the former indigo plantation near Eden's Meadow. He was several years older than the twins and had grown up with his widowed mother in France. The Ducoeurs of Joyous Garde were elderly and childless; upon their deaths, the estate would pass to Louis.

That summer, he had come to stay with his Louisiana relatives to become acquainted with the estate that would one day be his and had subsequently befriended the Fairfax girls. He was at that time an art student in Paris, though Eve described him as a precocious Renaissance man, having already gained credentials in music and the sciences at illustrious European universities, though he was not yet twenty-one. I was skeptical of my aunt's account of his abilities until I read that it was he who had painted the portrait of the twins I had uncovered in the cottage.

Near the description of the portrait, Eve included an account of a series of murals that Louis planned for Eden, once more using herself and my mother as models. He meant the pictures to represent the biblical story of the Fall. Eve's descriptions of the project were so enthused that I was almost sorry Louis had abandoned the idea, until I realized why.

Apparently, an adolescent love triangle had developed over the weeks the twins spent with Louis. Eve had fallen in love with Louis, Louis with my mother. My mother, for some reason she could or would not clearly define, disliked Louis from the first, "as intensely as I have ever loved my sister." Thereafter she alluded to Louis's attentions self-consciously, and never with any hint that she returned them.

Yet Eve, having begun her descriptions of the affair in the same offhand tone she had used when referring to her own Boston admirers, rapidly abandoned this in favor of a more vigilant examination of her own growing love. Consequently I began to take her observations more seriously. I came, ultimately, to feel sorry for this unknown aunt, trapped as she was between love and jealousy.

Early in the summer she wrote of Louis:

We speak easily of anything, of everything. We cover more topics in more depth during one conversation than I have in all the others of my life combined, and I am continually amazed at the way he seems to understand and articulate feelings and ideas that have always both possessed and confounded me, and which I would have thought, previously, to be unique to myself. Every word he says convinces me further how alike we are. Never before have I thought—rather, felt—that someone understood me so perfectly.

And yet it is Elizabeth he looks at first when he enters a room, Elizabeth whose words he hangs on, Elizabeth whom his eyes follow when she moves. We have never spoken of his feelings for her, but I know what he would tell me if I asked. A face as expressive as his couldn't hide even a lesser emotion; when he looks at her, love is in every part of his countenance.

And my own feelings? I only wonder how he can be so blind

to them. I feel them written on my face when I look at him, as clearly as his are when he looks at her. I could not claim to love him and wish him anything but happiness; yet, feeling as I do, I cannot honestly wish that Elizabeth will change her mind and return his love. I know for certain that she does not love him; at least I don't have that on my conscience. Yet would she feel differently if I spoke to her on his behalf? Do I resist doing so because of my own feelings?

God help me! I can't bear to love both of them so much!

Several weeks later Eve wrote:

I have been looking back at the beginning of this book—could I be the same person who wrote those pages? I used to look in the mirror and think of myself. Now when I look, I think only of Louis. Not more than half a year has passed, yet I can say that I was a child when I began this volume and, with as much certainty, that I am a child no longer.

I remember saying to Lizzie once that I didn't believe in love. I truly used to think that it existed only in novels and operas, because my own fancies shifted so quickly and continually. Now I am so full of love that I cannot eat or sleep; even music fails to distract me. It seems impossible now that I could not always have loved him, and I see no way to stop it. Yet I know that this love is wrong, formed as it is for someone who is my sister's, whether she values him or not.

She told me today that he has asked for her hand, and that Papa has made her promise to accept. Could she see that my heart nearly burst inside me when she spoke those words, that it was all I could do not to fly at her when she told me of her distrust and dislike of him in the same breath? She says that he is reckless, overly passionate—as if these, the very things I love most in him, could be reasons for dissatisfaction!

I know that she loves another, and this is what makes her speak so. But how can she distrust him when he so clearly feels for her what I feel for him? It seems impossible that one could reject such devotion, though he himself proves the possibility countless times every day, when he breaks off his conversation with me the moment she enters a room, when he smiles at her, or when he retrieves a blossom she has crushed, believing himself unnoticed. And to think that she has made him promise to wait for her until she comes of age—that's five years away! Though I imagine Maman had something to do with that, too. She would never say so, but I know that she is as wary of Louis as Elizabeth is, and of course Elizabeth is her favorite.

How can they be so blind?

I had not thought of it seriously before, but it seems now that I must go away to a conservatory when I am finished with school next year, and pursue a performing career, no matter what Maman and Papa say. I don't know how I can bear another minute with all of this so close to me, let alone the rest of my life.

The pages following this rather poignant piece of self-analysis were disappointingly bereft of the same feeling and eloquence. My aunt seemed to have sunk into a depression, and what little she wrote about her unrequited love was rancorous; she even stooped to admitting jealousy of her sister. Yet one passage in these pages stood out among their petty counterparts, sending my imagination off on a new tangent:

Maman has fallen ill. First she burns with fever and complains of a terrible dryness in her mouth and throat, then she appears well again; for some days now, this strange pattern has repeated itself. The doctor first diagnosed malaria, but the quinine does not seem to be working. Papa plans to call in a specialist if she isn't better soon. At any rate, we won't be leaving Eden until Maman is well enough to travel, and I am ashamed to admit that to me, this is the most dreadful part of her illness. I long to be away from this place and all its unhappiness.

I flipped through my mother's journal again to see if I had overlooked similar mention of my grandmother's illness there, but the entries stopped several days before Eve's. Returning to Eve's journal, I found only one more short mention of this illness, written a week or so after the first. It simply said:

Maman is better. We will leave within the fortnight.

The last entry in Eve's journal was in many ways the most affecting. It so clearly reflected the views that until recently had been my own, and the subsequent, similar re-evaluation I was facing in light of meeting Alexander—though even then I would have rejected the idea that my feelings for him were anything lasting.

At last Louis is gone. At last, though it gives me pain greater than I have ever imagined. I think of his face smiling at Elizabeth and imagine that the smile is for me—oh, but why torture myself this way? Why look for logic where there is none? Love cannot be logical, but I will never understand why it must be painful. It seems so ridiculous, the three of us madly pursuing what cannot be ours. For it is clear that Elizabeth is unchanging in her feelings for him: she may yet be his wife, but he will never have her love. And I, with the same face and form, so ready to give him mine, am merely tolerated. Poor Lizzie. Poor Louis. It seems there is no choice but to live these separate miseries we've made for ourselves.

On the page opposite she had pasted in a fragment of paper, filled with close writing in a different hand, the edges of which appeared to be scorched. A postscript in Eve's hand explained that it was a piece of a letter from Louis to Elizabeth, which my aunt had rescued from the kitchen stove, where her sister had deposited it. It read:

So much has awakened in me, so many new expectations, so much certainty and still more uncertainty. I feel that I am spinning, rushing toward a future that is at the same time clear and clouded, so close at hand yet still in the balance. There is so much to experience, and so little time. There are snow and rain, sun and stars, sea and sky and laughter and music, and everything in between; a chaos of faces, of feeling, of thoughts, worlds, loves, hates, all circling together.

And at the centre of this solar system, where once there was nothing, there is now a constant: there is you, with all your purity and beauty, with all your strength and frailty. How can you not see that to be this sun is your destiny, as to orbit you is mine? I know that in time you will see it. You must—just as, in you, I see the ancient circle of rock and water, fire and sky, of leaves that bud and then fall golden, all in the light of your smile, suspended within it, like the doorway to a moment that never began nor will end, but which we will always be free to pass into and out of—

Hurt me! Lash out, try for blood, you cannot refuse to love me…

Beyond this, the writing became illegible. I put the volume aside, chilled simultaneously by the sheer, mad passion of the final words and my mother's cold refusal of them. I flipped again through her own journal, looking for any intimation that she had seen and understood her sister's plight or in any way sensed the strength of Louis's love for her. Yet her only reference to the two of them together was that Louis was the first person who had successfully tamed her sister, and that in this lay his only worth to her. There were scattered remarks about how little she liked him, and one that fairly clearly stated that she suspected him of toying with her sister's affections, but she expressed no more powerful feeling for her lover, nor any understanding of his own.

How could the two sisters have such vastly different reactions to the same man? I wondered, and continued to wonder as I reread the journals over the days that followed. But there was nothing in either volume to give a clue to this variance of opinion, nor to the lesser question that Eve's entry about her mother's illness had sparked: whether it could have been the onset of the disease that killed her.

Like so much about my family's past, I had never before known enough to wonder about my grandmother's death. My grandfather had seldom talked to me about her, and certainly not about how she died. During my childhood the idea of her, like that of my parents, inhabited a completely different realm from the one in which I lived. The older I grew, the more they all seemed to be figures from a distant past that was no more real to me than a storybook. The little I knew about the nature of Claudine Fairfax's illness, and the suggestion that there had been a mental aspect to it, had come from snatches of gossip I had overheard during the society evenings of my childhood, and had never been supported by anything more substantial.

Now I realized I had one potential foothold in Claudine's portion of the mystery, if no other: the name of her doctor. And I knew who would know where to find him.

"Yes, I've heard of Dr. Beaufort," Colette told me over the bread dough she was kneading. "But it won't do you no good: he died ten years ago. If it's a doctor you're looking for, the best is Dr. Brown. He took over Dr. Beaufort's practice, right in Eden village. Nice man—he treats colored and white folks alike."

"Thanks, Colette," I told her, and then, to avoid suspicion and also to cover my tracks from Mary until I had decided whether or not to include her in this investigation, I said, "My insomnia medication from Boston hasn't been working. I thought a doctor down here might be able to suggest something else."

"No doubt he can," Colette answered, "but if you ask me, none of that new medicine works as good as the old. If you like, I'll talk to Callista Martin next time I visit my mother."

I knew from previous conversations with Colette that the said Callista was a self-proclaimed medicine woman, whose practices no doubt involved a sprinkling of voodoo. "I think I'll talk to Dr. Brown first. I need to go to town this afternoon, anyway. If she comes back before me, let Mary know I've gone on some errands, would you?"

"Of course, mademoiselle," Colette agreed, clearly free from any suspicion. For a moment I wondered why I cared what anyone thought; but I suppose I had enough pride not to want to broadcast the details of my grandmother's illness to the servants or, for that matter, the fact that I was interested in it.

I gathered my things, called for the car, and then settled in for the ride to the village, turning over the mild anxiety about what I might discover. I told Jean-Pierre to leave me at a dress shop and come back in an hour; when he had driven out of sight, I hurried across the street to the address Colette had given me.

There were only two other people in the tiny waiting room: a receptionist, to whom I gave my name, and an elderly woman who stared at me brazenly until she was called into the examining room, no doubt wondering why I had come all the way into town instead of calling the doctor out to Eden. In fifteen minutes she re-emerged and then let herself out, stealing glances at me all the while, which I had no choice but to pretend to ignore. Then Dr. Brown called me into his consulting room.

I was immediately disappointed by him, in that he could be no older than thirty-five: too young to have known any of the people I was interested in. Nevertheless, he had a kind, ruddy face and an affable manner that told me that even if he couldn't provide any answers himself, he would help as best he could.

"Good afternoon, Miss Rose," he said, shaking my hand energetically and showing me to a chair. "Very pleased to meet you."

"Thank you," I said, sitting down and self-consciously twisting the straps of my handbag.

"Now, what seems to be the problem?"

I looked into his solicitous, smiling face and realized I had no idea how to begin. I stared at him in silence for a few moments, and finally, still at a loss, I said, "Actually, I'm not ill."

I could see that he was repressing humor, but his kindness prevailed and he said only, "You're looking for advice, then?"

"Well, yes," I answered. "I imagine you'll think this is an unusual request, but, well...I wondered if you were at all acquainted with my grandparents, William and Claudine Fairfax."

He sat further back in his chair and answered, "Unfortunately, no. I grew up in a suburb of New Orleans and only moved out here a few years ago. I've certainly heard of your grandparents, but they had long since stopped coming to Eden by the time I arrived."

"I thought that would be the case. In fact, that has to do with what I meant to ask you." I paused, still shy of revealing the unpleasant nature of my grandmother's final years. However, the openness of Dr. Brown's face and his frank blue eyes convinced me that he would be the last to treat a sick person with contempt or, for that matter, to gossip. So I told him, "I never knew my grandmother. She died when I was only a baby. I didn't know my parents, either; my mother died when I was three, and my father…left. My grandfather, William Fairfax, raised me."

I looked to see how Dr. Brown would react to this information, but he only nodded, his palms together and index fingers on his lips.

Drawing another long breath, I continued. "He was quite reticent about discussing my mother and my grandmother. I know that they both died of illness, and he alluded to me that it might have been the same one." I couldn't look the doctor in the eye. Instead I focused on my gloves, which had replaced the handbag straps as the subject of my anxious attention. "My mother was not much older than I am when she fell ill. I don't know what she died of, and I have no records to refer to. But I thought that perhaps, since my grandmother was first treated here, at Eden…" I had never been good at lying, and now I lost my nerve; my face burned.

Thankfully, the doctor took this as embarrassment at requesting confidential information. He smiled sympathetically and said, "Generally we don't disclose medical information about our patients. However, as she was your grandmother and she's no longer living, I don't see what harm it could cause. I assume that Dr. Beaufort was the practitioner? His records should still all be here, and I'll show them to you, Miss Rose—I presume that was what you meant to ask."

Grateful, and flushing still more deeply, I nodded.

"However, I'll also insist that you have a full examination. If your mother and grandmother died of a congenital disease, there is always the chance that you could have inherited it." Again I nodded, feeling that to submit to an examination was a small price to pay for the information I sought.

Dr. Brown left the room. As I sat in the close, quiet heat of the little examining room, my anxiety grew. For the first time since I had read Eve's account of her mother's illness, I allowed myself to fully consider my impetus in pursuing this information. Of course, I was curious to know what had happened to this woman about whom I knew so little, particularly if, as my grandfather had suggested, her death might pertain to my mother's. I even had an idea that there might be something in those old medical records that would shed some light on Eve's fate. But deep down I knew that what was really driving me was a tiny, insidious idea that had worked itself into my mind sometime during my childhood, planted with my grandfather's challenge to me to avoid my mother's and grandmother's fatal melancholy, and fed on the gossip about the sinister turn that melancholy had taken in my grandmother's case. I had allowed the doctor to think that I feared an inherited physical defect, but this wasn't the whole truth. If something sinister had infected my grandmother's mind, I needed to know whether it threatened mine, too.

I had so succumbed to this thought that I didn't hear the doctor return to the examining room, and I jumped when he said my name. I smiled broadly to hide my discomfiture.

"I was in a dream," I apologized, but my smile died as I saw the serious expression his face had assumed. Slowly he sat back down at his desk, holding an old, discolored green file in front of him and reading intently. Finally he looked up at me, and his face was no less grave.

"Have you—have you found it?" I faltered.

"Yes," he answered slowly, "these are your grandmother's records. As you say, she did indeed fall ill here, in July of 1898, and it does appear that it was the beginning of the illness she died of. In the first instance, Dr. Beaufort diagnosed it as malaria. However, as Mrs. Fairfax didn't respond to the traditional treatment, he revised this diagnosis."

"What to?"

Dr. Brown shook his head. "At first it was unclear. Apparently, as is the case with malaria, she seemed to improve several weeks after the first attack of illness, and the family traveled back to Boston, where she remained well. But the records from the next summer show that her condition returned and worsened after they moved back to Eden, and by the time he was called in to see her next, she was extremely ill. The symptoms were no longer strictly malarial."

"What were they?"

"Well, much what you'd expect from a tropical disease: episodes of high temperature, interspersed with longer periods without fever but with overwhelming general malaise. There were minor symptoms such as dryness of the mouth, flushing, and pupil dilation, but these could all be side effects of the fevers themselves and therefore not directly related to the illness. The disease had definitely not progressed to the liver, as it does in the case of malaria. At any rate, the traditional quinine treatment was ineffective."

"And the fevers," I said, choosing my words carefully, "there weren't any other symptoms with them?"

Dr. Brown raised his eyebrows. "There's no mention of anything else."

Again I couldn't look at him, but I had to know the answer to the question that was nagging me. "There wasn't any delirium or...or anything of the sort?"

Dr. Brown's look turned graver still. "Why do you ask?"

I sighed. "I've heard rumors that made me think there

might be something to that effect."

The doctor studied me intently. "There are almost six years' worth of records here. It seems that after your grandmother fell ill, her family spent the majority of their time here. If anything like that had come up, it would be in these records.

"Of course, I don't have the records from the doctors she saw in Boston, but from what Mrs. Fairfax told Dr. Beaufort, their opinions were no different from his. And at any rate, they were mainly speculative, as her symptoms always improved during the winter. That is, until the last couple of years, when she was ill most of the time. They were all at a loss." He continued to look at me, and I could see that there was something else he wanted to say, but didn't know how.

"If there's more," I said grimly, "you'd best tell me."

Dr. Brown sighed. "It's nothing definite. But it seems that, toward the end of her life, Mrs. Fairfax's condition worsened dramatically. Dr. Beaufort maintained that there was nothing more to be done for her than what he was doing, but it seems your grandfather was concerned enough that he wanted a second opinion. He called in a Dr. Dunham, from New Orleans."

"And what did he think?"

He shook his head. "It seems Dr. Dunham kept his own records, and he and Dr. Beaufort didn't consult with each other."

"That's not so strange, is it?"

"It wouldn't be unusual in the case of two physicians. But Dr. Dunham isn't a physician. He's a specialist in mental illness."

I blinked at him in silence, unable to think of a response. What he had told me was no more than what I had prepared myself to hear, but at the same time, hearing it was a blow. Once again I thought of my grandfather's long-ago request that I avoid the life of melancholy that had killed my mother and grandmother.

Dr. Brown finally brought me back to the present with a sympathetic smile. "I know that this must be disturbing information, Miss Rose," he said, "but there is no proof here, or even in the fact that Dr. Dunham was consulted, that your grandmother's illness was indeed psychological in nature. Do you recall anything of the sort being said about your mother?"

"No—but she had been separated from her family for years when she died."

"Well, fatal diseases are common enough, and were more so at the turn of the century. If you have no reason to believe that your mother suffered from a psychological disorder or had an unnamed illness like your grandmother's, then it is doubtful that you would be in danger of inheriting one, even if your grandmother did suffer from one. But if it would make you feel better, I can contact Dr. Dunham and ask him for his records."

I thought about this and decided that whatever I might learn, it would be better than speculation. There was certainly no chance that I would forget the subject now, and I knew myself well enough to understand that the uncertainty would ultimately be as destructive as any truth could be.

"Yes, please, I'd appreciate that," I told Dr. Brown, and he said that he would write to New Orleans that day.

He proceeded to examine me from head to toe and found nothing wrong with me, aside from being a bit underweight and overtired. He renewed my prescription for chloral hydrate drops, promised again to write to Dr. Dunham straightaway, and then saw me to the front door. I shook his hand, then ran across the street to the dress shop to meet Jean-Pierre.

6

I had exhausted the journals' potential to enlighten me on my aunt's story, and there was nothing I could do but wait for Dr. Brown to contact me in regard to my grandmother's. This temporary dead end left me open to a different, if related, preoccupation.

Alexander's comment about the house on the hill having a hold on me had shaken me more than I cared to admit. The house's pull seemed to intensify with every day that passed, though this might well have been a result of my conscious efforts to ignore it. I held out for more than a week, not wanting to give in to superstition. However, on the morning the Trevozhovs were due to arrive, I awakened early, and after an hour at the piano, I realized that I wouldn't accomplish anything there that day.

I stood at one of the music room's open windows and looked at the lake spread out below me. I couldn't see the house on the hill, but its fairy-tale turrets, Alexander's veiled warning, and the newfound reality of Eve were all in my mind. Before better judgment could prevail, I made my way out of the room and down the corridor to the entry hall, opened the screen door, and stepped outside.

I took a roundabout path to the topiary garden, half hoping

to see someone to distract me from my plan, but the garden was empty. I followed the path hugging the lakeshore until it ended a little past Alexander's house, then began to thrash my way through the unbroken forest. The woods were thick with vines and mosquitoes, and the underbrush lashed out at my legs and hands. Before long I was covered with tiny scratches, stung by insects and nettles, and thoroughly convinced that the forest had a sadistic nature all its own. Still, I pushed onward, until I stumbled out onto what seemed to be an overgrown meadow. It took a minute for me to realize that it was the far left-hand corner of the lawn that preceded the house on the hill.

A hot wind rushed down the grassy expanse and pushed at my shoulders, as if trying to turn me away; but the house's magnetism, like its size, had increased dramatically with proximity. I was convinced now that it had been built more recently than Eden's plantation house. I wasn't an expert on architecture, but the turreted roofs and cluttered gingerbread ornamentation were clearly Gothic revival. A circular tower rose from the left wing; beside it, three old oaks stood in a triangle, their branches so entangled and matted with clusters of Spanish moss that they seemed to be one tree with three trunks.

About two hundred feet from the house, the ground leveled off, tapering toward a cobbled drive. The front door had a roofed carriage entrance. The elaborate entryway must have been beautiful in its day, but time and disuse had worn heavily on it. Curtains of ivy and Spanish moss hung over its open sides, swaying gently in the breeze. Narrow terraces ran the length of the house in both directions, but the railings had begun to crack and crumble in the ivy's insidious grasp, and the cherubs at their stair ends were covered with fine brown moss and corrugated lichen. Stone urns, rattling with the desiccated skeletons of ferns and a few of the tougher, ranker indigenous weeds, sat on either side of the front door. One had cracked in half, and part of it lay shattered on the stairs.

If I had felt sadness or the hint of a buried secret in my grandmother's house, it was nothing compared with the feeling of the house on the hill. I found myself wishing desperately that I could make it what it should have been. I wanted to throw open the windows and let the wind blow the cobwebs from its rooms. Its chimneys should spill smoke, its windows and doorways laughter. The sounds of children's feet should resound on its floorboards. Instead it was trapped in a wail for its own barrenness, a vacancy far more pervasive than its unoccupied rooms.

Drawing a breath, I stepped over the broken urn, placed my hand on the doorknob, then stopped, suddenly overwhelmed by the feeling that someone was watching me. I stepped back and looked at the windows on either side of the entrance. I tried to tell myself that unease was making me see what wasn't there, but at the same time, I was sure that the curtain covering the window to my right had twitched the moment I looked at it, as though it had been lifted and then dropped back into place. I shuddered, paused and then, taking a deep breath, turned the doorknob.

Anticlimactically, the door opened easily onto an empty entrance hall. The far end of the cavernous room was nearly lost in shadow. The few remaining pieces of furniture were covered by white drop cloths and rested on a faded oriental rug. French doors lined the wall on either side of the front door, all but two covered by faded blue damask draperies. I pulled the cords on several of the curtains, and the room flooded with light.

The white walls and ceiling were decorated with elaborate plaster molding, its gold leaf mottled but still shining softly. On either side of the room were several closed doors, and at the far end three dusty French doors opened onto what appeared to be another terrace.

Dimly illuminated, dual staircases curved from the far end of the room up into the shadows. The stairs were covered with a thick film of dust, and I felt irreligious leaving footprints in it, as I had felt walking in new-fallen snow as a child. At the first landing the stairways converged into a balcony that looked down into the room below. On one wall of the landing was a half-shaded casement. I uncovered this, dispelling more of the gloom. The original abandon with which I had entered the house was dissipating rapidly, leaving in its place an apprehension that, however childish, I could not shake.

Another stairway ran up along the far wall. A wide corridor opened to the right of the landing, a smaller one to the left, and a set of closed doors stood opposite the top of the stairs, at the base of the next staircase. I chose the wide hallway. At its end, sunlight streamed blearily through a large window; more doors opened off either side of the corridor.

Fear clutched as I opened the first of these, but the room behind it was empty. After that, my timidity disappeared. There was nothing in any of the rooms but antique furniture, dust, and spiders. After looking into a few of them, I abandoned the hallway. I even debated leaving then, putting the place out of my mind altogether. However, the feeling that the house was hiding something was still strong enough to overcome any remaining unease. I studied the stairs and the small hallway. Remembering the tower on the left wing of the house, I decided to make this my destination.

Though dim and murky, the hallway was not long. The

walls were painted deep red, and there were several small, arched, leaded-glass windows set in the left wall. Looking out, I saw that I was level with the tops of the three oaks. The lake seemed miles away, my house even farther. Quickly I looked away.

At the end of the passage was a heavy wooden door, which led to a surprisingly bright corridor. The left side was lined with windows, the right with closed doors. Sunlight lay in warped rectangles on the wooden floor. At the end of the corridor was an arched door, also closed. I had come to expect that all of the doors I found would open easily, but this one did not. I rattled the handle, to no effect. I could not fathom why an inner door would be locked when the front door was wide open to the world. One answer squeezed out of the back of my mind, but I wouldn't entertain it: the mustiness and pristine layer of dust belied the possibility that anybody might be living in the house.

I knew that I was on the second floor; therefore there had to be a ground-floor entrance as well. I went back through the corridors and down the stairs to the entrance hall, which seemed brighter and smaller and far less formidable than it had. I opened the first door that led to the left out of the entrance hall, and came into a sitting room with a large stone fireplace. Two doors opened off the room, one on the back wall, the other straight ahead.

Opening the door in front of me, I found myself in another wide corridor, this one also lined with long windows on one side and more closed doors on the other. The door at the end of this corridor had to be the entrance to the tower. I tried it, and found it locked as tightly as the first. I raced up to the third floor, found a comparable entrance, and when it, too, was locked, I nearly cried in outrage.

I inspected the lock carefully. Its keyhole was large enough to see through, but it was dark on the other side—either that, or the hole was blocked. Clearly, the lock would not be difficult to pick if I could find the proper implement.

I retraced my steps, looking for any such tool. Eventually I arrived back in the sitting room next to the entrance hall. It was empty except for a deer's head hanging over the fireplace on the left hand wall, an equivocal look in its glass eyes. The deer resurrected the uncomfortable feeling that I was being observed, and I turned away, toward the door I had not yet tried.

The room it opened onto was long and high-ceilinged, running at least half the length of the house, where French doors let in floods of sunlight. The walls were white, or had been; now they were discolored with age. The floor was a checkerboard pattern of black and white marble, and a balcony ran around the length of the room, lined with doors that must have belonged to second-story rooms. A stairway curved up to meet the balcony, its steps made of the same marble as the floor.

The arched ceiling was pale blue, painted with mythological scenes spreading from a yellow sun in the centre. Goblins danced with fairies; gods with severe faces and long beards chased nymphs in chariots drawn by swallows; satyrs played their flutes on clouds where butterflies fluttered in rings of gold and red and blue; Pegasus carried a boy to a girl in a pearly turret. Myriad species of birds and insects, both real and imaginary, fluttered in and out of scenes too numerous and intricate to extract from the whole.

It was the most beautiful room I had ever seen. I could imagine it decades earlier, lit with candles or gas, the light glinting on ornate costumes as the crowd swung to a waltz or reel. Then I saw the piano, and the imaginary dancers vanished.

It had been pushed into the far right-hand corner of the room and covered with a white cloth. I peeled this away, revealing an old Steinway. The keys were in perfect condition. I touched several of them gingerly. Though it had slipped, as my own piano did all too quickly in the Louisiana climate, its tone had no trace of the tinny dissonance inherent to instruments that have been neglected for a number of years. I sat down on the leather-covered stool, settling my fingertips on the keys. I did not know whether I meant to play; before I could really think about it, I was not only playing but utterly absorbed.

The music that emerged was a Chopin ballade, the one Alexander had played that night at the symphony half a year before. I had not played it in years—would have said, if I had been asked, that I had forgotten it. Nevertheless, the ballade poured forth, my fingers never hesitating. Only when the last notes had faded to an echo in the vast, empty room did my mind begin to work. I stared dumbly at my hands on the keys before me, as though one or the other would answer the questions that now churned in sickening circles, like the butterflies on the ceiling.

Outside, a cloud eclipsed the sun. Shadows crowded the room, pushing for space in the corners and the arched depths of the ceiling. With shaking hands I closed the piano and replaced the cloth.

My conviction that there was something wrong with the place was growing by the second. Yet I had come for a reason, and I told myself that it would be ridiculous to abandon it because of a piano that seemed to enable me to play a piece I believed I had forgotten.

Resisting the urge to look back, I walked up the stairs to

the balcony and opened the first door I came to. Inside was a surprisingly well-furnished library. Books lined the walls from floor to ceiling, some of them very old. They were of all sorts, written predominantly in English and French, though there were several in other languages. A ladder led up to a small loft on one side of the library. The loft held two bookshelves, and the bookshelves held Bibles, prayer books, hymnals, and various other books of a Christian nature. I pulled one from a shelf. Its brittle pages were filled with calligraphy and illuminations, the words in Latin. I chose two more at random; they were equally old and precious.

I stared at the books in my hands, unable to believe or deny what they seemed to be. They must have been priceless, yet they were rotting in this fetid place, abandoned with the house. Again the fear was creeping, for had this all been mine, nothing less than fear for my life could have induced me to leave it.

The mummy's-skin leather of the books' bindings began to repel me; it crumbled under my touch, leaving a dry, rotten-smelling dust on my fingers. I replaced them in their cases and climbed back down the ladder. I was still no closer to the tower, and the day was wearing on.

In the right-hand corner of the room, under a window, was a writing desk. In the top drawer I found a pair of cracked reading glasses, three rusted pens, and a sheaf of heavy, yellowed paper, all of it blank. In the next drawer down was a ring of keys. I closed the drawer and ran back down the stairs into the ballroom, through the sitting room, and down the bright corridor to the locked door. The first three keys did not fit. The fourth one slid easily into the lock. Something clattered to the floor on the other side.

I pushed the door open. A narrow stone staircase wound up

out of sight. The only light came from a slit of a window, high above on the curving wall of the stairwell. When I closed the door behind me, I noticed a key on the ground, identical to the one that had opened the door—my key must have pushed the other one out of the lock. I dropped the key from the floor into my pocket, slid the key ring in next to it, and began to climb.

Every few feet a narrow window was cut into the wall, but they shed little light. My legs began to ache from the slant of the tight spiral. As I climbed, I wondered again what I expected to find at the top. If there was something substantial, it would be likely to upset me, as Eve's portrait had done. What would I do this time, so far from home? I wondered. Worse still, what if the place was inhabited by someone demented or violent? Stubbornly I pushed the thought aside and climbed on.

After a time, I reached a narrow landing. The stairway continued up beyond it, and to my right was a door that must have been the second-floor entrance to the tower stair. The window across from it threw a blade of light that glinted dully on the nails in its cross-beams, the faded brass doorknob, and the key in its lock. The trepidation I thought I had dispensed with rekindled at that; I climbed up to the final landing.

There was a key on the wrong side of the third lock, too, but it barely registered, because what I saw in front of me was more unnerving still. The door to the room at the top of the tower was ajar, revealing a sitting room from an earlier era, neatly kept, without so much as a speck of dust anywhere. The room was round, with one large French door that opened onto a wrought-iron balcony. There was a sofa covered with cream brocade, and an old-fashioned mahogany desk. A matching wardrobe rested against the wall opposite the sofa. A trunk of the same wood was pushed against the wall on the side of the door, on the other side of which was a small table with an ornate old mirror over it, bisected almost symmetrically by a horizontal crack.

Opening the wardrobe, I found two pieces of antique women's clothing, not unlike those Mary and I had found in the attic. Both were dresses: one fluttery and white, the other of red silk shot through with gold. I looked at each dress carefully but did not touch them. I knew well enough where I had seen them before, and something in me balked at the idea of their immediate tangibility.

I shut the wardrobe and moved to the balcony door. It was unlocked. From the balcony, it seemed as though I could see forever. Eden's house was almost hidden by the trees, its driveway snaking through them toward the main road like a lifeline. Eventually the main road connected with the village of Eden: a huddled cluster of doll houses in the pristine expanse of jungle and swamp. To the north, a dingy smudge on the horizon marked Baton Rouge.

I could no longer ignore the angle of the sun. Alexander and Tasha would have arrived long ago, and I would be missed soon, if I wasn't already. I closed the glass door behind me. Perhaps the discovery of the room ought to have enticed even greater curiosity, but it had the opposite effect. For the moment the house had released its hold on me, and I grasped the chance to escape.

Before I left, I meant to replace the key I had taken from the ground-floor entrance to the stair. I refused to believe that the room could be inhabited any more than the rest of the house was, yet I was still superstitious enough to want to leave everything as it had been. I fished around in my pocket for the key but could not find it.

In an instant, mild annoyance solidified into horror. I stood benumbed, listening with every nerve in my body, because I had just heard what I could not have heard—and then I heard it again, too clearly to be denied. A faint strain of piano music twisted up from somewhere below. It was a Chopin ballade. It was the Chopin ballade I had played not an hour before.

The blood pounded in my ears. Don't panic, don't panic, I kept repeating to myself. I emptied my mind, thinking of nothing but those words, repeating them over and over until they had no meaning anymore save to block other thoughts. If I allowed myself to consider what was happening, I knew that fear would paralyze me.

I let myself out of the tower room, fighting hysteria all the while, and raced down the stairs. There seemed to be so many more now than there had been before, the stairway so much more confined. My heart beat in my throat as the minnows in the lake's shallows would beat against my toes when I stepped into their school. I reached for the doorknob, and panic turned to terror. The door was locked.

I was beyond wondering how this was possible. I tore the keys from my pocket, and was shuffling through them, trying to remember which one fitted the door, when I heard footsteps, still far away but moving in my direction. I turned from the door in front of me to the stairway, unable to decide which was the better choice. Then some still-rational part of my mind told me what I must have known all along: whoever used the tower room must have some other way of entering and exiting the stairwell. There was no other way that it could have been locked from the inside.

And so I saw what I might never otherwise have seen. In the shadow of the staircase, to its right, was a small door. It led to a narrow compartment with two more doors. One led downward into darkness. The other could only lead outside, but it, too, was locked. I remembered the keys then, opened my hand, and looked down: I had clutched them so hard that beads of blood sprang up on my palm and fingers.

My hands shook so much that I could hardly place the key in the lock. I tried every one, and none of them fit. The footsteps were closer now, and unmistakable. In one last, desperate effort, I threw all of my weight against the door. It sprang open, disgorging me into bright sunlight and a wave of sodden heat. Wrenching the keys free, I slammed the door shut, then ran to the shelter of the woods, where I slumped down against a tree, blinded by the brightness and sobbing for breath.

7

When I had collected myself again, I found an overgrown drive and followed it down the hill. Eventually it connected with Eden's own drive, and I was home in an hour.

I sat in the dim cool of the kitchen, trying to make sense of what I had seen and heard. It seemed unlikely that the house's tenant was a wanderer. She—I had decided the resident must be female, judging from the contents of the bedroom—could be deranged, but she could not be poor or uncultured. At any rate, she could not always have been: her playing was too accomplished for that.

Of course, the most obvious answer was that I had discovered the whereabouts of my mother's missing twin. Yet if Eve was alive and in Eden, I didn't see how she could have escaped everyone's notice for so long. More than that, if she had hidden from me all these months, it made no sense that she would then bid for my attention, particularly in so mawkish a manner.

The key ring from the library was still in my pocket. I pulled it out and lay it on the table in front of me. The keys were old and rusty, each more or less like the other, except for a small one which looked more like the key to a chest or cupboard than to a door. Something about this last key struck an ominous chord in me, though I was quite certain that I hadn't seen anything like it before. Like everything else about the house on the hill, it made no sense.

The fear I thought I had left behind began to return. I knew that I had to confide in someone before it took hold. It was past four, and the Trevozhovs were to have arrived by two. The house was clearly deserted, and I was about to go look in the cottage when I found Mary's note on the piano's music stand.

2:00

Eleanor, I looked for you, but you're nowhere to be found! The Trevozhovs were late coming in to Baton Rouge, and the car they'd called never came. I've gone with Jean-Paul to get them. We shouldn't be longer than three hours.

Mary

I went to stand by the long windows that looked over the lake. No wind stirred, no sound broke the insects' drone. Between the cypress' fluted columns, the water looked thick and smooth as mercury. I lay down on one of the couches facing the windows, gazing out at the drowsing afternoon. I only meant to rest for a while, then perhaps to practice, but within minutes I was asleep.

A full moon hung low on the horizon, its pallid light pouring through the open ballroom doors. The air was warm and still, saturated with the smell of roses and honeysuckle.

In the shadows, the fabric of my dress was the color of blood. Its heavy skirt crackled and dragged as I walked toward the piano in the centre of the room, sat down, and began to play. What emerged was a soft, dark melody that my ear didn't recognize, though my fingers knew it well, as if I'd played it all my life. It was lyrical and repetitive—nearly, though not quite, a set of variations over a basso continuo. In its lack of resolution, its superficial regret, it was not unlike the ballade's first theme. Yet this unnamed music reached deeper, calling up real, raw sadness and longing.

When it ended, I looked up. Alexander stood beside the piano. Everything about him was dark, except for his face, which was luminous as the moon. He smiled at me, then held out his hand. Standing up, I accepted it. It was surprisingly warm, seeping heat into my own cold fingers.

We stepped outside, into a small rose garden with a fountain at its centre. Water spilled from level to level, drops distinct as ice chips falling through the languid air. I wanted to isolate each facet, yet couldn't focus on any of them, and Alexander was urging me on, toward the ivy-covered wall at the far side of the garden. He let go of my hand and, reaching around my neck, pulled something over my head. It was a small silver key on a fine silver chain. He lifted the curtain of ivy to reveal a door in the wall underneath, which he unlocked with the key.

Beyond the door was another garden, circumscribed half by the wall, half by a high hedge, with a break at the far side marking the beginning of a path. Behind the hedge stood a row of trees, black and blue in the shadow and moonlight. The garden's only tree, standing at its centre, had the weeping branches of a willow and slick, dark, heart-shaped leaves interspersed with tiny pink flowers that smelled faintly of lemons. Beneath the tree stood a statue of a boy playing a flute. Except for his whiteness, he was not like a statue at all; he seemed a real child, caught out of time on the verge of a gesture. At his feet was a pool dotted with water lilies.

The heavens blazed with more stars than I had ever seen,

so many that the sky was ultramarine, like the firmament in a Renaissance fresco, reflecting in the pool by the statue's feet. Alexander knelt by the lily pond and cleared a space among the blossoms. As I looked into it, the stars began to change their configurations, spinning and zigzagging until I could not watch them anymore. When they stilled, they had arranged themselves on the dark mirror into two faces, which looked up at us like a distorted reflection.

I recognized the one beneath me at once: she was pale, with onyx eyes and a passionate look that distinguished it from the other so like it. The reflection beneath Alexander was like him as well, but for the fair coloring and the expression on his face. Yet something was wrong with the images. Eve looked sad and defeated, the man beside her bitter and calculating.

As I watched, Eve's eyes filled with tears, though her face remained inert. Then my own vision blurred, and suddenly I was crying too, weeping bitterly for something I could not name. Eve moved her hands to her throat, removed the ruby that hung there, and held it toward me. I reached into the water. As my hand closed around the hard little object, Eve's image faded, and the lilies moved back in to cover the space Alexander had cleared.

I held the jewel up to the moonlight. It glinted in shades of heliotrope and plum. The prism fractured Alexander's face like the Braque or Picasso of my childhood, sad and schismatic and, somehow, accurate. When I lowered the jewel I found him looking intently at me. He said, "Remember."

The moon was low now on the horizon, its chalky light fading fast. The stars held my eyes magnetically. They began to spin again, but this time I could not look away. The sky turned faster, so fast that the dark and the moon and the scatter of stars became a single blur. They were something terrible, something from which I knew that I must run and also that I could not. I felt the cold of complete and inexplicable terror.

I reached for Alexander, but he was gone. The sky had gone black. I began to fall, tried to scream, but I had no voice. I caught a flickering image of two figures standing together under what looked like a tree circled by a ring of light, holding something between them. Then they were lost in the darkness, and far away but clear, I heard the unmistakable wails of a broken-hearted woman.

I sat up gasping. For a moment I didn't remember where I was. Then I saw the piano in the corner and realized that I had fallen asleep in the music room. From the slant of the sun through the window, I knew that I had slept at least a couple of hours. My head pounded viciously, and every muscle in my body ached. I felt wretched, confused, and frightened. I was aware that I had dreamed, that it had been a nightmare, but what little I could remember flitted in and out of my muddled consciousness in unrelated fragments.

My right hand ached dully; it was clenched shut. When I opened it, the diamond that had been my mother's, the one I always wore, fell into my lap. I could not remember having removed it, but I was certain that it had been a part of my dream.

I rubbed my eyes and aching forehead. I knew that I was supposed to remember the dream, and the fact that I could not was infuriating. Alexander had been part of it, though I couldn't think how. There had been a piece of music—neither a nocturne nor a serenade, but like both—and a boy playing a flute. A rose garden, water in the moonlight, two faces I couldn't quite recall...I gave up. I fastened the diamond again around my neck, then went to find Mary.

The front hall was silent. I called for her, and then Colette, but no one answered. The hands of the grandfather clock stood at half past six; the silence between its ticks stretched thin. For a moment my eyes fixed on the paper on the wall behind the clock: a strident red Nouveau affair of vines and roses I had always found rather garish, and not at all in keeping with Eden's otherwise faded palette. It, too, seemed for a moment to remind me of the dream; but the feeling slipped away again as quickly.

I turned away and continued down the corridor, looking into the series of empty rooms until I reached the library. There, finally, I heard Mary's voice behind the closed door. She sat inside at the long table with Alexander and Tasha, an array of books spread before them.

"Eleanor!" she cried. "I was beginning to wonder whether you would sleep forever."

"Why didn't you wake me?"

"I thought that you must be tired, to sleep in the middle of the day. Did you go for a walk this morning?"

"A bit of one." I tried to smile, but Alexander fixed me with a penetrating look, and it faltered.

"I've just been acquainting Alexander and Tasha with the library," Mary said. "Jean-Pierre and a couple of the others are moving the Trevozhovs' things to the cottage."

"I wanted to help them," said Alexander, "but Mary wouldn't hear of it."

"She certainly shouldn't have," I said. "I hope that we can also convince you to stay to dinner. You can't be ready to cook at the cottage yet."

"I asked them already," Mary retorted.

"And they accepted, I hope."

Alexander smiled. "It didn't take much convincing."

"We usually eat at eight," Mary said. "That leaves time for Eleanor to give you a tour of the closer gardens, if you like. The rose garden is as old as the house, apparently."

"I'd love to see it," Alexander replied, so sincerely that I couldn't bring myself to decline.

When I turned, his eyes lingered below my face for a moment. I felt self-consciously for the necklace I had just put on. Simultaneously I remembered the beginning of the dream: Alexander had stood by the piano in the house on the hill, looking at me as intently as he did now. Then he had led me to a garden, where a child played a flute by a mirror. After that, the images became confused again.

"Eleanor?" I heard Mary say tentatively.

I looked at her for a moment and then smiled. "I'm sorry, I was daydreaming. Well—would Tasha like to come to the gardens, too?"

"Perhaps Tasha would be more interested in your mother's old doll house," Mary said.

"Which will it be, love?" Alexander asked her.

"I'd like to see the doll house, please," she answered, with a visible glow of excitement. Mary held out her hand, and the little girl took it readily.

"We'll be back in an hour," I told them, and Mary waved us on our way.

Alone in the hallway with Alexander, I was suddenly shy. "I'm sorry if Mary seems forward," I said, carefully avoiding his eyes. "She'd like to see me married off, I think..." I trailed off, realizing how coarse I sounded.

"Oh?" Alexander replied, obviously amused.

I blushed. "I didn't mean that as it must have sounded."

He had begun to smile. "Of course not."

I cursed myself and quickly changed the subject. "Actually,

I'm glad of the chance to talk to you."

"Tell me what happened."

I looked at him. "How do you know something happened?"

"You must stop jumping at your own shadow, Eleanor. I am not psychic, if that's what you're wondering. I am not even especially talented at guessing. But when you walked in here a moment ago, you looked as if you'd just seen a ghost. You still do. What happened to frighten you?"

Once again I found that I could not meet his eyes. "Let's not discuss this here," I said. I turned and began to walk. He followed me to the end of the corridor and out the open doors of the solarium, into the most expansive of the rose gardens.

"You won't believe me," I said as we strolled through the arbor of white climbing roses that ran along one side of the garden.

"How do you know that?"

"Because if the roles were reversed, I wouldn't believe me. I wouldn't believe it now if I could think of any way to talk myself out of it. But it's hard not to believe something you've seen. Heard, I should say."

"So where did you see this ghost, Eleanor?" Though he smiled, I could not tell whether it was in encouragement or derision.

"I haven't seen a ghost," I began, wondering how to explain something to him that I could not begin to explain to myself. "Or if it is a ghost, I haven't seen it, only heard it. Her, rather. I'm not making sense, am I?"

The more I tried to explain myself, the younger and less coherent I felt. He must have seen or sensed a bit of this, because he said gently, in the tone I had heard him use with Tasha, "Why don't you start from the beginning?" At that moment I wanted nothing more than to turn back to the house and leave him there with his condescension; at the same time I realized that I had come too far now to turn back.

We stepped out of the arbor, onto the pebbled path that circled a fountain at the farthest end of the garden. The basin was white marble, its sides low and wide for sitting. The falling water had dampened the seat; Alexander took off his jacket and spread it out, gesturing for me to sit down. I looked at him in surprise. The beginnings of a smile played around his mouth and eyes, and there was nothing in it of the mockery I thought I had heard a moment before. I smiled back, and his own widened. Another shadow of the dream flickered mothlike across the boundary between conscious and subconscious, and I felt something far from fear twist a knot in my stomach.

I sat down. "I don't know when the beginning was," I said, aware that I was speaking too quickly and without thought, in the panicked urge to hide Alexander's effect on me. I lowered my gaze to my hands, took a breath, and forced myself to concentrate on answering the question he had put to me. "Maybe it was the first time I saw Eden's Meadow, or the house on the hill. Maybe it began the morning I met you. But there's something telling me that none of this is a surprise, that I've known it…well, all of my life." I finally looked at him, but he was looking intently at the water's broken surface, his face unreadable as stone. "Do you understand?" I asked hesitantly.

"I think I'm beginning to."

His expression had not changed; I tried not to think too much about the portent of his words. "I suppose what you want to know is the immediate beginning," I said. "That was this morning, when I decided to go and see the house on the hill."

He looked at me quickly. "You went up there? Alone?"

I couldn't tell whether or not the words were meant as a reproof. "I had to know," I said defensively.

"So, you did find a ghost?"

I smiled feebly, wishing that I could read him even half as easily as I had been able to read the young men I knew in Boston.

"A lunatic, maybe. Even if she's that, though, I don't think she's particularly dangerous. Possibly tragic. What kind of madwoman would she be if she wasn't?" Alexander smiled back, but it faded quickly, leaving his face sad and myself inexplicably anxious. "I have a feeling she may have something to do with my aunt, Eve. My mother's twin."

This time his tone was openly incredulous. "Eve, of Eden's Meadow?"

"Granted, it's a bit theatrical."

"Not necessarily," he said. "Perhaps only religious."

"Mary tells me my grandmother was religious."

"You didn't know her?"

"She died the year I was born, and by that point my mother had left her family."

He paused before he continued. "What makes you think that your aunt is connected with that house?"

I plunged into the story of how I had learned of Eve's existence, the troubled relationship between my mother and grandfather, my grandfather's comments to Mary concerning the house. I described the house on the hill, the pristine tower room, the piano that had made me play forgotten music and then seemingly played by itself. Finally I told him about the footsteps I'd heard in the hallway and the hair's-breadth escape from my phantom.

When I finished, Alexander looked at me intently. This time

his eyes moved quite clearly over the diamond at my throat.

"Are you certain that you're not simply being visited by a tramp?"

"It seems unlikely," I answered, thankful for something to say. "First of all, the tower room was meticulously neat. Not a tramp's room, as far as I have the authority to say. Clearly, she knew where all the keys were kept. And she played the piano too well."

"Tramps come from all walks of life, and anyone could happen upon a key ring or a hidden door. It doesn't mean that the person in the house today was your missing aunt."

I looked at him, and he looked back at me. Nothing in his expression belied suspicion, but I sensed that he was waiting for me to tell him something more. I watched the spread of ripples on the pool's surface where drops fell from the fountain. All was still but for that falling water.

Again the dark moths stirred, fragments of the dream trying to settle into place. Then, all at once and without apparent impetus, it flooded back. The sneaking shiver began to creep up my spine. Like the twist in my stomach when Alexander smiled, it was rapidly becoming a sensation that was both familiar and unnerving.

"I know it's no coincidence," I finally said, clutching the rim of the fountain for courage, "because of the dreams."

"Dreams," he repeated, with the slightest catch in his voice.

"I've always had them."

"What do you mean?"

I looked at him to try to judge whether he asked the question with interest or scorn, but his eyes were on the water, and as opaque. "I dream of Eve. I've dreamed of her ever since I was a child. Ever since I can remember. Until a few days ago, when I saw the painting in your cottage, I thought that she was a confusion of my mother, who died when I was very small. I dreamed of Eve the night my grandfather died. The night I first saw you."

"Have you..." Alexander began warily, then paused. "Have you dreamed of her since then?"

I shook my head. "That was the last time. It was strange, because I hadn't dreamed of her since I went away to school, but I used to quite a lot." I paused again, searching for the words to explain it to him. "She warned me sometimes. About things...dangers...before they happened." Alexander was watching me steadily. "Once there was a boat," I blundered on. "My grandfather and I had been traveling in Europe and were on our way home from England. The night before we planned to leave, she told me not to go, because...Alexander, do you know of the Titanic?"

"Of course I do," he answered, looking at me in disbelief. "You mean you were meant to be on it?"

I nodded. "I still can't believe I managed to convince my grandfather to give up those tickets. Another time something similar happened with a train."

His eyes remained calm. "Are you saying that you have a guardian angel?"

I shrugged uncomfortably. "Then I had a different dream," I continued, determined now that he should know all that I knew myself, "different, but in the same vein. Just this afternoon, after I came back from the house, I fell asleep...as you know." I paused, looking again at his scattered reflection. "I dreamed I was in the house on the hill, in the ballroom—I mean, the room where the piano is. It was night-time, and there was a full moon. I began to play the piano, a piece I knew well in the dream, but nothing I've ever heard before. At least, I don't think I have. When the song ended I looked up, and you were standing there, by the piano. You were...you looked like..." I stumbled, looked at him, and knew that if he were telling this story, he would speak the truth.

"You were beautiful," I finished softly. My eyes did not move from his, but it was an incredible effort. His expression was unchanged. I drew a deep breath. "You looked like...like something not real. At first I didn't think that you were real, but then you smiled and held out your hand, and we walked out of the ballroom and into a garden. There was a fountain in the garden, and roses, and a wall with ivy. We walked to a door in the wall, and you took a key from around my neck and opened it.

"Inside was another garden. There was a statue, and a tree with pink flowers. I remember looking at the stars. They were so bright, and the statue looked so real, I thought that in a moment he would move...but that's ridiculous, I know." I laughed hollowly. "Then you made me look into a pool of water at the statue's feet, and there were two faces there, Eve's and a man's. He looked a bit like you, but he was fair." I shook my head, willing the spinning images to settle. "They were terrible. Terrible and...familiar." I paused for a moment, uncertain of the implications of the word I had unwittingly spoken. "Then Eve handed me her necklace, which was like this, only a ruby"—I touched the diamond—"and you said, 'Remember.'"

"Remember?" he repeated.

"Yes."

Alexander was watching me incredulously again, with the ambiguous half-smile I was coming to recognize as a characteristic.

"Is that all?" he asked.

"Isn't that enough?"

He looked down again, dropping a white stone from the path into the dark water of the pool. Concentric circles spread out from the place where it had fallen.

"You forgot a few things," he said. My eyes snapped upward. "In the first part of the dream, you were wearing a long red dress with a lighter pattern on it. Your feet were bare. The piece you played is a real one, though it's no wonder you didn't know it—it's mine, and it's unpublished. The key you had was silver, on a silver chain. And the faces in the pool were terrible because they were broken, and they were so much like our own."

I stared at him for a few moments, my thoughts and feelings an inextricable tangle. Most powerful, though, was the return of the chilling fear he alone seemed capable of inducing in me. Finally I managed to ask, "Are you psychic, then?"

He shrugged. "Not that I know of. But I must tell you that I have had the same dream." He spoke the words unemotionally; there was no hint of humor in his face. I waited for him to laugh, to somehow retract the impossible words he had just spoken.

When I finally accepted that he wouldn't, I could only think to ask, "What does it mean?"

"I wish I knew." He looked at me, and in that moment something shifted. His eyes, unguarded for the first time since I had met him, told me that he was as bewildered as I was, and this went farther than any words in bridging the oddly turgid gap between us. What I had taken for the mild contempt of an older man for a young girl was apparently his way of guarding some far deeper feeling that had nothing to do with me.

He sighed. "I suppose it's my turn to be honest," he said hesitantly, as though finding the right words to speak his mind in a foreign tongue was a greater struggle than he had anticipated; yet I also wondered if it was the subject matter rather than the language that frustrated him.

"The first time I had that dream," he continued, "I didn't know that you existed, but it was as if I'd known you all my life. In my dream, there was light all around you. I had different dreams of you, none so clear as that one, but the one element that carried through was the light: there was always a glow around you, sometimes faint, sometimes too bright to look at. I didn't know why until I learned your name. In its Greek origins, 'Eleanor' means 'light.'"

He paused for a moment, then continued in a less ruminative tone. "You can imagine how I felt when I saw you that night at the symphony. Yes, I did see you. It was only for a moment, as you were leaving, but I cannot express to you what it was like to see you standing there looking at me, to know that you were real. Then, when I came here and found you as well as that house, it was like coming back to something I'd once known well. In a way, I did already know you, as I knew the house, from the dreams. But you must understand that I was also afraid."

"Of what?" I asked.

"Not of you, Eleanor; only of the fact that you are real. Because if you are real, then that means the other one is, too."

"What 'other one'?"

The muscles around his mouth had tightened, making it look almost cruel. "Have you dreamed other dreams of that man? The one with Eve in the pool?"

"Why?" I asked softly.

I was surprised by the supplication in Alexander's eyes when he looked at me. "Is he someone you know?"

"No."

He paused, his jaw tightening again, then asked, "Did your aunt have a lover?"

The question took me aback, more because of its abruptness than because of its nature. "Not that I know of," I answered after a pause. "Unless you count a boy she admired when she was sixteen—a relative of the family at another plantation. Anyhow, I'd more easily believe she hated the man in the dream, if that's what you're getting at."

"What makes you think that the face in the dream was Eve's? Couldn't it as easily have been your mother's?"

I shrugged. "I suppose I assumed it was Eve's, because I've always dreamed of Eve and never of my mother."

"I also have seen the painting, Eleanor." He paused, again appearing to choose his words with difficulty. "It strikes me that Elizabeth would have been the more sensible of the two. But love and hatred are sometimes inseparable. They can certainly cause equal misery."

The reserve was gone from his face. In its place was a brooding kind of anxiety. I looked down with him at the surface of the pool, and our shimmering reflections looked back.

"Do you believe that she's alive?" I asked.

"I suppose it's easier to believe that she's alive than that she's a ghost. Anyway, it will be easy enough to find out." He turned away, his mouth grim. Yet when he looked back at me, he was smiling. "The first time I had that dream," he said, "I was depressed for days afterward. I thought you were a figment of my imagination."

"You wanted me to be real, then?"

"There was something in your face, in your eyes...a depth and an honesty that seemed so unusual. And then there was the light. But I think that most of all it was the fear: something like what you were describing earlier. I had to help you find something so that you could stop some other, terrible thing from happening."

"But what? And how?"

"Frankly, I'm more interested in why this is happening. Or is there a reason at all?"

"So you're a philosopher."

He smiled. "I've been accused of it." Alexander shook his head. "Anyhow, I don't know any more than you do, but I think that the answers to at least some of your questions are to be found up in that house on the hill."

I shivered in a sudden brush of wind. The sun had set, and twilight was deepening around us. Finally Alexander stood up and offered me his hand.

"Come, now," he said. "It won't do to worry over it. If you want to find out who is in that house, you can do so easily enough. But the choice is still yours. Some secrets, Eleanor Rose, are better left as such."

It's true: the choice lay before me then, still uncomplicated. To this day I wonder what my life might have been had I chosen differently.

I looked at him. His face was full of resignation, but I had never believed in fate. I shivered again, and stood up quickly to receive the hand he offered, which closed tightly about mine for a moment, as warm and alive as I had dreamed it. It made me realize how cold I had grown, despite the heat. Then convention intervened, and Alexander let my hand go, offering me his arm instead, and together we walked back toward Eden.

8

Mary and Tasha were upstairs playing with the doll house when we returned.

"There you are!" Mary said.

"We thought you'd never come back," Tasha added.

"What time is it?" I asked.

"A bit past eight," said Alexander, looking at his watch. "I'm sorry...we lost track of time."

Mary waved away our apologies. "Come downstairs and eat before it all gets cold." We moved into the dining room and sat down at the great mahogany table, which had not hosted so many people in years.

Over dinner, Alexander related some of his story to us. His family had been well-to-do before the revolution. Like most White Russians at that time, they were hounded continually by the Bolshevik government, and when one night their house was torched, burning the family in their beds, no one was surprised.

Alexander and Natalya had been out that night at the ballet. They remained in the country only long enough for Alexander to clean out one of the family's bank accounts and buy black-market visas for France and transportation to Poland, where their long journey to the west began. They had arrived in

America a little over a year ago, after nearly two years of a transitory existence in western Europe.

"It must have been awful," Mary said softly, "especially for the little girl. To see her home and family destroyed that way; to leave everything familiar behind."

We all looked at Tasha. She sat happily oblivious to the topic of conversation, stirring a melting pool of ice cream around the bottom of her dish.

"I suppose," Alexander said, "it wasn't so bad as it could have been. She was barely four when we left. She won't remember much."

"But the poor child, her mother—"

"It wasn't as you imagine," he interrupted sharply. Seeing Mary's surprise, he quickly said, "Forgive me. It is only…it is not a simple story." He paused, composing himself, then said, "Natalya's father was my older brother. In middle age he married a beautiful young woman, who I'm afraid had little else to offer in the way of redeeming qualities." His face had hardened as he spoke. "Anya was a silly, social girl, only a few years out of school. Natalya was her only child, and she died in childbirth, leaving my brother to despair and Tasha to the care of nursemaids."

He paused again, looking at the child. She stared into the dish of melted ice cream, her lips slightly parted. "Why don't you go play with the doll house again, Tasha?" he told her gently.

"All right," she agreed. She slid down from her chair.

"Do you remember which room it is?" I asked.

"At the top of the stairs, to the right."

Mary smiled at her, and Tasha disappeared.

"She shouldn't hear these things," Alexander said, not looking at us. Then he continued, "No one ever imagined she would live to see her first birthday. The poor child was skinny and sickly, and she went unloved and unwanted through that first year of her life. Her father wouldn't look at her, thinking that she'd killed her mother. Our only other family were my politically crazed younger brother and a blind great-aunt who was acrimonious enough in her own right.

"I was playing in public a great deal at that point and was rarely at home. I had cares far more important to me than a sickly little niece. Then one day I overheard Tasha's doctors speaking together. One of them said to the other that he was going to advise my brother to put her into an asylum, since she would probably not live long, and if she did, she was certain to grow up slow or deformed. The doctor's words seemed particularly cruel to me. I went directly to the nursery to see if they were true." He smiled. "I found a perfectly normal child, if a little undersized. She was sufficiently well looked after, but her face was sour and pinched. She wailed when I picked her up, and kicked her legs as if she would have been happier to have me drop her. By then I pitied her. I carried her out of the nursery, ignoring the doctors and nursemaids who said it would only make her ill again. I took her to the only place I knew of that might help her, because it had so often helped me."

"The music room!" I said.

Alexander nodded. "I recall that she was still shrieking when I set her down on the carpet and began to play. Beethoven." He laughed. "I thought the music of that troubled soul must catch her attention, and it did. She stopped crying and her face smoothed out maybe for the first time in her life, and I saw that in fact she was a very pretty child. After that day I never let her out of my sight. I had her nursery moved to a room next to mine, and I took her with me whenever I went out, no matter where I was going. I suppose it was a strange life for a child, maybe not the most suitable. But, you see, she had come to think of me as her father even before she lost her own. Sometimes I wonder whether she even remembers that she once had one."

"Neither you nor Tasha has anything in the world to call your own but each other," Mary mused.

Alexander looked up at her, shaking his head. "It may have been like that once, but we're well on our way to having a life in this country—a life as rooted as our last. You must not feel sorry for us." He smiled. "We're far from being lost souls."

"Oh, no, that's very clear." Mary smiled back. We sat in silence, sipping the last of our coffee. Then she said, "Alexander, won't you play for us?"

"Oh, please do!" I agreed.

He looked at me. "I'll play if you will. After all, you have heard me, but I have only heard about you."

I shrugged. "That sounds fair."

We called Tasha downstairs again and moved to the music room, where one of the maids had already lit the lamps. Alexander conceded to play first: Schubert, on Mary's request. He played the first of the second set of impromptus, and the fourth of the "Moments Musicaux", so beautifully that for the first time in my life I was afraid to take the bench.

"I don't know what to play," I said, realizing even as I said it how silly I sounded.

"You said you were working on Chopin's études," Alexander suggested.

"Oh, no!"

"Well, then, play your favorite piece."

I thought for a moment, then smiled. I began to play, and everybody else smiled with me.

"'Children's Corner'!" cried Tasha when I'd finished the first, clapping her hands in excitement. "Oh, play the rest!"

When I was finished, everybody clapped, and then Alexander said, "Come, won't you play one of the études for us?"

I sighed, fingering the keys. "Which one?"

"The fourth of opus ten?"

"I don't think I'll ever be able to play that one very well!"

"Well then, I've always liked the last of opus twenty-five."

I played it, though I was painfully aware of its flaws.

"Lovely," said Mary.

"Not as lovely as it ought to be, I'm afraid."

Alexander only looked at me thoughtfully.

"You've said you compose," I said quickly, before he could request anything else.

"A little, on the side," he said, but his quick glance told me he knew exactly what I was getting at.

"Oh, do play one of your pieces for us!" Mary said, before I had to.

He stood up with a sigh and took the bench, and before I had time to wonder, he was playing the piece from my dream. I found it no easier to classify than I had previously. It had the rippling quality of an étude, the repetition and variation of a nocturne, the fluidity and nostalgia of a serenade. Mary's eyes went dreamy; Tasha watched Alexander with quiet composure. Several of the maids crowded in the doorway to listen. My own thoughts wandered a spectrum from études to abandoned houses, and I was hardly aware that Alexander had finished playing until Mary's entreaty for another piece cut through the silence.

"Why not play the ballade? The Opus 23?"

Alexander and I looked up at her simultaneously. He smiled, but not quickly enough to hide the sadness. I watched Tasha absorb that look in her silent, incisive way, and I knew why Mary had said that she was not a child.

"Forgive me if I postpone your request," Alexander said, smiling at Mary as he rose from the bench. "The ballade requires more concentration than I am capable of tonight."

"No, forgive me," Mary answered. "I'd forgotten how far you both have traveled today! You must be exhausted, and we've kept you too long."

"No, no, it's been a pleasure. But you, Natashenka"—his look arrested Tasha in the middle of a yawn—"should be in bed. Say good night to Mrs. Bishop and Miss Rose."

The little girl thanked us obediently, then stretched out her arms. As Alexander lifted her up, she asked, "Will we come back?"

"You're welcome any time," I said. "Both of you."

"Thank you again for dinner. You've been so very kind."

"It's you who've done us the kindness," Mary insisted.

"It's far too late to begin a battle of civilities," I interrupted. "Come, I'll see you to the door."

"Better see them to the path home," said Mary. "It wouldn't do to lose them in the woods on their first night!"

I led them through the kitchen and grape arbor to the top of the topiary garden. By the time we reached the steps where we had first spoken, Tasha was asleep on Alexander's shoulder.

"Will you be all right from here?" I asked.

"Of course," he said. "It's just a short walk, and the moon is bright. The ghosts won't be walking yet." He smiled. "Thank Mary for her kindness to Tasha."

"I think she might be just what Mary needs."

"And likewise. People always need the company of others."

I nodded, and wished for once that I had the subtlety to avert my eyes, or at least to blush. Instead I looked at him steadily. He reached out and took my hand.

"Don't worry, Eleanor," he said. "All of it has an explanation."

"I won't. I'll try not to, anyway."

"I suppose that's all anyone can ask. Good night, then. I wish you pleasant dreams."

He lifted my fingers to his lips and then let go of my hand, disappearing into the shadows of the topiary garden. In his absence, the darkness had the vast silence and desolation of an empty cathedral. I looked toward the house on the hill, where all was black and still, and shivered despite the heavy warmth of the air. Turning my back on it, I retreated to the light of Eden's Meadow.

It's odd to recall that Eden was still a haven then.

9

Many consider Chopin's ballades the most beautiful of his compositions; certainly they are among the most varied and musically intricate. Until the night I heard Alexander play the G minor ballade at Symphony Hall, I had never thought much of them, nor of Chopin, for that matter. When I was a young girl, he seemed hackneyed to me. My grandfather called me hopeless when he heard this opinion, and Mary looked at me with pity. Despite them, I could not be swayed from the mathematical intricacies of Bach, the thundering passion of Beethoven.

After I heard Alexander play Chopin that night at the symphony, I began to discern the quality in the music that had such a hold on most people. I thought about the ballade a good deal after that. In the days following my exploration of the house on the hill, it began to occupy my thoughts obsessively.

A ballade is by definition a story told in music, and despite the fancy of it, I could not stop thinking that this particular ballade's story must hold some clue to the strange occurrences of the past few days. Since Chopin never recorded the stories in words, I hunted down my old copy of the score and attacked it, dissecting it measure by measure for whatever meaning I could construe.

Typical of Chopin, its first theme carries on for pages at

either end, haunting, illusive, and dark even for him. What captivated me about this theme now was the same quality that had originally irritated me: it is really nothing more than a phrase that keeps repeating until the second theme moves in to replace it. The more I played over the first few pages of the piece, the more this disturbed me. Chopin couldn't resist a heart-wrenching melody, and he generally ended such passages with a final twist of the knife, particularly in major works. The more I thought about it, the more the ballade's major theme seemed to miscarry rather than move toward any kind of conclusion. After an hour I shut the book in frustration and looked up to see Mary standing in the doorway.

"You know you can come in," I said, more shortly than was necessary.

She moved in a trail of rose-colored gauze toward one of the couches. "It was so lovely, I didn't want to disturb you."

I fingered the right-hand melody absently, stealing glances at the bruised sky over the lake. Overcast days had always vexed me; in Louisiana, accompanied by humidity and heat, they were practically unbearable. "You wouldn't have disturbed me. I'm disturbed enough as it is." I stood up, pulled the cover over the keys, and went to sit beside her.

Mary smiled. "A bit more difficult than you remembered?"

I looked away from the leaden scenery, back at her myopic eyes. "What makes everybody love it? Don't you hear the sickness in it? He couldn't even finish that phrase, he just kept repeating it until he had to go on to something else."

"Eleanor, what's really troubling you?"

"That theme!" I got up and began to pace the perimeter of the worn oriental carpet. "It's infuriating!"

"I'd never thought of it quite in that light," Mary said slowly, "but I can see how it might strike you that way."

"But not me," I said, stopping in front of her. "It never used to strike me at all, yet now it sickens me. And most people seem to love it. You love it—how come? What makes you want to hear it over and over again?"

Now it was Mary's turn to look at the brooding lake. "Maybe the same thing that bothers you: that it never answers the questions it raises. Such mystery can't help but intrigue. I think quite a bit of Chopin is like that."

"But not in the same way." I turned away again, this time dejectedly, and resumed pacing. "He never leaves anything hanging in quite the same way. It's as if he wanted his unanswered questions to drive people out of their minds."

Mary raised her eyebrows but didn't turn her face from the window. "Perhaps it was his way of keeping his own." She reached out as I passed by her, gently caught my hand, and guided me to the couch. I sat down next to her.

"What do you think it's about?" I asked.

She pressed her lips together, studying the grey and green landscape framed by the windows, and finally answered, "I've always thought that it's about two lovers, one of whom dies."

The succinctness of this answer left me at a loss for words. The two of us kept our silence for a time, watching a landscape we weren't really seeing. After a moment I shook my head, looked back at Mary, and only then saw that she had two letters in her hand.

"What are those?"

She looked down at the envelopes. "I'd forgotten about them. They came for you this morning." I took them from her. One envelope was institutional manila, the other of heavy, pale blue paper. My name and address were written on this second in a small, neat hand.

I opened the manila one first. Inside was a short letter from

Dr. Brown. Its news was disappointing. He had written to Dr. Dunham in New Orleans, and though Dunham had answered his letter promptly, he had refused to give Brown access to the files. Brown concluded by saying there was little hope that a direct petition from me would be any more effective.

"What is it?" Mary asked.

I had never told her about that visit to Eden village. Now that I had reached a dead end, there seemed little point in explaining it all, and told her that it was bank correspondence.

I opened the blue envelope expecting another complication of my grandfather's scrambled estate, but what I found was entirely unexpected. I read it quickly once, then went back to the beginning and read it to Mary.

Dear Miss Rose,

My name is Dorian Ducoeur. My family originally comes from New York, but we are relations of the Ducoeurs of Joyous Garde, of whom you no doubt have heard. At one point I enjoyed an acquaintance with the family Fairfax, of which I am certain that you have heard—you are the daughter of one of the twins, Elizabeth or Eve, if I have figured correctly.

When I knew them, the Fairfaxes did not spend much time at Eden's Meadow—only summers, as I recall. My own family often traveled abroad during the summer holidays. As a result, our immediate families did not have much overlap on the plantations. However, I do retain certain vivid memories of the Fairfaxes from one childhood visit.

We met at an informal recital, featuring your grandmother Claudine's playing. When Claudine finished, someone called for her daughters to perform. They were children then, about my age. Elizabeth declined to play, being shy of the crowd, but Eve leaped up to the bench and plunged into the "Pathétique".

I was moved by her beauty and her talent. When she had finished the sonata and several encores, I went to congratulate her.

That was the beginning of our friendship. For the rest of that visit, the Fairfax twins were my playmates. Though I lost touch with them in subsequent years, I never forgot them. Sometimes I imagine it was Eve's playing that set me on my own career: I now teach at an English conservatory.

But please excuse my long-winded reminiscences. I return now to the object of my letter, which is to say that I am sorry to have fallen out of contact with your family, particularly as I have spent so much time in Boston of late, practically your neighbor. You can imagine my surprise when I saw you take the bench at Martha Kelly's November recital last year—excepting your fairness, the very image of the twins. Another engagement required my early departure from that recital, and I could not introduce myself to you as I had hoped.

As coincidence has it, the last owner of Joyous Garde, an elderly cousin, passed away several weeks ago. As none of the Louisiana Ducoeurs cares to take on the responsibility of such a large old estate, Joyous Garde has fallen to myself. I travel to Baton Rouge in a few days, to set the estate in order. Afterward I will come to the plantation, and if it would not trouble you overly much, I would dearly love to see Eden's Meadow again. Of course, it would also be a pleasure to meet you and renew my acquaintance with the family I have missed so long.

Yours sincerely,

Dorian Ducoeur

I looked at Mary. "It's barely believable."

"It is coincidental timing...but really, it would almost be

stranger not to meet someone here who knew the twins."

"But a Ducoeur!"

Mary picked up the pages, shuffled through them. "Well, indeed. Perhaps he knew the mysterious Louis. You ought to invite him for a chat. The letter's dated a week ago, he could be in Baton Rouge already."

I was still holding the envelope in my hand. I had been looking at it for several moments with the feeling that something was amiss. Now I realized what it was. "Mary—the letter wasn't posted."

I flipped the envelope to show it to her: the stamp wasn't cancelled. "No, it wasn't," she agreed, apparently unconcerned.

"But you say it came with the rest of the mail. It doesn't make sense."

"Maybe he meant to post it and forgot, and gave it to the mailman directly."

"Which would mean that he's at Joyous Garde now."

She shook her head, smiling. "Honestly, Eleanor, you're jumping at shadows these days! There are far fewer mysteries in the world than you imagine."

"Eden isn't the rest of the world."

"Well, Mr. Ducoeur isn't here to tell us how he sent the letter, so it's no use speculating."

I nodded, still looking at the pages in my hand with the vague feeling that I was missing something obvious in their contents.

"Well, then," said Mary, standing up, "I'll leave you to your practicing."

I shook my head. "I think I'll lie down for a while. My head aches."

“It’s the heat. Get something cold to drink before you go.”

I tried to smile. “All right. Ask Alexander and Tasha to tea, if you like.”

“Already done. They’ll be here at three-thirty. I’ll get you up at half past two, if that gives you enough time.”

“Plenty. Thank you, Mary.” I went upstairs, trying to ignore the heat pressing down under the lowering sky.

Once again I found myself in the ballroom of the house on the hill. Honey-colored sunlight poured in through the open French doors, stretched across the checkered floor. The twins, wearing their dresses from the portrait and flowers in their long, loose hair, danced an exaggerated waltz through the columns of light, to the music of the grand piano and their own happy laughter. The instrument stood at an angle against the wall of French doors that led to the rose garden, its open lid and long brocade scarf hiding the pianist, who played a waltz.

The twins turned in widening circles through the rich sunlight until finally they collapsed, panting, at the centre of the room. Elizabeth leaned back on her bare white arms, face to the sunlight and heavy lids drooping against it. Eve lay down with her head in her sister’s lap and began to disentangle the flowers from her hair. She pulled them out one by one, and their petals scattered across her bodice, the floor, her sister’s white skirt. The pianist played on, oblivious to the intimate beauty of the scene so close to him.

Then Eve disengaged a pink rosebud from a clump of curls, looked at it for a moment, and with a face suddenly serious she sat up and proffered it to her sister. The twins’ eyes met, and their faces all at once seemed older, their expressions more complex. As Elizabeth accepted the blossom, there was a sadness in her eyes that did not match the rest of the scene or the joyful impetuosity that had preceded it. Elizabeth held the rose for a moment, looking intently at Eve, and then, for no apparent reason, dropped it. It fell languidly, but when it finally touched the floor between the two girls, the sunlit ballroom vanished. It was replaced by the dark void that had ended my last dream of Eve. The same bitter wailing filled the darkness. It rose and crested, and then all was silence, leaving my ears ringing with its suddenness.

Softly, from far away, came a whispered word: "Remember."

10

When Mary shook me awake, it was after three.

"Are you all right, Eleanor? I tried to wake you earlier, but you were too soundly asleep."

I shook my head in an attempt to clear it. "I keep having such strange dreams."

"Of Eve?"

I looked at her, fear on the point of clamping down again, until I saw that she was smiling, undiscerning. I tried to smile back. "I suppose," I said. The doorbell rang, and then Tasha's excited chatter floated up the stairwell.

"Don't hurry. We have plenty to occupy us until you're ready."

Once she had gone, I inspected myself in the mirror. I was pale, and there were half-circles under my eyes, as though I had not slept for days. I hoped I wasn't getting sick; I had that slow, heavy feeling that precedes illness. I washed my face and changed my blouse, then rearranged my hair. Whether or not I looked it, I felt better.

"And how does today find you?" Alexander asked when I came into the front hall.

"Well, thank you," I said, willing my smile to widen enough to cover the lie. "And you?"

"Lovely!" Tasha answered for him, dancing away from me, her pale dress streaming. "We've been walking in the gardens, and we saw the horses, and I'm going to ride a pony."

Alexander raised his eyebrows, instantly sobering her.

"If Miss Rose and Mrs. Mary say it's all right," she added.

"Of course it's all right," I said. "That's what we bought them for. We'll take you tomorrow morning if you like. And please, call me Eleanor."

"Thank you, Eleanor," she said carefully, though the boundless joy at the prospect of a ride was clear beneath her composure.

"Come with me, sweetheart," Mary was saying. "Colette's baked cookies just for you. Let's go to the kitchen and find them." Tasha readily slipped her hand into Mary's, and they disappeared.

"She's at it again," I said.

"I think both of them are," Alexander observed. "Though Tasha will go along with anyone who seems ready to spoil her. Her Mrs. Mary is a prime target."

I shrugged. "Maybe she needs to be spoiled for a while. Of course, if you'd rather not—"

"No, no," he said quickly. "I think it's wonderful that they get on so well. Anyhow, I don't think that Tasha could be spoiled irrevocably."

Colette had laid out a table with iced tea and lemonade and more food than we could possibly eat. I poured two glasses of tea.

"Let's take it out to the gallery," I said.

We went out and sat on two of the rocking chairs Mary had bought.

"Did you dream last night?" Alexander asked, looking toward the woods.

"Everyone dreams every night," I told him. "Most of the time we don't remember it."

"Is that your way of telling me that you don't remember?"

I sighed. "I remember. It wasn't last night, though. It was this afternoon." I told him about the dream. He looked not at me but at the dark trees, a grim and resolute expression settling on his face.

"What do you think?" I asked when his silence had become uncomfortable.

"It's so vivid, it's hard to believe that your Eve wasn't trying to tell you something. What do you think? After all, it was your dream."

I shook my head. "It was all so cryptic." Alexander waited for me to continue. I swirled the melting ice around the bottom of my glass. "I don't know. The sudden change in their expressions, the way that Eve looked when she held out the flower, my mother when she accepted it—I agree, it must mean something, but I can't imagine what."

Alexander considered this for a time, then finally said, "Remember, the flower was a rose. Perhaps it represented you."

"Perhaps," I agreed. "But she looked too young to have had me yet. Of course, she met my father when she was very young. Maybe it was about him."

"Did he die young, too?"

"I don't know. He and my mother separated not long after she had me, and I never heard from him again." Alexander looked perplexed by this information, so I added, "It's all right. I never think about it anymore, and I don't remember him to miss him."

He was silent, apparently uncertain as to how to move past the subject.

Finally, I said, "I have some musical questions for you."

We both smiled, and again the pall was shaken, though not so completely as it had been in the sunlight. I left the glasses on the tea table, and we moved to the music room.

"Musical questions," he repeated, indicating that I should sit down at the piano. "The études?" he asked.

I thought for a moment, then nodded, deciding that the ballade was better left alone at present.

"The fourth of opus ten," he suggested, opening the book that lay to the side of the music rack and studying the piece. "You said last night that it was giving you trouble."

"Worse than that, I'm afraid."

He pulled a chair up near the bench, setting the music before me on the piano. "I would ask you first," he said, "why it is that you want to play these pieces."

"I've never loved Chopin," I said slowly, "but the études have always appealed to me. I suppose because they're so meticulous."

"And this is perhaps the most meticulous of the lot. The most mathematical, at any rate."

"The most difficult."

"In some senses."

"I've been trying to learn it for weeks, and I haven't even got through the first page."

He scrutinized me. "It is difficult, Eleanor, but so is the last of opus twenty-five, and you played that beautifully. I am certain that your problem is psychological rather than physical. Position yourself at the bench." I sat up straight, near the edge of the seat, resting my right foot on the sustain pedal, my heel firmly planted on the ground. "Now play," he demanded.

I smiled at him incredulously, and he looked back, ingenuous. "I told you, I can't play it," I said when it was clear that he really meant it.

"I think you can."

"Alexander, this is ridiculous. I've been trying for months—"

He shrugged. "I can't possibly help you if I haven't heard what you can do."

I looked at the music for a moment, then began to play tentatively, far short of tempo. I stumbled over the fourth line and glanced at Alexander helplessly. His face was devoid of expression.

"Well?" I asked.

"Well what? Is that all you're going to do?"

"Isn't that enough?" I was beginning to be irritated.

He laughed. "With all due respect, Eleanor, I'm glad I never had you as a student." I raised my eyebrows haughtily. Apparently unperturbed, he asked, "Is this your approach to every piece?"

"What approach?"

"Try once, give up if it doesn't come immediately?"

"I told you," I cried, "I've worked and worked on this piece, and it never moves!"

Alexander stood up, began pacing the room. "Because you approach it as an adversary, a trial—something to be defeated. A piece of music is not an adversary but a vessel. An implement. Without you, it is a jumble of hieroglyphs. I am not so trite as to deem music your friend, Eleanor, but it is certainly not an enemy. Rather, it is something poor and malleable, dust and water under your fingers. Don't you see, you hold its soul in your hands! Human beings are flawed creatures, but some are gifted as well, and within a piece of music, you can be God. Now, play!"

His eyes had caught fire; patches of color burned on his pale cheeks. He was looking not at me but through me, and for the second time I realized that I was in the presence of a man more gifted than I could imagine. Obediently I turned back to the piano and played. I did not stumble until the sixth line, then looked back at him in exasperation. He had resumed his pacing and did not look at me.

"Now then, those lines were perfect; a little short of tempo, but that of course comes with time. Think of the rest of the piece as repetition of those lines, albeit with variation. Have patience."

"Something in which I'm sadly lacking."

"I can see that. And I understand, it is frustrating to know what a piece should sound like and not be able to play it. But you must stop trying to do it all at once. You can't."

I laughed, shaking my head. "You sound just like my teacher from Boston. He was always telling me not to rush, to correct the old mistakes before I went on to the new parts. And most of all to make myself read it, even though I knew how it should sound."

"Why didn't you listen to him?"

I shrugged. "Impatience, I suppose. Or just plain conceit."

He came back to the piano and sat down, the passion draining gradually from his face. "Well, with music, you must channel the one and quell the other. May I?" He gestured to the bench. I got up. He took my place and began to play. The first five lines of the étude spilled fluidly from beneath his fingers before he broke off.

I shook my head. "I'll never play so beautifully."

He looked at me, honestly puzzled. "You already do."

"Well, then," I conceded, "never so easily."

"That's not true, either. I only have a different approach."

"Are you going to enlighten me?"

He studied the music for a moment, then said, "Let's try something. I want you to look at the first line. Study it until you can close your eyes and see it." I studied it until I couldn't look at it anymore, then I looked at him.

"Now play it. Don't think about making a mistake. Don't think about anything and don't look at the music, except inside your head."

I began to play. I made one mistake, then another, and another, until I threw up my hands in despair.

"You thought about it."

"I can't help it!"

He walked to the window and stood with his back to me, a dark silhouette against the turgid rain clouds. I found myself paying more attention to the line of his back and shoulders than his words. "You see, it's a chain reaction," he explained. "You make one mistake, then you begin thinking about the next one you will make, which causes it to happen. Soon you are mis-stepping in all directions, and you can't stop."

"It's so difficult."

When he turned back to me, I had the feeling that he had momentarily forgotten I was there. "Of course it's difficult! Learning anything is difficult. But you cannot give up because of that. Now, try it again. Clear your mind. Close your eyes if it helps, and don't think of anything but the music. Think always a step ahead, to the next measure, and you won't be able to think about making mistakes in the one you are playing. Come, try it."

I took a deep breath and set my hands on the keys. I looked at the music once, then cast my eyes down, focusing on my left hand, which has always been the weaker of the two. I began to play, tentatively at first. I was aware only of the music, its intrinsic movement. All of a sudden I stopped in surprise: I had played the entire first page, too slowly, but without stumbling once.

"Why did you stop?" asked Alexander.

"You were right!"

He shrugged. "It's a good system. I think, though, that part of the reason this worked so well is that you've listened to the piece so much. You have a very good ear. I'm better at sight reading, so the more I study the music before I play it, the better I play. It's all relative, like I said. Here"—he sat beside me on the bench—"I'll play the left hand, you play the right."

We began to play, stumbling in some parts, laughing at our clumsy coordination, stopping when our hands ran into each other and starting again, finally reaching a shaky cadence. We laughed, and then stopped abruptly, startled by applause. Simultaneously we turned toward the door.

For a moment time seemed to stop. I felt Alexander's body tense beside mine. Then the man in the doorway began to laugh. I tried to smile back at him, but I was cold, the muscles of my face frozen.

"This is unexpected," the man said in a resonant voice with the faintest British clip. "I have never before elicited quite so dramatic a reaction." He had been leaning against the doorjamb. Now he straightened and removed a cream-colored Panama hat. Alexander stood slowly, and I scrambled to my feet as he moved toward us.

"I am Dorian Ducoeur," he said, taking my limp fingers in a firm grasp and kissing them. "You must be Miss Rose." His blue eyes flickered toward Alexander. "And you, sir, I do not know, but I can say that your lesson was one of the finest I have ever witnessed, and I flatter myself that I have witnessed some of the best."

Alexander and I looked at each other, and I hoped that my dismay was not as clearly stamped on my face as was his own.

Looking back and forth between us, his smile fading, Mr. Ducoeur said, "I hope that my call isn't unwelcome?"

11

I no longer recall any preconceptions of Dorian Ducoeur; I only know that the actual person would have defied any. To begin with, he was neither young nor old. That is, he fell into the group that is past thirty-five but not yet fifty, for which it is often difficult to pinpoint an exact age. He had symmetrical European features, neatly trimmed grey-blond hair, and eyes of an unnervingly bright blue, even through his wire-rimmed spectacles. In the vein of the hat, his clothing was precise and expensively made. He wore a natural-colored linen suit and white shirt, a red silk kerchief around his neck, and he carried a grey raincoat over his arm.

The overall effect of his person and his face was pleasing to the eye—inoffensive in its predominantly neutral color scheme, while small bright flashes such as the kerchief and the eyes continually recalled one's own eyes to him. Yet it was curiously difficult to pinpoint a deeper reaction to him. Though his eyes were bright and attentive, they were fundamentally expressionless, and though he smiled, I had the feeling that it was as superficial as his clothing. Moreover, his appearance was familiar in the infuriating way that makes the resemblance impossible to place.

I finally recovered myself enough to say, "I received your

letter this morning. I hadn't expected to see you so soon." I felt Alexander's eyes on the side of my face but didn't turn to meet them.

"My fault, Miss Rose," Mr. Ducoeur soothed. "I didn't send the letter until I arrived here yesterday."

"In Baton Rouge?"

"No, at Joyous Garde. You do know it?"

"I've heard of it," I said, trying not to sound overly eager, though I was overwhelmed with questions I wanted to ask him. "We couldn't figure out…I mean, without the postmark…"

He was laughing, yet I had the uncomfortable awareness that the laughter didn't penetrate the surface. "Of course. It must have seemed mysterious to you. But there's little mystery to Dorian Ducoeur." He waved a hand abstractly in the air, indicating that he wished to change the subject. "Now, who is your friend?" He regarded Alexander calmly; I was surprised to see Alexander return the look with decided coldness.

"I am Alexander Trevozhov," he said, not offering his hand.

For an instant Dorian's mouth thinned and tightened. Then he was smiling coolly again, apparently unruffled, but it was too late. In that moment I had seen in his face the fair man from the dream I had shared with Alexander, and I understood Alexander's coldness. I, too, felt cold.

"You are Russian, then," Dorian was saying, still addressing Alexander, though it seemed that many minutes had passed since Alexander had introduced himself. "From St. Petersburg?"

Alexander raised his eyebrows. "Is it so obvious?"

Dorian smiled again. "The accent is distinctive, but I admit, I have heard your name before, and something of your origins; I believe in musical circles?"

"I'm a concert pianist."

"Splendid!" Dorian cried, but this time I quite clearly detected a note of insincerity in his bravado. He turned back to me. "I hope that my forwardness hasn't offended you. Your housekeeper showed me in."

"No, of course not," I faltered. "We've just had tea...I'm sure there's plenty left..."

"Thank you, but I had a late lunch."

There were footsteps in the hall outside, and Tasha's golden laughter. In a moment she entered, leading Mary by the hand. Both of them stopped short at the sight of Dorian Ducoeur. Tasha clutched Mary's skirt, and Mary put a reassuring arm around her.

"And who is the little beauty?" asked Dorian, turning the brilliance of his smile onto them.

"Mary," I said quickly, "this is Mr. Ducoeur. The one who sent the letter. Mr. Ducoeur, this is my friend, Mary Bishop, and Mr. Trevozhov's niece, Natalya."

Mary looked at me questioningly for a moment and then smiled. "Of course." She offered her hand, and Dorian kissed it, flustering her further. "We hadn't expected you so soon." She turned to the little girl. "Tasha, there's no reason to be frightened. Mr. Ducoeur is a friend of ours." Tasha tilted her auburn head closer to Mary's hip, regarding Dorian with silent suspicion, not unlike her uncle's.

Dorian was speaking again, this time to Tasha in a softened tone. "Do you like flowers?" he asked. She watched him silently. "All little girls like flowers, perhaps because they look like them, in their pretty pale dresses. You yourself look rather like a white rose."

When the compliment failed to win a smile, he continued: "Do you know that you can grow roses?" He didn't wait for a response. "Right here." He extended one arm, untied his red kerchief, and draped it over his fist. "Blow a kiss to warm the seeds." He watched the child's uncertainty mix with curiosity. "Go on, see what happens," he coaxed.

Reluctantly Tasha kissed her hand to the covered fist. Dorian flicked the kerchief aside, and in his hand was a bunch of ivory roses. Tasha's face melted into a smile as she accepted the bouquet. Dorian laughed at her formality; Mary and I couldn't help smiling. Conscious of the many eyes on her, Tasha ran to Alexander's side, slipping her free hand into his. He looked down at her, smiling faintly through the consternation.

"Time to go home now, Natashenka," he said. "You must rest."

"Oh, surely you're not going already!" Mary cried.

"I'm afraid so."

"Will you come again for supper?" I asked, searching his face for an explanation of his strange and sudden reserve.

"Thank you," he said, the formality in his tone unmistakable and crushing, "but there is work I ought to see to tonight."

"Well," I said, "if you're set on going now, I'll walk you to the door. Mary, try to persuade Mr. Ducoeur to have some tea." I turned and followed Alexander out of the room.

On the doorstep we hesitated, looking at each other over the sudden, subtle barrier Dorian Ducoeur had erected between us.

"Why don't you go and pick some more flowers, Tasha?" Alexander said. She nodded, still clutching her roses, her hair catching the sunlight as she ran into the long grass by the driveway. We watched her for a moment, I snared by her fragile loveliness, Alexander doubtless by something more powerful.

"He looks so like the man in the dream," I said.

He didn't answer me immediately. The silence between us expanded until he asked abruptly, "Why didn't you tell me about the letter?"

It was undeniably a reprimand, and I fluctuated between a woman's anger and a child's wounded pride, answering with a little of each. "I...I forgot all about it."

His face was grave, and the set of his mouth had the tinge of cruelty I had seen in it before. "Will you tell me what it said?"

I shook my head and laughed flimsily, further unnerved by the look on his face. "Nothing, really. It was a letter of introduction. Apparently he spent a summer at Joyous Garde as a child. He remembered the twins, and wanted to introduce himself."

Alexander's lips tightened into a stubborn line. "I wouldn't be so quick to trust him."

"Why would you assume that I trust him? And even if I did, you can't condemn a man you've just met for resembling someone you've dreamed of."

He only looked at me, but there was an accusation in his eyes that made me lower my own.

"You can't think that he really is the man in the dream?" I asked.

"At the moment I think only that he cannot be trusted," he repeated.

I was annoyed by his cryptic look and tone. "What would you have me do? I couldn't tell him to leave without good cause."

Alexander sighed, his eyes moving again to Tasha's bright form in the swaying grass. "You needn't have asked him to stay." Before I could answer, he said, "Be careful, Eleanor."

Powerful emotion moved beneath those words, but when

he looked at me again the anger was gone and he was smiling gently, his eyes elusive. I nodded, my own anger dissipating as quickly as it had arisen. He took my hand and squeezed it once before he turned away.

I watched the Trevozhovs until they disappeared around the side of the house, then went looking for Mary and Mr. Ducoeur. I found them seated on the terrace overlooking the rose garden where Alexander and I had spoken that first night, laughing over glasses of tea.

"Oh, Eleanor!" Mary cried, pulling up another chair. "Mr. Ducoeur is telling stories about your grandfather—"

"I didn't know you knew him well," I interrupted peevishly, more troubled by Alexander's reaction to Dorian than I had realized.

He looked at me and flashed another wide smile. The extraordinary brightness of his eyes struck me again. "He was a well-known commodity here," he answered. "Any Yankee is. You yourselves are the topic of much speculation among local society."

"But why?" Mary asked, clearly already snared by his charm.

"Because you are Yankees won over to the beautiful South. The musical talent adds to the intrigue, along with the fact that you apparently don't need local society. It rankles them bitterly…and piques their interest."

"Oh, dear," Mary said. "I knew we ought to have given a party by now. We've been so wrapped up in our own affairs, I'm afraid we haven't got around to it."

"Think no more of it now," Dorian soothed. "I assure you that you are better off without the company of those who are offended by your discretion. The Baton Rouge ladies have always secretly worried about their inferiority to the

Ducoeurs and the Fontaines. But I can see that Miss Rose's mind is elsewhere." He turned to Mary. "Do you think that I could make her speak her thoughts?"

Mary laughed and shrugged. "You can try, but I've never known anyone to succeed in making Eleanor do anything."

I glared at her, but answered nonetheless, "I was wondering whether Mr. Ducoeur, who seems to know so much about our history, could enlighten us on the matter of a certain Louis Ducoeur. He must be your cousin?"

Dorian considered for a moment before he answered. "I believe he grew up in Europe," he said slowly, "which would explain why we never met. I'm certain I've heard the name in connection with one of the Fairfax twins, though I can't recall which one...I believe there was some talk years ago of his engagement to one of them."

"Was there?" I replied, careful to hide my eagerness to hear more.

"Yes; but I suppose it came to nothing, or we would all know of it."

"Perhaps. But I don't know much about my aunt...or even my mother, for that matter."

Dorian shrugged. "I'm afraid I can't be of help."

"Well, then perhaps you could shed some light on the matter of the house on the hill just there." I indicated the direction.

His smile disintegrated. "What do you know of that house?" he asked.

"Nothing but what I've seen."

"I hope you haven't been up there alone," he said, then added quickly, "It could well be dangerous."

"Mr. Ducoeur," I said in my best practical-Yankee tone, "I'm mistress of this estate now. If there is something I ought to know about it, you had best tell me."

"I don't know the specifics of that house," he said ruminatively, "but it wouldn't surprise me if they were unfortunate."

"Why do you say that?"

He sighed. "Have you heard of the Fontaines' curse?"

"No...but it sounds interesting."

"Sit down, then."

He indicated an empty chair between Mary and himself. I didn't take the seat he offered, but sat on the balustrade instead. He contemplated the melting ice in his glass for some minutes before he began speaking.

"It's an ancient theme," he said slowly. "Even a cliché, though it's common enough wherever two powerful families live in proximity to each other.

"Ours came here from France, when Louisiana was little better than a jungle and French was still its native tongue, voodoo its religion." He smiled humorlessly. I tapped my fingertips on the railing in the rhythm they refused to forget.

"They came together. It wasn't affection that bound them, but a blood feud begun when the Fontaines were a peasant family on one of the Ducoeurs' estates. Apparently a cruel Ducoeur baron had evicted the Fontaine patriarch, a stone carver, over a money dispute. Dispossessed, the family scattered, and the patriarch sickened and died. The dead man's wife, who was commonly thought to have knowledge of the dark arts, cursed the baron's family to be bound unhappily to her own forever. In this way, she meant to ruin his line as she believed he had ruined hers.

"Whatever people thought of her threat at the time, they remembered it a year later when the baron and his wife both died in mysterious circumstances. An heir was found, but he too died mysteriously before he had had time to enjoy his new title.

"However, this second baron had been wary of his apparent good fortune. When his will was opened, his family found that he had done something unheard of in those times, ostensibly to try to circumvent the witch's curse. Rather than leave his title to any of several male relations, he had left it unconditionally to the younger of his two daughters, who was only fifteen.

"He may have been trying to protect his family, but in the end it came to nothing. Not long after her inheritance, his young daughter fell in love with the Fontaine's son, and she married him despite the unsuitability of the match. Before they had been married a year, she died in childbirth, leaving Fontaine the fortune that set his family on a social level with the Ducoeurs, and the child who would bind their families together always.

"Those were superstitious times, and people whispered that Madame Fontaine and her son had been in league to acquire the estate all along, but of course this could never be proved, and the speculation only soured relations between the families further. Yet as neither would relinquish custody of the child, they were bound."

"Assuming such a preposterous fable was true," I interrupted, "wouldn't the witch-woman and her son simply have been hanged, or burned at the stake, or whatever was done to witches once upon a time?"

Mr. Ducoeur smiled. "I see Miss Rose is too astute for a fairy tale. As it happens, yes—people did become suspicious of both families and the rumors surrounding them. It was then that they were driven from their homes, and they fled to America to avoid persecution. Once again they settled near each other… right here, in Iberville parish."

Dorian paused, tapping his fingers on the table speculatively. He looked up at us finally, an abstruse irony veiling his bright eyes. "It seems, though, that even in the wilds of Atchafalaya they couldn't outrun their bad fortune. The Fontaines, the Ducoeurs, and later the Merciers of Chênes, with whom they both intermarried, have suffered misfortune after misfortune, right down to the time of your mother and aunt, it seems."

"What a legacy, Eleanor," Mary said, with what sounded irritatingly like envy.

"Witches and murderers," I replied caustically, "don't seem much to aspire to."

Mary shrugged, clearly unfazed. "It's only a story, as Mr. Ducoeur has said."

"So you don't know anything specific about the house on the hill," I said to Dorian.

Dorian looked up at me, his eyes searching my face. "Why the interest?"

I looked back at him squarely. "It just doesn't seem to belong here. It looks to me like the kind of late-Victorian house you'd find up North. And then, Mary and I haven't been able to find any record of it. We don't even know who owns it."

"Well, there I can help you. In the documents I received with Joyous Garde, there's a deed that states that the property on the hill is owned jointly by my plantation and yours. Perhaps, if I decide to stay at Joyous Garde, we can come up with a joint use for the place. At any rate, I have no intention of carrying on our families' differences."

He smiled at me, and I found myself smiling back, for once without thinking of the effect it might have. "Nor do I, Mr. Ducoeur. Besides, I'm not really a Fontaine at all."

"No," he answered, tilting his head as he studied my face, "you are, in every aspect, a Rose."

Mary and I laughed, exchanging a look. "I'm afraid compliments will get you nowhere with Eleanor," she said.

"It doesn't seem Miss Rose is of a mind to be won at all," he agreed, shaking his head.

"Honestly!" I cried.

"At any rate," Mary said, "Mr. Ducoeur was telling me about his musical career before we got off on the tangent of houses. It seems this place is a magnet for aspiring musicians. Or perhaps the music is due to the influence of the place?"

"Probably a little of each," Dorian answered. "At any rate, I wouldn't go so far as to call myself an aspiring musician. I'd rather say that as a teacher of music, I have come to the fullest realization of what talent I was born with. Surely you, Miss Rose, are the one with aspirations."

"Of a sort. What did you say you taught, Mr. Ducoeur?"

"I didn't. Most recently I have been involved in vocal music, but my first love is the piano."

"Where do you teach?"

"Tetbury Conservatory—a small place in the Cotswolds. I don't expect you will have heard of it."

"No, I haven't."

"Anyhow, you're a musician," said Mary, smiling at him. "It means you belong here."

"I'm afraid not," Dorian answered. "That is, having spent so much of my life abroad, I would not claim to belong to any one place anymore."

Mary looked back at him vaguely, as if her eyes were not quite focused. "But it feels as if you belong here now. With us."

He shrugged. "Perhaps. I've been away from Louisiana a long time, and I've forgotten the way of it. Besides, I'm afraid I haven't made the best of impressions, arriving unannounced and filling your ears with ghost stories."

"We asked you to tell that story," I reminded him, hoping

to keep to less abstract topics. The low clouds bore down like a consequence. My head was beginning to ache badly again; I had heard and seen too much to absorb in one day.

Dorian smiled with all his former brilliance. "Then perhaps you may reintroduce me to my beloved, beautiful South. Now then—" He stood up, began to gather his things. "I really must be going. I hadn't meant to stay so long; there's still so much to be seen to."

"Could we persuade you to come back for dinner?" Mary entreated, standing as well. I looked at her sharply. Dorian, catching my look, replied, "I think we'd best postpone that until I'm more settled. Besides, I'd hate to wear out my welcome so soon. I do hope, though, that I might entice you to visit Joyous Garde in the near future." He turned his eyes on me. "There's a lovely old piano begging for competent fingers."

"Thank you." I smiled as graciously as I could. "Of course, you're always welcome here."

Dorian was watching my discomfort with a subtle humor that raised my ire again. "Mary," I said, never taking my eyes from his, "would you mind showing Mr. Ducoeur to the door?"

"Don't trouble yourself," he told her as she stood up. "I remember the way out." He kissed her hand. "Good day, Mrs. Bishop, and thank you for the tea." He took my own hand but only pressed it, to my further chagrin. "And you, Miss Rose, thank you for bearing my prattle. I hope that it hasn't offended you."

"On the contrary, it's been most interesting. I do hope that we have the chance to speak again in the near future."

This answer apparently was acceptable to him. He let go of my hand and took his leave.

12

The clouds kept their hold on us throughout that day and the next. I had not expected to hear from Alexander right away, but when the second evening passed with no word from him, I began to worry that I had offended him in some way I hadn't understood. This worry preoccupied me so much that I was a poor companion for Mary at dinner and absolutely useless in the music room afterward.

The rain, when it finally came, was a welcome distraction. It began at dusk, a few heavy drops spattering the windows as prelude to the downpour that followed. Mary and I watched from the music room as the lake and the cypress grove and finally the gardens were obscured by dark sheets of water, the likes of which we had never seen before.

Mary went to bed an hour after dinner, but a restlessness had come upon me with the change in the weather, replacing the torpor of the past two days. I sat up late at the piano, with the renewed intention of practicing. It was not long, though, before my fingers were again forming that redundant phrase, the theme never developed, my thoughts lost in a maze of haunted rooms and gardens.

From there they ran to Alexander. The more I thought about the events of the previous day, the less certain I was of my behavior, the more convinced that somehow I had affronted him. Finally my fingers stopped moving. I sat watching the rain trace tortuous patterns on the window screens, listening to the deep silence beneath its whisper. It seemed a brooding silence, waiting for something to break it.

I stood up and closed the piano. Before I let myself think about it, I was in the kitchen, shivering as I drew Mary's raincoat over my thin dress and stepped out into the sodden darkness. I had a vague idea about the impropriety of what I was about to do, what society would say, indeed what I myself would have said in the world I had left behind. My only explanation, then and now, is just that: I had left the world behind. The thought of walking a half mile through the rain at midnight to visit a man twice my age, who I barely knew, would have been unimaginable six months before.

I felt my way down the path through the grape arbor, keeping my thoughts and my eyes carefully aimed straight ahead. I navigated the steps of the topiary garden as best I could, grateful when my fingers finally encountered the rough wooden railing describing the margin of the lake. I ran along the water's edge, wary of the silent expanse to my right.

Just before I entered the woods, the clouds thinned. For a moment the rain was illuminated by the moon's murky flood lamp, and I had the disorienting sensation that the lines of water were running up from the lake rather than down from the sky, like stringy umbilical cords feeding the swollen clouds. Shuddering, I turned my back on the rainy lake and entered the dripping vault of the woods.

Among the forest's undiluted dark, I tried not to feel the singing power of the tree roots deep in the earth beneath my feet, the slick wet caresses of invisible vines trailing across my face and neck. The air was close and funereal with the smell of flowers. I was overwhelmingly relieved when finally I saw light through the trees, casting a dim glow on the grass beneath it.

Then I heard the music. It washed through the shadows huddled beyond the rim of light, enveloping, beckoning. It was a piece I didn't know, though it bore similarities to the piece of Alexander's I had played in the dream and was, as that had been, curiously familiar. But there was a darkness to it more insistent than the shadows flitting beneath the sunlit surface of the first piece. The longer I listened, the more intimate the melancholy became, and I began to feel the guilt of an eavesdropper. I knew that I was listening to the ruminations of a broken heart.

Before cowardice could waylay me, I stepped toward the open casement, where once again I was arrested by the graceful elegance of the lines and planes of Alexander's back and shoulders. The only light in the room emanated from a small lamp on top of the piano. Against its gentle glow, his profile stood out with keen precision, his hair forming a dark halo. I lifted my hand, hesitated as the silly anxiety twisted in my chest, and then tapped softly on the windowsill.

Alexander snatched his hands from the keys, but his eyes were calm when he turned around. Hesitantly I smiled, the light of his reciprocal smile making me forget the rain that was drenching my hair and running into my eyes. The next moment he was gesturing me toward the door, helping me take off the saturated coat, asking whether anything was wrong at the house. I could see now by his paleness that I had startled him more than he wanted me to know.

"Nothing's wrong," I assured him, suddenly shy. "I...well, I know that it's late, but everything was getting to me, I couldn't sleep, and I didn't like to be alone anymore...I hoped that you might still be up."

His eyes searched mine before he smiled. "So, I am not the only chronic insomniac here. Of course you're welcome any time, though you might have picked a less inclement night to venture out."

"Indeed. Alexander...I couldn't help hearing you playing. I hope I haven't interrupted something important."

He turned away from the lamp light, perhaps in an attempt to hide the caustic smile. There was a decided bitterness in his tone when he answered, "What you heard was nothing but my own damned self-pity." He looked at me again, the lamp's light reflected in his eyes. "It happens, especially at night." He shrugged, then looked at me more carefully. "You're shivering."

"I'm all right."

"Come." He put a hand under my elbow and led me back into the study. I glanced at the twins' faces before accepting the seat he offered. He shut the window and handed me a blanket, which I wrapped gratefully around my shoulders.

"Do you drink brandy?" he asked.

"Sometimes." In truth, I had not yet learned to drink anything stronger than table wine with any degree of grace, but I would have died before telling him that.

He lifted a decanter from a book-case full of volumes with Cyrillic titles, beautiful and inscrutable as runes. Pouring two glasses of deep amber liquid, he passed one to me, then settled with the other into the chair across from my own. He looked at me with eyes so direct I could not possibly make small talk.

I took a tiny sip of brandy and didn't quite manage to hide the difficulty of swallowing it. "Alexander—" I began, putting the glass aside.

"Don't say it," he entreated, looking at me earnestly. "It is for me to apologize to you. I blamed you yesterday for something you could not control, something for which you were as little prepared as I. I let my shock run to anger, and you bore the brunt of it. It's a contemptible tendency of mine."

I smiled. "Are you finished berating yourself? Because that wasn't at all what I intended."

His look turned to one of embarrassment. "You didn't come here because of what happened yesterday? Please forgive me also for the presumption."

"Now you're embarrassing me."

He had begun to smile in earnest. It gave his face a luminous, ingenuous beauty. "No, you've done nothing wrong. It's I who have the confession to make."

"Confession?" I repeated, suddenly flustered.

"Yes. Of a far less innocent offence than anger." When I made no reply—I couldn't think clearly enough for one—he said, "Jealousy, Eleanor. I can see what Dorian Ducoeur would be in a woman's eyes. I could not help but imagine what your reaction to him might be. I stayed away because I didn't want to impose my own opinion of him, or my presence, for that matter, on what might have been the beginning of a mutual attachment."

I laughed. "I'm not in danger of forming any attachment to him!"

He smiled. Then, recalling my still ambiguous relation to Dorian, he said, "Forgive me if I persist in my distrust of him."

I looked down at my hands. "I suppose it's indelicate to say so, but I'm flattered by your jealousy."

"As far as I'm concerned, you are no more wrong to be flattered by it than I was to feel it." We looked at each other for a serious moment, and then laughed together. For the first time in days the anxiety lifted. Alexander settled further back into his chair and looked up at the overgrown shadows on the ceiling. "I suppose I should ask you about him."

"There isn't much to tell. He's a music teacher, and heir to a nearby plantation. A bit self-important for my liking."

Alexander sighed. "Why am I not surprised?"

"But he did tell us an interesting story."

"What was that?"

I began hesitantly, but soon enough the tale was pouring out, seeming so much weightier now in the wavering shadows.

When I had finished, Alexander said, "The ironies are as thick here as the atmosphere."

"Perhaps. But I've had the feeling for a while now that more is happening here than irony or coincidence."

"What do you mean?" His face was expressionless, his eyes and tone guarded. This put me on edge, but I stumbled on.

"It seems almost that we're expected to take part in something. But at the same time, I can't help feeling that everything's already being done. That whatever is happening at Eden, whether or not it involves any of us, is far beyond our control."

Alexander was silent for a few long moments, then said abruptly, "I would like to see your house on the hill."

I shook my head, only mildly surprised at the tears I felt in the corners of my eyes. All I could think of was that cloying melody drifting through dim corridors, traversing stagnant shafts of sunlight, winding up the chambered nautilus of the staircase. Alexander must have understood my reaction, because the next minute he was leaning forward, taking my hand in his. A part of me wondered how we could have come so close so quickly, yet at the same time, like the clues to the twins' history that kept falling into my path, it seemed right, or at least inevitable.

I shut my eyes, and time suddenly seemed many layers removed from us, and the present we inhabited. I do not recall the fear passing, only my own growing awareness of Alexander's body near mine, of its great strength and greater frailty. When I looked at him again, his eyes were waiting to catch mine, bright within their darkness. I knew that nothing of myself was hidden from him or ever had been; also that I did not begin to understand him, as he apparently understood me. It was at that moment that I realized I loved him. All I could think of was that first night at the concert hall, when I knew that he was gifted beyond any talent the opulent crowd could imagine, and that hearing his music had altered my life irrevocably.

"Alexander, I—"

"Don't," he interrupted, letting go of my hand again. "You don't begin to know what I am." He was distancing himself, his eyes furling inward like severed morning glories, leaving me with a sense of loss as terrible as the fear.

"Maybe not, but I know you!" The tears I had suppressed were still dangerously near the surface. "I knew you the first time I laid eyes on you. And you knew me. You saw me, and you knew me. Alexander—you can't deny it." The words were as much an appeal as a statement of fact.

He watched me for a moment more, then looked away. His hands fell back to his sides slowly, perhaps with resignation. My throat was clogged with the words I couldn't speak, confusing my thoughts. It had been a misunderstanding: a terrible misunderstanding. I was on my feet, turning away, not wanting him to see me cry. After all, he had never promised me anything, never said that he shared my feelings.

"I'm sorry," I managed to blurt out as I stumbled toward the darkness of the doorway. The images of the room dissolved, blurring as the tears rose. For once I longed to be out in the living silence of the forest, but I was not halfway through the adjacent living room when he caught me, his hand closing firmly around my wrist. I stopped at the edge of the strip of light the study lamp cut through the darkness, sobbing and resigned.

"Eleanor," he said, with unmistakable tenderness. He reached out and turned my face toward his, and what I saw there was very far from indifference.

"There are parts of me," he said, "that you cannot begin to imagine. You heard me playing tonight, and it frightened you. Don't argue; I know that it did, and what you heard was only the edge of it." He sighed. "I wouldn't flatter myself by giving you advice, but for my own conscience I must tell you to turn around right now and leave me and this haunted place, and don't look back. You deserve much more than this."

"Then why did you stop me from leaving?"

My words faded into the hush of rain in the trees. Their echo died, leaving nothing in its place. When Alexander finally looked up, the defiance in his face had faded too, leaving something that looked oddly like remorse.

"Because," he said, "I love you as I have never loved anyone."

The words seemed to come not from that moment but from a distant past. I took his hands in mine, and at the moment of contact there was a flicker of images: a fire that reddened the night sky, a woman's white face with a red gash across it, the sound of heartbroken weeping. It was only a flicker, barely enough for me to register, yet the words I spoke next seemed a response to it as much as they were to what he had said.

"If you do love me," I said, my voice dreamily detached from myself, "then please don't ever speak of us parting again."

Looking at me with those unfathomable eyes, Alexander said something in Russian; and then, in English, he said, "Never again."

All at once I was acutely aware of the silence. The rain had stopped as suddenly as it had begun. There was no sound of insects or birds, no breath of wind, nothing but the rustle as we shifted, his arms slipping to my waist as he leaned down to kiss me.

13

I make no moralistic pretensions. So strong was my feeling for Alexander that I would have given myself to him that night. It was his own restraint that kept us from an act that perhaps would have been premature then.

I admit that I wondered about his hesitancy, particularly after I left him early the next morning. However, I was too tired and confounded by all that had changed in the last few hours to ascribe much meaning to it. I tiptoed upstairs and fell asleep in my clothes, only to be awakened what seemed moments later by Mary, who told me anxiously that Alexander had come to the house to use the telephone because Tasha was ill.

Apparently Mary was too overwrought by this news to notice that I had slept in my dress. As such, I never had the chance to discuss with her what had happened between Alexander and me. It was one of those seemingly trivial oversights that bore more repercussions than I could ever have imagined.

Mary, like the rest of the household, was immediately caught in the suspense of Tasha's sudden illness. By afternoon the child was complaining of stomach pains and was having trouble breathing. Mary and I both went to the cottage to offer help. A local doctor—thankfully not Dr. Brown—was called in, and after listening to her chest, he determined that her breathing wasn't consumptive. Nonetheless, he left several bottles of medicine and explicit instructions to phone him at the slightest worsening of her condition.

We took turns trying to distract Tasha from her discomfort all afternoon, and in the early evening she finally drifted into a fitful sleep, aided by a hot drink mixed with a tablespoonful of sweet rum—a remedy Mary had used on me during my own childhood illnesses. Once she was soundly asleep, we sat at the kitchen table and spoke in whispers about what was to be done.

"Should I call the doctor back?" Mary asked.

Alexander shook his head. "Not yet. Since the illness, I panic every time she sneezes. It's likely that she only has a cold."

"It can't hurt to have the doctor in, anyway." Mary was off to the house to call without waiting for a reply.

I reached across the table and squeezed Alexander's hand. He looked up at me and smiled, though it didn't begin to mask his anxiety.

"I'm sure it's nothing," I said, forcing myself to sound steady and sincere. "It was probably the change in climate. I always catch colds when I travel."

"I cannot bear to think of her becoming so ill again," he said, and was lost once more in a world of his own.

An hour later the doctor arrived. He listened to Tasha's chest, took her temperature, and diagnosed the illness as Influenza He told us to watch her carefully and to call him again if she seemed any worse.

We all stayed up with Tasha that night, watching her as she tossed and moaned, trying to make her drink water which she only vomited back up, finally calling the doctor again early in the morning. His look at the end of the examination was graver than it had been the previous day, and he no longer made any pronouncements about the cause of the illness. He gave us a number of new medicines, which Tasha swallowed with the obedient resignation of a practiced invalid.

That night Alexander finally managed to persuade Mary to sleep, though she insisted on staying at the cottage. I was as far from sleep as Alexander. The two of us stayed in Tasha's room, to read to her and sing to her and keep all of our minds from dwelling on darker anxieties until she, too, fell asleep.

In her stillness she was like a porcelain doll, her lashes silken fringes against the fever-flushed cheeks. When I looked up from my musings, I saw that Alexander had fallen asleep in his chair. As I reached to turn off the bedside lamp, my arm brushed a bunch of roses that stood beside it, sending a shower of faded petals and dusty pollen onto the linen cloth beneath.

I hadn't noticed the roses before, but it occurred to me now that they must be the ones Dorian had given Tasha. They weren't like Eden's roses, but bigger, with fleshy ivory petals. There was something corrupt about them, as there had been about the rotting leather bindings of the books in the house on the hill. I was wondering why Dorian had chosen them as a gift for a little girl, when another clump of petals broke away, revealing crimson sepals and tough, dark stems from which the thorns hadn't been clipped. Then I could only wonder how I had been so naïve. Dorian could never have known there was a little girl at Eden.

Shivering with repugnance, I picked up the jar and the fallen petals in the linen cloth, opened the window screen, and dropped the lot outside, shaking the cloth well. Then I leaned on the sill, gratefully breathing the cooler air. Clouds covered the stars; the darkness was nearly complete.

Pulling the screen back into place, I stepped across the room and out the door, through the narrow hall, and into the dark of Alexander's bedroom, where Mary lay asleep. The speck of light high up on the hill elicited no surprise, only a sinking kind of acceptance. I don't know how long I would have stood watching it if Tasha hadn't whimpered in her sleep.

Back in her room, Alexander was still deeply asleep. Tasha had not awakened, but she was no longer sleeping peacefully. Her head had fallen to one side, her lips were parted, and periodically her forehead creased. I smoothed the hair back from her face. Her skin was still too warm. When I touched her, she recoiled and cried out, "No!" and then she began to speak. At first it was only a jumbled whisper, but soon I could discern specific words. Then, quite clearly, she said, "Dorian."

Almost simultaneously her eyes opened. When she saw me looking down at her, she seemed at first confused, even frightened. Then she blinked, and smiled. "Eleanor," she said, reaching frail arms toward me. "It's you."

I got up on the bed beside her, and she snuggled into my arms.

"Do you remember what you said just a minute ago, love?" I asked her.

She looked up at me, her eyes wide and puzzled. "I didn't say anything."

"You don't remember saying anything when you woke up?"

Slowly she shook her head. I smoothed her hair. Her eyes were already drooping again, and I was about to resign myself to yet another mystery, when she said, "I was dreaming."

"What were you dreaming of?"

"A man."

"What was he like?"

She thought for a moment, then answered, "He was the man with the magic roses."

I smiled encouragingly at her, though I shuddered at the mention of those flowers. "Did you speak to him?"

Again she seemed to be contemplating something carefully before she answered. "He didn't see me. He was looking at you."

"Was he?" It was a strain to keep the trepidation out of my voice, but I must have succeeded, because the child remained relaxed.

"Mmm," she answered drowsily.

"That's all right," I told her, and hugged her tightly. "It was only a dream, anyway. Go back to sleep, now."

"Will you sing me a lullaby?"

I began to sing the first lullaby that came to mind, a French lullaby my mother had sung to me:

Dans les monts de Cuscione la petite a vu le jour
Et je fais dodelinette pour que dorme mon amour
La bercait avec tendresse lui prédit sa destinée...

I wondered for the first time where the song had come from; if it had passed down through the generations of my enigmatic ancestry from some region of France where once two families had lived side by side, locked in feud. The lullaby trailed off; I couldn't remember the rest of the words. Perhaps my mother had not even known them, and anyway, the theme of motherless girls was too prevalent for me to be comfortable singing a mother's words to a child who wasn't my own.

I tried to stop the flow of morbid thoughts. I told myself that my aunt had been an impetuous girl who clearly had done something to displease her family, but the story was common enough among affluent families. After all, my mother had done the same: I had never known of the existence of a grandfather before he appeared at my mother's funeral. As for the house on the hill, it was as haunted as any old, abandoned house. More likely than not, its inhabitant was some wayward vagrant, as Alexander had suggested.

But at Dorian Ducoeur, logic faltered. There was something amiss about him that not only Alexander and I, but also Tasha could sense. I recalled what she had said about him looking at me, and shivered again.

I looked down at Tasha, asleep again in my arms, and decided two things then and there. First, I would take Alexander up on his suggestion of visiting the house again, and flush out its mysterious inhabitant once and for all. Second, I would resurrect my grandparents' abandoned tradition and bring society to Eden—in particular, Dorian Ducoeur. His mystery could not be watertight, and I was certain that I was capable of unraveling it. With those resolutions I pulled the coverlet over Tasha and myself and settled into deep and dreamless sleep.

I awakened long after the sun had risen over the hazy tops of the trees. At first, finding the bed empty, I was seized by fear for Tasha, but then I heard her laughter somewhere below, and I settled back into the pool of sunlight on the pillow. It streamed through the gauzy curtains to touch my face like a blessing. I felt like a child myself, ready to smile at the sun. I lay for a time like that, with the sun on my face, listening to the humming world outside, for once not bothered by the mounting heat.

Then a thought fluttered into that bright, placid void, like a samara carrying nightmare seeds. It was the name Tasha had spoken last night from her dream: Dorian. Somehow, inexplicably, he was infecting all of our lives, and despite my resolutions of the previous night, this thought troubled me again in the light of day.

"You're awake." Alexander's voice cut into my musings.

I scrambled to my feet. He stood smiling in the doorway. "You should have awakened me sooner."

"Tasha told me that you were up with her in the night. I thought it was only fair to let you rest, as you seem to have cured her."

"So she's better?"

"Much—thanks to you."

"I didn't do anything."

He came and sat down on the side of the bed, taking my hand in his. "You were kind to her. Sometimes such things are more powerful than any medicine."

"Well, she's better now. Let's not ask why."

We were quiet for an awkward moment, realizing that we were alone for the first time since the night of the rainstorm. Then Alexander said, "You must think me a brute for ignoring you these past two days."

"I understand how you must worry about her," I said.

He leaned down and kissed my forehead. But when he looked up again his smile was gone, eclipsed by sadness and anxiety.

There must have been a similar expression on my own, because he asked, "What is it, Eleanor?"

I sighed. "I've been considering what you said, and I think now that we should go back up to the house on the hill."

"Why the sudden change of heart?"

"I had a lot of time to think last night." I shuddered, remembering Tasha's voice speaking Dorian's name. "Besides, I don't believe in ghosts. If someone is in that house, I want to know about it."

He paused, looking out the window. He turned back to me with the inscrutable grimness I was coming to dread. "Eleanor...please don't take offense if I say that it's important that you know what you're looking for up there, and that you are prepared for whatever you might find."

The anxiety in his eyes made me speak impetuously. "Do you know something I don't?"

He only said, "Who knows anything, really?"

"I ought to have known you'd bring in the philosophy!"

"I only meant that mysteries have a nasty habit of losing their glamor when one pursues them. Anyone, or anything, could be hidden away in the house on the hill."

We looked at each other for a moment. Then I said, "Let me go home and change."

He nodded, then followed me downstairs. At the door, I said, "I'll come get you sometime in the afternoon. I'm sure Mary will stay with Tasha."

Again he nodded, his stance oddly resigned. Then, as I turned to go, he pulled me back into the doorway and kissed me. "Don't be long," he said.

Mary was pleased with the prospect of spending the afternoon with Tasha, particularly when I told her that Alexander and I wanted to go for a walk. I didn't like to lie to her, but I wanted more information before I let her know that the house might be inhabited. Or so I told myself.

Mary sat down with me at the breakfast table. There were a few letters by my plate. On top was a pale-blue envelope I recognized immediately. I picked it up, looking at the stamp, the Baton Rouge postmark.

"At least he sent it by the conventional route this time." I slit the envelope.

Mary raised her eyebrows. "From Mr. Ducoeur? What does it say?"

I looked up into her cornflower eyes; as always, they melted the sarcasm on my tongue. "It's an invitation to a party at Joyous Garde. Two weeks from Saturday. For all of us: you, me, Alexander, and anyone else we care to bring. As though we know anyone else to bring!"

"He's only trying to be kind, Eleanor," she said gently. "Why are you so suspicious of him?"

"I'm not!"

"You certainly seemed to be when he came to see you."

"Honestly, Mary!"

She shrugged, sipped her coffee. "Will you accept?"

I tossed the invitation back onto the table. "Would you let me do otherwise?"

Mary laughed. "Eleanor, you're impossible sometimes." She leaned down to kiss my forehead on her way toward the door.

"Mary, would you mind writing the acceptance? I've got some things to do before Alexander and I go out."

"I'll have Colette or Marguerite write it," she answered.

"Are you busy, too?" I asked absently, glancing up from the other mail.

"It's not that," she answered. "My eyes have been bothering me the last few days, and when I focus on small writing—"

I dropped the newspaper, interrupting, "Why didn't you tell me? We should have had the doctor look at you while he was in for Tasha."

"No, no." She waved my protests aside. "I've been sewing, and the close work always makes my head ache."

"Mary—"

"Don't worry, Eleanor," she said, and hurried out of the

room before I could protest further.

Tasha was outside in the garden when Mary and I arrived at the cottage later, with enough dolls and picture books and puzzles to entertain a princess. She was oblivious to the toys and games, trying to weave a wreath of flowers instead.

"Oh, no, sweetheart, you can't do it that way," I told her. "And roses? You'll prick yourself! Here, let me make the frame, and then you'll have an easier time."

"We shouldn't be gone more than a couple of hours," Alexander told Mary.

"Don't worry about us," she assured him, smiling down at Tasha.

"You'll promise to bring her in when the sun goes out of the garden? And don't let her pester you otherwise?"

"Dyadya!" Tasha protested.

"Tasha, you'll listen to what Mary says, please." He raised a menacing eyebrow at her.

The protest still lingered around her mouth, but she answered, "I will."

Alexander watched them for a moment, then turned to me. "Are you ready?"

"As much as I ever will be," I answered. I handed the ring of roses to Tasha, then waved good-bye to the two of them.

14

"The first time, I went through the woods," I told Alexander when we were beyond Mary and Tasha's hearing. "I looked at the maps of the estate and all through the twins' journals for any information about another way up there, but there wasn't anything."

"Journals?" he asked sharply.

"I suppose I never thought to tell you. Eve and my mother kept journals one summer and left them here. Mary and I found them around the time I first found out about Eve."

"Would you mind if I had a look at them?"

"Of course not. I would have offered sooner if I'd thought of it. Though I'll warn you, most of their contents are about a teenage love triangle."

"Involving whom?"

I shrugged. "A young man called Louis Ducoeur—one of the Joyous Garde Ducoeurs. I asked Dorian about him, but they've never met." I looked at Alexander, but he made no reply to this. After a moment, I continued, "At any rate, I went through the woods last time, but I came down by the old driveway. It joins Eden's driveway near my house. It's easy to miss unless you're looking for it."

We continued in silence along the path by the water, through the topiary garden, and onto the driveway. The sun was brutally hot, but the trees shaded the road's edges. I found the opening to the house's driveway without too much difficulty.

When we stepped onto the overgrown driveway, my head swam for a moment with a strong sense of déjà vu. The heat wreaked havoc on clear thought, leaving only a heightened capacity for sensation. Once again, I felt that Eden was pressing its own mentality onto me. However, I couldn't turn back now. I stepped with Alexander out of the bright lane, into the deep green twilight of the forest.

When we reached the house, I walked boldly up to the front door. Alexander followed more slowly, studying the front of the house, as I had the previous time. I turned the doorknob, to no effect.

"It can't be locked!" I cried.

"Let me try," he said. I stepped out of the way, and Alexander satisfied himself that it was indeed locked.

"Who could possibly have locked it?" I said, though I had at least one idea of who it could have been. Without thinking, I reached into my pocket and pulled out the key ring I had picked up on my first visit; I had brought it along as an afterthought.

Alexander watched me incredulously. "Where did you get those?"

I looked down at the keys again. "I found them the first time I was here."

"May I see them for a minute?" he asked, his mind clearly working on something. He took the keys from me, and a small smile, almost cynical, turned his lips upward. "I thought so," he said softly.

"You thought what?"

"Look at this key. No, the little silver one. Don't you recognize it?"

"I suppose so," I answered. "It's the one from the dream. I'd forgotten about it, with all the other strange things that have been happening."

"Hmm. Let's try the rest of them." The third key he tried fit.

Everything was precisely as I had left it, a new layer of dust already filling my footprints.

"What now?" I asked.

Alexander shook his head. "You choose what to show me."

He followed me out the door to the left, through the study room with the deer's head, and into the ballroom. I brought him up to the library.

"Did you look into any of the other drawers?" he asked, indicating the desk where I'd found the keys.

"Just the top one."

He began to rummage through the others, while I looked at the titles in the nearest bookcase. When I turned around again, Alexander was holding a piece of water-stained paper, covered with close writing.

"What is it?"

"Do you read French?"

"Well enough."

I put aside the book I had been holding. He laid the paper on the table. I leaned over it and began to read. At first I was confused by the formality of the language. When I realized what I was looking at, I could barely believe it. The paper was a death certificate for a woman named Elizabeth Ducoeur, née Fairfax, who had died of typhus fever in Paris in 1905.

"But Elizabeth Fairfax was my mother," I said, "and her married name was Rose. She didn't die until 1907, and then it was consumption, not typhus, and she certainly wasn't in Paris."

Alexander rubbed a corner of the paper between his thumb and forefinger. "It's interesting," he said speculatively.

"But it's false," I reiterated. "My mother, Elizabeth Rose, was living in Massachusetts in 1905."

Finally Alexander looked at me. His eyes were serious and perhaps a little sad. "Something is certainly amiss; but we should not jump to conclusions. Are you certain, for instance, that your mother was married only once?" "She was twenty when she married my father. How could she have been married prior to that?"

"It's unlikely, but possible." His tone was troubled, as though he was trying to work something out.

"Even if the certificate is correct, why would it be hidden up here? It ought to be filed somewhere public—a courthouse, or a town hall."

"Unless it's a copy." He paused, then said, "Or if the death was factual, but not the identity."

"What do you mean?"

"Do you know why your aunt left her family?"

"You know that I don't."

A glint began in his eyes. "Do you remember when I asked you how you knew that it was your aunt's face in that dream, and not your mother's? Are you still so certain that you dreamed of Eve?"

The apparently rhetorical questions were beginning to irritate me. "As certain as I can be," I began impatiently, "considering—" I stopped short, realizing the implication of what I had been about to say. Considering that they were twins. It all began to make a terrible kind of sense. "You think they switched."

Alexander was looking again at the certificate. "We have an official document stating that your mother died at a time and place which you know could not be correct. It appears senseless, unless you imagine that the woman who died was really Eve, posing as Elizabeth."

"Why would she do that?" I asked peevishly.

"Come, Eleanor," he said with a touch of impatience. "If you seek the truth, you must be willing to accept it."

I looked out the window, at the light trapped in the frowzy tangle of forest. He was right, of course, about all of it. I drew a breath, turned back to him and said, "Louis Ducoeur grew up in Europe. He was educated in France, so it's quite possible that he would have returned to Paris if he married. Given that, I suppose the only reason Eve's death certificate would have my mother's name on it would be..." I found I was still unable to speak the words I knew I must accept.

"Would be if she had adopted your mother's identity so completely that even her husband believed she was Elizabeth," Alexander finished for me.

I thought of that sweet, bright face in the painting over Alexander's piano. She didn't seem capable of a plan so devious, to say nothing of my own mother's part in it. And yet, to switch identities, preposterous as it might look to me now, might have seemed to the twins the only solution to their problems. Eve would have married the man she loved but couldn't win honestly, and my mother would have been free to marry my father.

"Something's still wrong," I said, nervous energy coiling in me until I had to begin pacing. I paid no heed to Alexander's worried eyes. "I can understand why my grandfather would have disowned a daughter for running away with a poor musician. But he never talked about either of his daughters. If he believed that Elizabeth had married Louis Ducoeur as he wished, then it makes no sense that when she died, he effectively disowned her, too."

"Unless he discovered what the twins had done," Alexander suggested.

"But then he would have told someone."

"Do you think a father would want to disclose such a thing?"

"Do you think he would have kept it from me?" I demanded.

Alexander reached out and stopped me. "I don't think we should stay here any longer," he said. "I forget how close it all is to your life."

"We can't stop now!" I cried, more vehemently than I meant to. "There's a reason for the dreams, and it has something to do with all of this—with what happened to my mother and her sister. Maybe my grandmother, too."

"Your grandmother?"

As soon as I said it, I wished I hadn't, but now it was too late. "She died of an undiagnosed illness," I said, "which first came on her here. Some say...that is, I've heard rumors to the effect...that she was mad when she died."

"Eleanor," Alexander said, taking the death certificate from my trembling hands, "I can't speak for your grandmother's mental state, but as for the rest, it's all here. The twins switched identities and married, their father found out and disowned them, Eve unfortunately died of a common illness, and that's the end of it."

"Then why am I dreaming of her?" I asked. "I dream of her only when something's wrong. And then there's all that happened to me here the other day. I have to know what it means!"

Alexander sighed. "Well, I imagine we'll find out easily enough who was here, if you're determined. As for the rest, there's only one thing to do."

I looked at him questioningly, and he answered, "Write to the hospital in Paris where she died. Locate the other copy of the certificate, or some other evidence of what happened. Prove to yourself that it was all as this paper claims..."

I looked at him, and I was painfully, almost physically aware of the two obvious words that would complete the statement. Or not. But we both shied from that fraught possibility for the moment.

Instead I answered, "I'll do it right away," seizing greedily on the task for its practicality and the means it gave me to occupy myself, if only for a little while, with something concrete in the midst of so much obscurity. "Now, let's try to find out who was here the other day."

Again Alexander sighed. "If you're certain."

"I am."

Alexander put the certificate back into the drawer, then took my hand. We walked out of the library and back down to the ballroom.

"Have you been outside yet?" he asked, and I shook my head. We turned toward the French doors.

The rose garden outside of the ballroom was a shadow of the one in the dream. Its fountain was dry and cracked, with tendrils of a honeysuckle vine dripping from basin to basin in place of the streams of water that had mesmerized my dreaming eyes. The bench next to the fountain was also broken: one half lay shattered on the ground, the other rested, lopsided, on top of it. Roses ran wild over the broken stones. I should not have expected it to be as I had dreamed it, but the extent of the ruin still came as a shock.

I looked around the perimeter of the garden, which had not been visible in the dream's night. To my left, a high stone wall overgrown with ivy converged with the far end of the ballroom, extended some ten or fifteen yards, then turned toward the nearer end of the ballroom, creating a kind of enclosed courtyard roughly the dimensions of the room it adjoined.

We passed the broken fountain and moved to the ivied wall in front of us. The door was invisible beneath the shroud of vines, but Alexander moved them aside and found it just where it should have been, locked as it had been in the dream. He took the key I proffered and turned it in the lock. The ivy's creepers gummed the hinges, but Alexander forced the door open and we stepped through.

Though the jungle had encroached on the second garden, it had not marred its beauty. If anything, the dense trees and vines seemed to have drawn protective walls around it, sealing it from the ravages of time and elements that had destroyed the previous one. The tree in the centre was not in bloom, but the clusters of waxy leaves were thick and dark with life. The grass was knee-length and silvery green, sprinkled with buttercups, Queen Anne's lace, and many more flowers I could not name. Wild roses had clambered over the evergreen hedge, choking out much of the original growth and replacing it with cascades of red and white.

It was the statue, though, that captured my attention. He was encrusted with dark moss and pale blue lichen; in places he was water-stained. A tendril of ivy had begun to wind up his right leg. Other than that, the years had not touched him. He was not cracked or broken; his face as he raised the flute to his lips was as lovely and serene, his smile as melancholy, as I had dreamed it. I wondered what he would have played, if he had not been caught in stone.

Standing in the hazy repose of that garden, I felt more than ever that I was missing a vital piece of information. I tried to think clearly, but the heat and strangeness of the surroundings made it impossible. I don't know how long I stood there, but after a while something touched my shoulder. I whirled around, frightened until I realized that it was Alexander. I smiled at him uncertainly, then turned back to the statue. When I spoke, my voice sounded alien and jarring:

"What is this for?"

"The statue?"

"The whole thing. Why is it here? What made us dream about something we've never seen until now?"

He didn't answer. I turned away from the statue. "Let's go."

Alexander and I explored the rest of the house, both the parts I had looked at and those I hadn't. The majority of the rooms were empty, and those that weren't contained only decaying pieces of furniture. As often as not, they gave no hint as to what the original purpose of the room had been.

One or two, though, had once had obvious uses; among these was the observatory. It was small and square, with a window in each of its three outer walls. Next to these were metal stands fastened to the floor. It was Alexander who realized that they had once held telescopes. The walls still displayed a few water-stained star maps. There was also a trap door in the ceiling, with a ladder of iron pegs leading up to it. Alexander went first, hoisting himself through the hole, then pulled me up after him.

We emerged on a platform built on a flat part of the roof. Moving to the railing, I looked out over the gardens where we had walked not long before. To the right was the ivied wall with its hidden door, the child flautist and the weeping tree. Now I could see that beyond that little round garden were others, running at parallels and perpendiculars to each other, all enclosed by overgrown, vine-strewn fir hedges. I was still trying to make sense of the jumble when Alexander said:

"It's a maze."

It was hard to believe I hadn't seen it at once. I said, "I wonder what it's for."

"What makes you think it's for anything?"

"Everything here seems to lead to something. I can't stop feeling as though someone else is controlling what happens... as if we're part of a play and we don't know it." The words sounded less ironic than I had meant them to.

"Shakespeare did say that all the world's a stage."

"Honestly."

"Honestly? This house is dead, and the dead leave nothing behind: no desires, no questions, no secrets. Certainly no answers."

I looked again at the gardens. "You don't really believe that."

"Perhaps you are right." He sat on the railing. "In fact, sometimes I wonder whether I believe anything. That anything is purposeful, at any rate."

His nearness to the edge of the roof made me uneasy. "Then why do anything at all? Why go on living?"

He smiled wryly. "I don't think you understand my meaning. I am not a nihilist. I suppose there are reasons why things happen, or happen the way they do. But the span of one life is so short, it seems senseless to spend it searching for meaning."

"That's an awful way to see the world."

"You still think that I am denying, rather than accepting."

Alexander leaned back on the railing, tipped his face to the sun. He hovered for a moment against the blank air beyond, and in that moment he reminded me of nothing so much as the angel in the Public Garden. Then he looked down again, with kind, troubled eyes.

"Just then, a moment ago, nothing was so real or so true as the sun on my face. And now, in this moment, it is the way that it turns your eyes to gold. But that truth too will pass. The only absolute truth is the moment in which we are living, the only certainty that it will be eclipsed by the next. Time is the one god, and we are sand grains in his flood. Why struggle to understand, to exercise will or judgment? Why not just let go, and tumble?" His eyes flickered to the drop behind him.

"Do you really believe this?" I asked softly. "Or are these only speculations?"

He looked at me again, and I felt his eyes reaching out, enveloping me in their particular emotion as they had that night in the shadows of his study. As on that night, I was aware that those eyes opened not onto the glorious light I sometimes sensed in him, but onto the shattered columns of a broken heart.

When he answered, his tone was barren. "I believe that we live in a world where terrible things happen without explanation or justification. What use are reason or free will when they neither afford explanation nor rescind mortality?"

"How can you say that?" I cried. "You, with all your gifts? Most people live and die longing for a tiny part of what you've been given! You have no right to play music to the world, to make people love you for it, believing what you do. Don't flatter yourself that they don't know it, either. I heard that betrayal the very first time I heard you play."

He watched me in stunned silence for a moment; then he blinked, a prolonged motion, almost ludicrous. When he looked at me again, his eyes were full of tears. They were like tears leaking from a statue's eyes: his face, though miserable, was inert. It was my turn to watch him in surprise, at a loss, until he took me in his arms. The urgency in that embrace was very like fear. For the first time it occurred to me that Alexander might be as frightened by all that was happening as I was.

"I'm sorry," he said finally.

"Why?" I asked, pulling free to look at him.

"Because there was no reason to say those things to you, and I don't mean them as you think I mean them..." He looked away, bemused. "Eleanor," he said suddenly, urgently, "is there no way that I can convince you to leave Eden? This place cannot be healthy for any of us, especially you. It's too unlike what you know, too secluded. Let's go back to Boston—or New York, or Europe, wherever you like. We can go together if you want to, I'll take a permanent post—"

He must have seen the futility of his pleas at once, because he allowed me to interrupt him.

"I left all of that for a reason," I said, "like you did. Maybe later things will be different, but I have to stay here now. I need to know all of it: everything that happened to my mother and her sister. If I don't, I'll always wonder. But go if you want to, or need to. Don't let me be the cause of more unhappiness in your life."

He was already shaking his head. "I promised not to leave you."

With his words, the fear returned; I could only nod in reply and will it to relent. Then, for the second time, an image darted into my head along with the fear, as clearly as a memory would have. One of the twins was writing by the furtive light of a single candle. Intermittently she paused to look behind her, as if she feared being detected, or to dab the page in front of her with a torn strip of blotting paper. I had long enough to see the fear in her face, and then the image was gone.

"Alexander," I said, and then paused, wondering how to explain it. "I...I just thought of something."

"What?"

I shook my head. "It was almost as if I remembered something. A dream, maybe. It was one of the twins. She was writing, and she was afraid." I shuddered, hating the ominous sound of the words.

His look had turned incredulous. "What made you think of this?"

"I don't know. It was just there suddenly, as if I'd seen it before."

His eyes narrowed. "Maybe you have. You could have dreamed it and remembered it only now."

"There's something else," I continued. "Sometimes, when I dream of Eve, I hear crying. A woman crying."

He looked out toward the hazy horizon. The sun was midway down the afternoon sky; our shadows on the flagstones were slowly lengthening. "How many times have you dreamed this?"

"Only a couple. Have you dreamed it, too?"

He shook his head. "Nothing like it."

We stood in silence for a few moments. Finally, Alexander asked, "What now?"

"Let's look at the maze," I answered. He nodded, and followed me back down the ladder.

We went back outside to the walled garden behind the ballroom, through the circular garden with the statue of the boy flautist, then out through the break in the hedge at the far side. This led us to a narrow corridor with tall evergreens on either side.

"Maybe this isn't the best idea when nobody knows that we're here," I said, looking up at the strip of robin's-egg sky beyond the tops of the overgrown hedges.

"Don't worry," Alexander said, taking my hand. "I'm fairly sure I saw the way to the centre from the roof."

Hesitantly I followed him along the corridor to the left and into the first two turns.

"It's like a storybook," he said after a time.

"Or a horror novel," I replied. "Jane Eyre." He smiled in the manner he did sometimes—the manner that told me as clearly as words how many years it had been since he had read Jane Eyre. I felt myself blushing, but he squeezed my hand and my anger dissipated.

After one more turn we emerged into a clearing about the size of the garden with the statue of the boy. At its centre was what must once have been a fish pond: a glorified stone bowl set into the ground, with a few inches of stagnant water and rotting leaves at the bottom, and a carving of an Aeolian harp in the middle. There was a stone bench next to the pool, an abundance of overgrown grass and some wildflowers, but not much else. At the far end the path continued.

"Let's go on," I said before Alexander could suggest anything else.

Again we entered a narrow path bordered by tall hedges, their tops taking on a golden cast in the lowering sunlight. Alexander remained as certain of the turns to take as I was muddled.

Finally I said, "If I didn't know better, I'd think you'd been through this maze before."

He shook his head. "These types of puzzles have always been easy for me. Think of it this way: however confusing, the configuration cannot be random, because it is man-made.

There's always a pattern to things like this...a bit like music, I suppose. Here there is a definite sequence. We take two right turns and one left, twice, then reverse the pattern. But if, when it comes time to reverse the sequence, the corridor we are in leads east, then we take one left and one right instead. And if we come to a clearing, then we go back to the beginning of the sequence. I believe that the clearings mark the way to the centre. Do you see?"

Theoretically I did, but trying to hold all of the information in my mind was taxing enough that I gladly left navigation up to him.

Soon we rounded a corner and came into another garden with a statue. This one was a willowy girl holding a violin by her side and looking down into the basin of another dry fountain.

"These people certainly loved the neoclassical," Alexander observed.

I tilted my head, studying the serious face of the stone girl. "I think she's pretty."

Alexander smiled. "She looks rather like you."

I could not help smiling to myself at this.

The next garden held a statue of Diana sporting her bow and arrow and a hunter's horn. The horn was hollow in the middle, and in its day had spilled not music but water into a pool at her feet. Looking at her, I began to see an order to the gardens. The more I thought about it, the more it made sense.

When we finally reached the centre of the maze, however, my theory collapsed. The clearing wasn't really a garden at all, just a rectangular patch of overgrown grass with a tree-trunk in the middle. The blackened streak on its rotting bark suggesting it had been struck by lightning.

"Damn," I said under my breath.

"What?" Alexander asked.

"I thought I saw a pattern, until this."

"What do you mean?"

"Every clearing in the maze has a musical statue. The Fontaines have always been musical. It seemed that the small gardens would lead to some kind of bigger one, with statuary depicting their union with the Ducoeurs, and then the rest would keep to some Ducoeur theme. But there's only this." I indicated the burned stump.

"Remember, when the house was built, that would have been a living tree. An apple tree, by the look of it."

"It doesn't tell us much about our haunted dreams."

Alexander considered this, then answered, "Perhaps it does. What is any haunting but an unhappy spirit looking for peace? Maybe it is as simple as your aunt wanting us to know what happened to her, and this place has something to do with it."

We stood in the silence of the clearing, considering this. Sunlight streamed through chinks in the top of the hedge, dropping bright spots like pennies into its shadow.

"Come," Alexander said, taking my hand, "it's getting late."

"There's something I want to show you before we go."

I followed him back through the maze to the rose garden outside the ballroom. I had my key ready in case the door was locked again, but this time it opened easily. I thought that I was prepared to find anything at the top of that spiral stair, but when we reached the tower room, what I saw struck me so violently I had to grab the door frame for support.

It was empty. Except for the little table with the cracked mirror, the furniture was gone. The floorboards were filmed by the same snowfall of dust that covered the rest of the house. Its dull grey surface was inviolate, but for the faint, skittering lines drawn by the dry leaves that had blown in through a broken pane in the French doors. Alexander looked at me incredulously.

"But—it's all gone!" I cried. "The couch, the desk—" I turned to him. "Alexander, I wasn't lying to you! It was all here. Please believe me!"

He looked from my face to the panes of sunlight lying across the carpet of dust. "I know that you didn't lie. But could you have been mistaken? Could we have come to the wrong room?"

"That's ridiculous," I snapped. "There's only one tower, and only one room at the top of it."

He sighed. "All right, then. I suppose the likeliest explanation is that whoever you heard playing the piano that day knew that you had been here and covered her tracks."

"But the dust? And the broken window? It's as if no one has come here in years. Besides, why would someone go to the trouble of moving the furniture out if they knew I'd already seen it?"

Alexander bent down to study the dust on the floor, touched it, and rubbed his fingers together absently. Then he stood up again, his eyes on the cracked mirror, and made as if to enter the room.

"Don't!" I cried, catching his arm.

"Why not?"

"I just—don't think that it's meant to be touched."

"Eleanor, don't be silly."

"Please...Alexander, this is frightening me. I've had enough."

"All right," he said.

I let him lead me back down the stairs and out of the house; I didn't even look back. But I knew very well that we had not seen the last of the place.

15

The next two weeks passed like as many days. My attachment to Alexander grew until it seemed impossible that we had not always known and loved each other, as it always seems when one falls in love for the first time.

We did not talk about the house on the hill. Privately, I wrote to the hospital in Paris that had been named on the death certificate, requesting verification, and then tried to put the matter out of my mind.

What I couldn't put out of my mind, however, was Dorian Ducoeur. I dreaded seeing him again, but his party was rapidly approaching. I had thought that Alexander would not accept the invitation, but he hesitated only a moment when I asked him to go with us. We arranged for Tasha to remain at Eden with Colette.

The evening of the party I stood before my closet dejectedly, realizing that what fashions had sufficed for Boston society would be inadequate for Louisiana. The fabrics were too heavy for the climate, the styles too spare for the decrepit decadence around me. There wasn't time to go shopping, even if there had been any decent stores in the village.

"Stop worrying," Mary said as she came into the room with a box in her hands. "I knew that it would never occur to you that you might need something new to wear tonight. I told Colette to find you something in New Orleans when she went to visit her mother. I had to trust her judgment." She opened the box and lifted a dress out.

"Oh, Mary, it's beautiful!" I hugged her and then took the dress from her. It was the latest style, rose-colored, the bodice glittering with beads and sequins, the skirt made of layers of gauzy fabric.

"Here, try it on," she said, and helped me into it.

What I saw when I turned around surprised me. I couldn't remember the last time I had really studied myself in a mirror. I saw now that I had regained some of the weight I had lost after my grandfather died, yet I was still thinner than I had ever been before. I seemed to myself unnaturally angular, but it made me look older, and I was glad of this. The color of the dress lent color to my face, which was apt to be pale. As for the dark eyes, the shape of my nose and mouth, suddenly I saw the twins in them, or rather, I could no longer not see the twins in them. Not only the features but their expressions were there, the two melded like a stereoscopic image.

Mary touched my shoulder softly and said, "You don't have to wear it if you don't like it."

"I love it, Mary. I'm just not used to seeing myself like this."

"No," she agreed. "You used to look at yourself often, but I don't know that you ever saw. Look now, though, Eleanor, and see yourself, because you are beautiful now, and someday you'll be like me."

I studied our images. They were not dissimilar: Mary was the same height and build as I, she wore her hair long, like mine. Her eyes were brilliant as Venice beads in a face so serene that it seemed timeless, despite its fine tracery of lines. One day, I thought, I will awaken from another period of inattention and find that I have aged. I hoped that I could wear the years as Mary did, and smile in the glass at whatever I became.

I shook my head. "I think you're more beautiful than any girl could be."

Mary smiled and kissed my cheek. "It's a gift to be able to lie artlessly," she said, then retreated in a trail of pastel gauze and sandalwood perfume.

Not for the first time, I wondered what she thought of the change in my relationship with Alexander. Though I knew she saw it, we had never spoken of it; by now I suspected we would not. The moment for it, after that strange, rain-soaked night at Alexander's house, had been eclipsed by Tasha's illness. By the time Tasha recovered, there was no easy way to open the subject.

Or so I told myself; in retrospect, I wonder if it was actually fear. Up until recently, mine had been a façade of impermeability, no doubt founded on the loss of my mother, to avoid being hurt again. But my grandfather's death had weakened it, and in those first weeks of declared love, the last of the girl I had been dissipated, leaving a stranger in her place. Moreover I had not been in the society of anyone except Mary, Tasha, and Colette since I had fallen in love with Alexander, and I didn't know how I would fare by it, without my slippery wall of wit and easy banter.

Sighing, I turned back to the mirror and debated putting on jewelry and makeup that would match the grandeur of the dress, and which in the old days I wouldn't have dreamed of forgoing. In the end I wore only my mother's diamond and a sprinkling of powder. I put my hair up with a plain gold clip that my grandfather had given to me as a twelfth birthday present, then went downstairs to wait for Alexander.

Mary was standing by a window at the back of the entrance hall in the fading light. "Eleanor—you startled me!" she said when I came up beside her.

"Why don't you turn on the lights?" I asked, moving toward one of the wall fixtures, but she put out a hand to stop me.

"Look up there," she said. "Do you see that light, or am I imagining it?"

I walked back toward the window with mounting trepidation. In the direction of her extended finger, far up on the hill to the left of the water, a light shone through the trees.

"I see it," I finally said.

"What could it be?"

"Maybe Dorian's been up there," I suggested, more to soothe myself than answer her. "Maybe he has people doing repairs."

"Still, don't you think it's odd at this time of night?"

The lights in the room came on suddenly, and we both turned. "I almost missed you in the dark," Alexander said. His eyes didn't falter when they reached mine, though he must have heard our conversation.

"Why, Alexander," Mary cried, "you look wonderful!" And he did. He wore the black tails of that long-ago night at the symphony. His hair was combed back; his eyes were velvety in the soft light. He wore a rosebud in his lapel, one of the barely pink roses particular to Eden. He held a bunch more in his hand; these he offered to Mary and me.

"How pretty," Mary said. "They look so lovely near your dress, Eleanor. You ought to wear one."

I took one from the bunch and began to tuck it behind my ear, then stopped. "Will you pin it on?" I asked Alexander.

"Of course," he said, smiling. "I even have a pin." He bent over me, squinting to see, and wove the pin carefully through the delicate fabric of the dress. Then he flinched and drew his hand away, but it was too late: he had pierced his finger, leaving a spot of blood on the fabric beneath it. "I'm sorry—" he began.

"Don't be," I said. "The spot will come out. But we should go now, or we'll be late."

The drive to Joyous Garde was quiet. There were few other cars on the narrow road that wound around the lake and hill. When we reached the house, though, we found it ablaze with light. Elegant cars lined the sides of the drive, and hordes of people moved about the downstairs rooms, the sounds of their laughter and conversation pouring with contrasting strains of music through the open front door.

I had never visited Joyous Garde, and I had expected it to be more or less like the other plantation houses I'd seen, but it was as different from a typical plantation manor as the house on the hill. The gardens had been bludgeoned into submission, with low, orderly evergreen hedges describing the margins of equally methodical flower beds. White-pebbled paths ran among them, up to the main entrance.

The house itself was made of the pale stucco particular to French country houses; it had weathered to a dingy shade of grey over the years, and the torrential rains and humidity had left spreading stains of a dark greenish brown. It was also built in the style of the grand châteaux, with elaborate decoration over the windows and doorways, lacy wrought-iron balconies, and curving swags of steps. These ornaments had the effect of lavish jewelry on an old woman's corpse.

"I thought this was supposed to be an exclusive party," Alexander said.

Mary shrugged. "Perhaps they define these things differently here."

Alexander took my hand as I stepped out of the car, and

squeezed it once. I looked at him to see what he was feeling, what might have prompted the gesture, but his smile was as serene and impermeable as Mary's.

"Shall we?" he asked. Rather than antipathy, I sensed anticipation in his demeanor. Knowing what he thought of Dorian, this made me uneasy. I nodded, and then he unsettled me further: he leaned down and kissed me, long and deeply. I stood blinking at him in surprise, but he had already turned back to the house, his look of expectancy too clear now to ignore.

Dorian stood just inside the door, greeting guests as they entered. His blue eyes glinted with humor, and perhaps with the contents of the champagne glass he held in his hand. I couldn't help but pay grudging respect to the splendor of his appearance. He was dressed in the ivory linen he seemed to favor, the shirt open on a kerchief the color of his eyes. This, coupled with the gold-rimmed spectacles, gave him the consciously casual air of a gentleman explorer.

He was talking to a dark-haired woman in green silk, who held a glass in her slender, violet-gloved hand. When we entered she turned her lazy green gaze on us, looking us up and down unabashedly. I wished then that I had thought better of the cosmetics and jewelry.

"I don't think I know these guests," she said to Dorian in a drawl as slow and audacious as her look.

"Dominique Fauré," he said, "may I introduce you to the newest tenants of Eden's Meadow: Eleanor Rose, Mary Bishop, and Alexander Trevozhov." She looked with pointed interest at Alexander, clearly noticing our hands as we disentangled them to shake hers.

"Welcome to Acadia," she said, raising her eyebrows. "We've all heard so much about you; we've been wondering why you haven't joined us sooner."

"We've had a lot to see to with the house," Mary said graciously, but there was a haughtiness in her eyes and tone that both amused and pleased me.

"On reprendra plus tard, Dorian," Miss Fauré said with the perfect Parisian accent I had always envied in my better-traveled peers at school, and slipped away into the crowd.

Dorian turned his radiant smile on us. "Don't mind her," he said, "or, for that matter, the likes of her, whom you will no doubt meet this evening. They're only envious." He glanced down. "Perhaps with good reason," he said pointedly, his smile losing a little of its brilliance, and I knew that the clasped hands had not been lost on him, either. "Make yourselves at home. There is plenty to eat and drink; this ridiculous Prohibition does not reach its fingers to Joyous Garde."

He threaded Mary's arm through his own. "Be gregarious," he said. "Everyone is dying of curiosity about you. Oh, and don't be surprised if they call on you to play later on." He winked at us, then wove his way into the crowd with Mary, despite her blushes and protests.

Alexander still seemed intent on something; more than that, he was beginning to radiate the captivating presence a crowd seemed to draw from him, the same that had dazzled the concert audience the past winter. I followed him into the room, half-dazzled myself. He took two champagne flutes from a laden table, handed one to me, and touched its rim to that of mine. They rang together with a sound like a child's laughter.

"To life," he said. His eyes were lustrous, his cheeks flushed as though he was already drunk. He looked like a figure out of a Renaissance panel painting, bright and beautiful and larger than life. He leaned down and kissed me again, softly and quickly. Those closest to us took in the gesture carefully, and I had the feeling that he had been as studied in making it. Again he had my hand in his, and for the moment I stopped trying to understand his behavior, as he led me through rooms each more splendid than the last.

I had grown up with money, yet even the best of Boston houses could not compare with this relic of a golden age founded on decadence, or Boston society with this crowd, which was even now under the spell of the past. My grandfather's Saturday night soirées had been nothing to the carnival of sounds and colors before me. I was awed by the opulence as a child is awed by the majestic grandeur of a cathedral.

Unlike Eden's watercolor palette, Joyous Garde was all rich colors and fabrics, elaborately designed, heavily gilded. One room was covered with frescoes of mythological scenes, similar to the ballroom ceiling of the house on the hill. Another seemed to be made of gold and mirrors, in obvious reference to Versailles. Dorian's guests danced, strolled, or stood about in groups, all sparkling, shining, dripping with color and light like their surroundings, so that they seemed part of some rich medieval tapestry.

Dorian had been correct in his prediction: his guests were intrigued by us. We could not walk a few feet without being snared by somebody or other. I was soon separated from Alexander, but the liquor had given me courage, and I was grateful enough for it that I didn't consider how it might betray me. It was no longer champagne that I was drinking, but a pale, opaque liquid with a distinctive herbal taste I could not place. I didn't know what it was, but I no longer cared. I let the crowd pass me from one group to the next. I spoke of everything from music to war, paintings to poison—conversations that seemed richer and truer than any I had had before—until the words were a blur and, as if Alexander had indeed cast a spell with his toast, I was drowning in the sheer exuberance of life.

Finally it was too much. Following a trill of fresh of air through one of the close-packed rooms, I made my way onto the back gallery. The corner where I stood overlooked a garden pool where fish glanced silver in the light of the declining moon. I was relieved to find this garden as unkempt as Eden's. I leaned against the railing, looking down at the swirling fish, sipping the dregs of my glass as I tried to regain my equilibrium.

I had been there some time when, above the murmur still undulating outward, I became aware of a conversation in the room beyond. My spinning head made the speakers seem first quite close and then miles away, but I knew at once who they were.

"The truth, now," Alexander demanded. "Why are you here?"

"I might as well ask the same of you," Dorian answered.

It was the supplication in his tone rather than his words that snared my curiosity, rooting me in silence when I knew that I ought to reveal myself to them at once. I edged closer to the door, completely careless of the indiscretion I was committing.

"Come now," said Dorian, "I mean you no harm."

"No, indeed," Alexander said grimly. "But you wouldn't hesitate to use her."

Dorian's laugh was mellow as a piano's middle tones. "You misunderstand me. I involve myself with no one who does not desire it."

Though I knew that the words I was hearing were significant, I could not fully comprehend them. It seemed as though a haze beyond that of the alcohol had enveloped my senses. A stone chimera, one of a pair framing the doorway, loomed out of the shadows beside me. Its downcast eyes seemed sympathetic; I put one hand on its back for balance, and leaned closer to the doorway.

"You speak as though you don't know the power of your charms," said Alexander.

"On the contrary—I know that no charms of mine have any real power at all. You would do well to consider that yourself. We are all players in a plot whose outcome no one may imagine, not even you or I. But that isn't what concerns you now. Your concern is entirely altruistic. Or is it?"

I pressed still closer to the carved portal. The night was dissolving into darkness, like a photograph left too long in the developer. It was difficult to hold on to that strain of conversation, even to a strain of my own thought. I touched the empty glass to my forehead, willing its cool tangibility to disentangle my thoughts.

"She is not your affair." Alexander's voice was resonant and determined, yet not quite definite. A moment later Dorian echoed my thought.

"You do not trust your own words, mon cher." I felt the golden tone seducing me, despite the fact that his words were not meant for me. "You brace at that endearment," Dorian persisted, "yet once you did love me. You can't have forgotten."

I started from my hypnotic lethargy, thinking only that it could not be. As in waking from a feverish sleep, it was impossible to tell whether I had heard the words or imagined them.

"You betrayed me," Alexander answered, and the terrible sadness in his voice confounded me still further.

Dorian's laughter continued to roll and gather, imperturbable as beads of mercury, though now there was as much sadness in it as there had been in Alexander's words. He said, "You may place your righteousness again between your love and the inevitable, but I assure you that you will not escape a second time intact; nor will your sacrifice save her."

In the ensuing silence I lost myself again in waves of something like a dream. I thought vaguely that they had gone away, but Dorian spoke again, this time without a hint of humor, and with a curious shortness to his words:

"Despite what you may imagine, I work as much in her interest as you do."

There was another short silence, and then Alexander replied in an acrid voice: "You lie. You always have lied."

"Ah," said Dorian, the expression like a protracted sigh, with more than a hint of wistfulness in it, "there you are wrong. I tell the truth—the sad fact is that few want to hear it. Perhaps that is the root of your misunderstanding of me."

"I understand you perfectly. I hate you."

Dorian began to laugh again, and the sound was so hollow, so awful that I shrank back against the wall. I found myself looking into the face of the stone incubus opposite me, grinning and nodding in a twisted semblance of life. I shrieked and raised my hands to cover my eyes, remembering too late the empty glass I held. It fell to the ground languidly, almost mockingly, and shattered on the flagstones. I looked for what seemed many minutes at the jagged shards glinting in the moonlight. Then came the sound of quick footsteps, and Alexander's solicitous face appeared before me, blue-white in the irresolute moonlight.

"Eleanor, what are you doing here?" There was no remnant of the tone he had used with Dorian, only concern.

"I...I came for air...I'm afraid I've drunk a bit much—" I took a step toward him and stumbled. He caught me, and I looked up into his face. All of the earlier bravado was gone, leaving him looking pinched and anxious. "What were you talking about?"

"Talking about?" he repeated absently.

"With Dorian, just now. I heard you talking."

Without answering, he bent down for one of the shards of glass, touched the liquid that clung to it, then tasted it. "Who gave this to you?" he demanded. Without waiting for me to answer, he said, "Damn him! He must have known you were listening."

He rubbed his eyes, suddenly seeming very tired. After a moment, he turned his attention on me again. "I ought to have explained it to you before this, and I wish that I could explain to you now...but I can't. Not because I don't want to, or don't think that I ought to, but simply because I am no longer certain myself of what I know."

He sat down on a stone bench by the railing and drew me down beside him. He took a deep breath, then said, "What I can and must tell you is that I have not been honest with you. I let you believe that I did not know Dorian Ducoeur before we met him in your house. In fact, I have been acquainted with him before, under vastly different circumstances. I know him to be a designing man of the most dangerous kind, for he has great sway over people's sensibilities. And I fear that he may harm you, because you have connected yourself with me."

"But those things you said...the way he spoke to you...it didn't seem to me that he hated you...."

"Things often are not what they seem, Eleanor," he said softly. "Forget what you heard; it will only trouble and deceive you further. Believe what you see."

I looked at him, and the concern in his face could be nothing but honest. I reached up and kissed him, and met the reserve that until that night I had considered characteristic. But only a few hours before, I had felt something different. I knew that he was capable of passion, and I would not accept his denial of it. His kisses deepened under my persistence, and gradually his body relaxed. His lips traveled to my neck, soft as butterflies' wings over my throat. The milky whiteness of the alcohol I had drunk rose in the darkness behind my lowered eyelids, drifting lazily, a glow that moved under the surface of my skin—then he pulled away, breathing hard.

"Not here, Eleanor," he whispered. "Not now."

His eyes were conflicted. Bits of the overheard conversation drifted back. "Alexander—" I began.

"Don't be deceived, Eleanor," he interrupted. "I have loved others, but you are something entirely different."

His eyes never wavered from mine, and I knew that whether I wished it or not, my heart was laid bare before him as his never would be before me.

"You are my only love," he said, "and I will not take you for granted. Come," he said, standing up and raising me gently, tucking my arm through the crook of his own. "Let's go home."

But we were not to escape so easily. The crowd closed in around us when we returned, demanding music. Alexander looked at me helplessly, and I shook my head—I could not possibly play. Sighing, he turned back to the crowd and then forced a smile.

"Miss Rose declines," he said, "but I would be honored to play for you."

We were pushed toward the conservatory in a soft, hot press of bodies. The first of the crowd flocked to the chairs; the rest gathered in the corners and spilled out into the corridor. As Alexander took the bench, the shifting and whispering abated. I tried to retreat to a corner of my own, but he stopped me, indicating a chair near him. Gingerly I sat down, aware of so many eyes on us, for they watched me with as much curiosity as they did Alexander. I caught sight of Mary standing in a group by a door at the far side of the room. Dorian stood at her side. His eyes met mine, and he smiled a tight, ironic smile. I looked away quickly, just as the first chords of a Rachmaninov prelude split the silence.

It was the Opus 32 in B minor, a piece I knew well, but listening to Alexander play it was like hearing it for the first time. As on that winter night at the symphony, he ignored the composer's dynamic markings, playing the first chords loudly, then subsiding into a far quieter interpretation of the piece than I had ever heard. It worked: every set of eyes in the room was arrested, each listener an instant prisoner of Alexander's intensity.

I have heard that, like so much of Rachmaninov's music, that prelude was inspired by the sound of Russian church bells, which haunted him throughout his life. That night, though, I heard something more in it than the horror of civil war and oppression. It went beyond sadness, beyond longing or even the solace of tears; it was a wail for an ultimate and absolute meaninglessness. In that music, the stirrings of madness twined with the understanding of a terrible, universal truth.

To be able to draw that out of someone else's music, to find a livable insanity buried in those mute marks on paper, Alexander must himself have lived it, must have been living it still. As I listened, I began to realize the magnitude of the blight on his soul, which his bitter, despairing litany on the observatory roof had intimated. I realized that I understood him even less than I had thought. Of one thing, though, I was certain: whatever constituted his prison was surely something greater than his lost and divided homeland.

The last notes of the piece withered in a stunned and perfect silence. Before it could be broken, he began to spin more music, this time soft as snowflakes, ephemeral as frost patterns on glass. Suddenly I was five years old again, looking down from my nursery window through ivy tendrils and a soft curtain of falling snow at the wings of the stone angel. The piece could only be one of Alexander's own.

He played softly enough to mandate the silence of his audience, almost too softly to be believed. The control required for such exquisite tone was as maddening to consider as the imprisoned impetus of the Rachmaninov. I thought that he intended the piece for Tasha, but then he turned his eyes from the piano to smile at me.

When the piece ended he paused again, then moved into the next before the silence could break. It was an étude, the one I had struggled with, and I felt the tension dissipate from the room as the audience found themselves back on the solid ground of a virtuoso showcase piece. For this one they applauded. Afterward Alexander played two more études, rather perfunctorily. Then he stood up, smiled and bowed, took my hand firmly, and left the room.

Mary caught up to us in the hallway and began to protest, "Oughtn't we to say good-bye to Dorian, at least?"

"Eleanor isn't well," Alexander told her, his look asking me not to contradict him, though I would not have thought of it.

Someone else had taken up at the piano in the room behind us, playing a popular song. People were singing, laughing, and I heard the sound of their footfalls as they began to dance. These faded as we twisted and turned our way through the empty rooms, strewn with glasses smudged with fingerprints and lipstick, bits of feather and ribbon, crushed flowers and the burnt-out ends of cigarettes.

"At any rate," Mary said as we stepped out into the sweet darkness and slid into the car, "we'll see him again soon enough."

"What do you mean?" I asked absently as the car lurched into motion. Alexander slipped an arm around my waist, and I was glad to lean against his comforting warmth.

"Dorian said that this party was such a success, he's already planning another. I told him that you had been thinking of entertaining at Eden, and he suggested that we have a joint party up at the house on the hill. Of course, it's ultimately up to you." She was clearly oblivious to our discomfort.

"The house can't be fit for guests," I said faintly.

"Eleanor, you're not going to be tiresome, are you?"

She was half-joking, but the serious half concerned me. I hadn't seen her this excited about anything in ages. The mark of Dorian's seduction was on her face like a brand, and suddenly I was frightened, for myself as well as for her. I had relied on Mary as an anchor of reason; yet if he won her over, we would be divided, and I would be cast adrift in a tide of dangers rising far too fast.

I sighed. "I'm sure he doesn't need me to go ahead with it."

Mary's eyebrows drew together, as they did whenever I scorned her beloved Chopin. "Really, Eleanor, I think you're a bit unfair about him."

I sighed again, leaning my head on Alexander's shoulder, closing my eyes for a moment. "I'm sorry, Mary. I'm just so tired, and my head aches." The last of my drunken euphoria had drained away, leaving leaden pessimism in its place.

"I know," she said after a moment. Her tone had softened

again, and I relaxed. The drone of the engine, the warm breeze touching my face from the propped-open vent, the total darkness beyond the twin dim pools of yellow light on the road ahead all combined into a drowsiness I couldn't fight. It wasn't long before I had drifted into sleep.

16

It was as if the dream had been waiting for sleep to release it. I found myself at the centre of the maze behind the house on the hill. A full moon brightened the night sky, so that the apple tree in the centre of the garden, young and strong and replete with golden fruit, cast a shadow on the ground beneath it.

I stood in this shadow, circumscribed by fire. It ran around the tree in a ring, making an island of the small mound where it stood. The twins stood on either side of me, blindfolded, gagged, and bound hand and foot. They wore robes and veils like medieval nuns, one red, the other white. The white one's head was like a wilted flower, the red's high and defiant.

I tried to cry out and to run, but I had neither voice nor the ability to move. I looked at the twins, and then at the moon above them. Its white light condensed and brightened until I was no longer looking at the moon, but at the sun.

Now the ring around the apple tree was of water. Birds and butterflies swooped and dove against the azure sky. To my left, a white horse grazed on the young grass. To my right, a black-haired woman gathered flowers, singing the lullaby I had sung to Tasha. Her skin was white and pink as the roses she held. As she neared the stream and the island, a man alighted from the tree's lower branches, and said with a sardonic grin that reached right up into his summer-blue eyes—

"Eve!"

The afternoon dissolved. The smell of burning was strong, and with it came dread. There were two more figures in the garden now, both outside the ring of fire. One stood near the woman in white, his features obscured by shadow, his back to the tree. The other stood by the woman in red, and his features swam in the firelight.

The wind shifted in my direction, carrying with it the acrid smoke and its accompanying dread. I tried to scream, just as the red-veiled woman lurched toward the fire. Dorian reached across it and stopped her, then untied her gag.

"You've killed them," she cried piteously. "Let me die!"

Dorian's eyes were hard and cold as pearl, but he loosened the woman's blindfold. As it fell away, Eve's passionate face looked out from beneath the veil. When she saw Elizabeth and Alexander, relief flooded her face.

"Don't think yourself saved," Dorian said to Eve, each word falling with resonance and finality. "You have sinned, and you must pay for it."

"I have deceived you, yes," she answered, her voice clear despite her obvious terror. "But I have always been true to myself, so I cannot have sinned."

"You have sinned," Dorian repeated. He looked Elizabeth and Alexander, then turned away. "All of you have sinned, and all of you will pay!"

The tears on Eve's face had dried. When she spoke, it was with authority. "Only I have deceived, and only I will answer for it."

"I've passed my judgment," Dorian replied shortly. He moved toward my mother, but Eve called to him to stop. He looked at her, this time with anger lighting his eyes. "Isn't your original sin enough? Do you cross me in my judgment as well?"

"It's not your right to judge us," she said.

Dorian struck Eve across the face. She barely flinched, though a line of blood sprang up on her cheek. "That is for your passion," he said to her. "Now, for your sin—"

Elizabeth turned her white-hooded head toward them, as if she wished to speak. Eve cried, "Unbind her!"

Dorian seemed confused for a moment. Then, dazedly, he did as Eve had ordered.

"If there is sin here, it is mine," Elizabeth said, as soon as her tongue was free. "Eve only did what she thought she must do. I complied with a deception when I knew better."

A tear spilled down her cheek, and collected in a drop on her jaw; on Eve's was a congruous drop of blood. The two hung momentarily, then fell with the suspended languor of autumn leaves. In that lengthened moment Alexander broke from his torpor at last, and caught a drop in each hand. When he opened them, he held two jewels: a ruby and a diamond. He regarded the prisoners, then looked at Dorian, whose face was frozen in an expression of disbelief.

"How is it," he asked Dorian, "that you are not moved by the one's honest admission of her mistake, or the other's willingness to shoulder the transgressions of another?"

"Their sin remains unaccounted for!" Dorian cried, pointing an imputing finger at the twins.

Alexander looked at the jewels in his hand. "Let each of them carry her own burden. That is punishment enough."

I blinked, and the jewels hung from fine chains. Alexander stepped across the fire. He gave the diamond to Elizabeth, the ruby to Eve. Each took the proffered jewel and hung it around her neck. Then Alexander began to untie the rest of their bonds, while Dorian watched in silent fury.

"Understand," Alexander said, "that Eden is lost to you."

As the last of the bindings fell away, Dorian leaped across the fire, and reached for Eve with unguarded fury. I tried to scream, but still I had no voice, no ability to move, no way to counteract the impending horror. The fire flared, stretching high into the night, trapping us. My ears rang with a woman's wails. Then all was darkness.

I started awake in the backseat of the car. We were at Eden, parked by the front door. Alexander and Mary were hovering over me, their faces anxious; Alexander's hands were on my shoulders. As soon as he saw my eyes open he let go of me. I sat up, my hair coming loose from its pins and tumbling down around my shoulders.

"I had a nightmare," I gasped, every image etched horribly into my mind. "A terrible nightmare..."

"I know," Mary soothed, smoothing my hair back from my forehead. "You were crying and calling—"

"We tried to wake you," Alexander interrupted, clearly as shaken as I was, "but you wouldn't respond."

"It was as if you were in some kind of trance." Despite her carefully controlled tone, I could see that Mary had been frightened badly.

I rested my forehead against my palm, trying to regain composure. I was hot, too hot to blame it simply on the warm night.

The lights of the house spilling across the lawn were like knives driven into my eyes.

"It was so awful," I said, "and so real...as if I had really been there. But I couldn't have been...could I?"

"Let's go inside," Mary said gently. "I'll make some tea, and you can tell us all about it."

I nodded, and Alexander led me to an armchair in the library. By the time Mary came back I was calmer. I sipped the tea and related to them the basics of the dream.

When I finished, Alexander's look was grave. "I know that you don't want to hear it, Eleanor, but I really think that Eden is not good for you. I can't believe you aren't at least half-frightened of the place, and I can't understand why you persist in staying here."

Mary was studying me closely. The fine lines I had noticed on her face earlier that evening were more pronounced now. "I have to agree, Eleanor," she said. "You've been excitable and peevish since we came here, sleeping all day, pacing all night. Perhaps it isn't a healthy place for any of us."

"I can't believe it!" I cried. "Both of you speak to me as if I were an invalid—a child! The rest of you are free to go anytime, but I won't leave! Not yet."

"Good God, Eleanor," Alexander said with the beginnings of anger, "you can't still think that digging into this mysterious past of your family's can lead to anything but misery?"

There were tears in my eyes; I wiped them away angrily. "Misery? My family is all dead! I've never even had a photograph of my mother. I don't know who she was or what divided her from her sister; everyone has tried to keep it from me all my life. And as long as I don't know what happened, then I don't know who I am!"

Alexander and Mary looked at me as the words settled, and then, furtively, at each other. After a moment Mary stood up, and I saw tears glimmering in her own eyes.

"You know that I'll stay here as long as you need me to," she said. "But I can never be happy with something that causes you grief."

I shook my head, already regretting my words. "I know that, Mary. I'm sorry."

"Don't be. I should have seen what all of this would mean to you." She kissed my cheek. "Is there anything else you need now?"

"No, thank you. I'll be fine."

She looked at Alexander, then smiled at me again. "Good night, then, both of you."

"Do you believe it?" I asked Alexander when she was gone.

"What?"

"The dream. Do you think that Eve did something terrible, and we're all part of it?"

He smiled ruefully, twining his fingers with mine. "It was a dream, Elenka. Nothing more. As for the past—let it be, for now. It's almost morning." I looked toward the arched window. The night beyond it was still bright with stars, but there was a faint trace of color in the eastern sky. "Come, I'll see you safely to bed. I can let myself out."

I turned from the window. Alexander's face was irresolute. I leaned forward and kissed him. After a moment he pulled away and looked at me again, and the conflict was gone.

"I'll see you to bed if you like," he repeated softly. "But only if you are certain."

"I was certain the first time I saw you," I answered.

Alexander looked at me a moment longer. Then he took my hand, and we tiptoed up the stairs by that first faint light in the sky. We made love in the twilight, lay watching morning break, and then slept in the sun, dreamless.

Nobody disturbed us that day. We lay in the dappled light that sifted through the leaves of the trees outside the window, talking and laughing softly between embraces. When twilight fell again, Alexander finally left, but before he went, he picked up the pink dress from its crumpled heap on the bedroom carpet. The rose he had pinned over my heart was still fresh and perfect. His eyes fell on it, and stayed. Finally I took the dress from him and unpinned the flower.

"It's as if it's only just been cut," I said, holding it up to study it by the dim light.

He ran his hand over my rough hair. "It's your magic," he said. I shook my head at him, but he repeated, "It is. Eleanor Rose—why not?" His smile waned as he fell to studying my face. "May I have it? To remember this day?"

I turned the little flower over in my fingers once, and then handed it back to him. "Consider it a token of my undying love." I smiled. "Or an undying token?"

His eyes were serious, though, as he accepted it. "Do you understand what you say?"

I nodded, suddenly as serious as he.

"I'll love you always, Eleanor," he said, clutching me in an intense and oddly clumsy embrace.

"Will you come tomorrow?" I asked, a little anxiously.

He smiled again. "Nothing could keep me away," he said, then kissed me good-bye.

Part Two

Prologue

NOVEMBER 1905, THE DUCOEUR HOUSE, IBERVILLE PARISH, LOUISIANA

Night time in a small, round, candle-lit room. The candle's flame reflects in a mirror over a small table; the only other furniture are a couch and a desk.

A dark haired woman sits by the candle in a dress the color of blood. There's a writing desk on her lap, and her hand moves furiously across the page. From time to time she turns furtively to look around the room, as if assuring herself that she is alone.

When she finishes writing, she blots the page with a torn strip of blotting paper, then seals it in an envelope. She scrawls something across it, then gets up and knocks quietly on the door. A young, frightened-looking Creole girl in maid's cap and apron unlocks the door and enters.

"He's coming, Madame," she says. Ascending footsteps sound below.

The woman presses the envelope into the girl's hand. "Send it as soon as you can, Jeannie. It must reach my sister as quickly as possible."

"It will go with the morning mail."

"Thank you," the woman says tremulously, and kisses the girl's cheek. "Now go! Use the second-floor doorway, and don't tell anyone that you were here."

The girl goes, locking the door behind her. The woman hides her writing desk under the sofa, then returns to her chair and takes up a piece of needlework. By the time the key turns again in the lock, she appears to be engaged in it.

A man enters the room. It is clear from his flushed cheeks and shiny eyes that he has been drinking. A lank piece of fair hair hangs over his face, and his jaw pushes sullenly forward. He lists in the doorway, watching the woman until she can no longer ignore his presence. She looks up at him. Her face is the thin blue-white of skimmed milk, but her eyes are still full of the smoldering passion that distinguishes them from her sister's. The man's pout dissolves into a leer.

"So innocently occupied, Elizabeth," he says with a faint French accent. Eve only looks at him with large, frightened eyes. "Has a day in here changed your mind?"

Her eyes flicker away from his, down to the embroidery in her lap. Nonetheless, her voice is resolved when she answers, "I've told you, she's with my sister, and there she'll stay until you've come to your senses."

His face hardens. For a moment his body, too, is frozen. Then he crosses the room and strikes her across the face. "Don't lie to me," he says, his voice low and menacing. "She's with him, isn't she?"

"Whom?" she asks dully, her face hidden by a dark tumble of hair.

A tight, ironic smile tugs at his lips. "We both know whom I mean."

She doesn't answer him, just turns her face to the wall and drops her head into her hands. He watches her for a moment, then he takes her hand—the one with the wedding ring—and turns it toward the candle's light, exposing the ink spots on the fingers.

"What have you been doing?" he demands.

"Writing letters," she answers after a pause.

"Where are they?"

She points to the desk, and he examines the three envelopes he finds there. He pockets them and leans against the wall she faces, crossing his arms languorously across his chest.

"You know, there is still a distance for you to fall...for the child, a much greater one."

She finally raises her head. Her hair falls away from her face, revealing a red welt under her right eye. The skin beneath it is already discolored. "Stay away from her, Louis," she says, her voice low and ominous.

Louis looks at her with impotent fury, then turns to go. However, as he is about to close the door again, something catches his eye. He moves back across the room and picks up the strip of blotting paper that lies by his wife's foot. She rises and tries to take the paper away from him, but he holds it out of her reach, his face freezing into a brittle smile as he reads the words imprinted there. He looks at them for a long time—too long—and then, still smiling, he raises his hand and strikes her again across the face, so hard that she falls backward into the stand with the mirror, knocking it to the floor. The candle expires, but the full moon sheds enough light to distinguish the crack that bisects the fallen mirror, and Eve supine before it, until Louis drags her to her feet again.

"That's for him," he says, raising his hand again. "This is for you."

For a moment the light picks out her terrified eyes, then his hand falls.

1

I have wondered whether Alexander would ever have spoken again of the peculiarities surrounding us if I had kept my silence. I suppose it is useless to speculate: as much as I wanted to forget the morbid allure of the dreams and the house and the mystery of the twins, I couldn't.

One evening several weeks after Dorian's party, Alexander and I took a walk through the topiary garden. When we reached the water, I could not help looking up at the house on the hill; and then I couldn't look away. Its dark angles stood out like stencils on the fiery sky.

"What is it?" Alexander asked, kissing my cheek, my neck.

I felt like crying. The past few weeks had been so peaceful, and it seemed wrong to destroy that peace. But I had known all along that it wasn't real, and if there was any hope for a future with Alexander, I had to know the truth. So I said:

"We can't pretend forever that there's nothing wrong."

"I don't know what else we can do," he said. "There don't seem to be any more records of anything concerning your aunt and mother."

"I'm talking about Dorian," I said. "I want you to tell me how you know him, and what it means that he's here now."

He seemed to be studying me, but his eyes were distant.

Finally he said, "Why trouble yourself with this, Eleanor? It can only hurt you."

The tone of his warning sounded too much like condescension. "A secret is always worse than the truth," I said shortly.

The sun had set, leaving the sky slate blue, the cypress trunks fluted shadows. The house on the hill was hidden again.

Sighing, Alexander turned away from the water. "Come, then," he said, and started toward his house.

Tasha was at Eden with Mary, so the cottage was quiet. Alexander turned on the lamps in his music room and poured two glasses of wine, handing one to me. He took a sip from his glass before he began to speak.

"I first met Dorian Ducoeur nearly fifteen years ago, in St. Petersburg. I had been playing in concert a good deal, and as goes along with that sort of thing, I had spent much time celebrating." He smiled wryly.

"One day, I became aware of him. That sounds strange, I know, but I can't explain it in any other way. Nobody introduced us. He did not appear in conjunction with any particular event that I recall. But walking the streets at night, coming late out of a party, stepping into a coffeehouse, I would catch glimpses of him. He was always alone, always meticulously and expensively dressed, and he always made sure to catch my eye before he disappeared."

Alexander paused, then drew a deep breath before he continued: "I suppose it is only fair to add that there was a woman, a well-known ballet dancer, who was my lover at that time."

"If that was your only objection to telling me this story—" I began, but he silenced me with a look.

"Anna cultivated mystery as some women do roses. It kept me infatuated far longer than I ought to have been. In that,

Dorian was like her. He seemed to appear and disappear out of nowhere. He seemed to know me, though I knew nothing of him. He began to haunt me: not in the way that Eve haunts you, but only in the ordinary manner in which one is plagued by the beautiful." He paused to refill my glass; he had barely touched his own.

"Several times I tried to approach him, but he always managed to disappear before I could reach him. It was so deliberate, it began to madden me. He would smile as though in recognition, making certain that I saw and acknowledged him before he vanished." Alexander shook his head.

"I asked around, but none of my friends had noticed him. Some thought that I was deluded, but not Anna. She laughed and pretended to be jealous, but I could see that this mention of a handsome stranger intrigued her.

"It went on like this for months. Then one night, walking along the river in a heavy snow, I looked up to find him walking beside me just as naturally as if we had known each other forever. As soon as I had thought it, he said: 'It feels as though we have, doesn't it?'

"He had addressed me in excellent Russian, but with an obvious French accent. 'Allow me to introduce myself,' he said. 'My name is Antoine Fontainebleau, and I am a great admirer of your playing.'"

"Antoine Fontainebleau?" I could not help repeating.

"That is the least of it," Alexander answered, "but his intentions seemed innocent enough that night. He has that way about him. He is beguiling. He beguiled me." These last words were bitter, but when he spoke again, his voice was low and calm.

"He told me that he was a drawing master from Paris, come for a few months to study the old buildings of St. Petersburg.

We talked that night straight through, walking the city, moving from restaurants to coffeehouses. When the last of those was closed, we went back to my family's house and sat in the parlor talking until the sun rose. You'll wonder what we spoke of, and I wonder too." He smiled humorlessly. "Most of our conversations were like that: deeply engaging while they lasted, yet an hour later I could not have told you what we discussed.

"Our subsequent meetings were of a similar nature. He would seek me out, and then we would talk and talk. I would have said that we were great friends, but I could not have told you on what it was based. I never even knew where he lived. It never occurred to me to wonder. So much about him was like that. His charm made me forget to ask the right questions...to ask any questions." He shook his head.

"As you can imagine, Anna was greatly angered at this sudden intimacy. So when she demanded to meet Fontainebleau I didn't dare refuse, and this was a great mistake. For as you have no doubt guessed, she fell in love with him. Completely and effortlessly. As for Antoine, well, she was a diversion."

"So is Anna the 'she' Dorian was talking about that night?"

"No," he said slowly. He paused again, then continued, "Anna changed under his influence. She had always been gay and energetic, wanting nothing more than to be the centre of attention. Once she met Antoine, she seemed only to want his.

"She kept up a pretence of her relationship with me, I don't know why; perhaps to convince herself that she didn't really need Antoine. And I didn't know how to extricate myself. It was bizarre, and miserable...and it was about to become much more so."

He sighed. "One night, Antoine and I were drinking absinthe."

"I thought it wasn't made anymore," I interrupted.

"It is, in places, but it would have been better for us all if it weren't. It's dangerous; not for the reasons you might think, but because it transcends the senses and moves straight into the deepest sensibilities. I half believe the old legend that a green fairy inhabits that drink. One can almost feel him uncurl and stretch into one's limbs, cause one to see with his eyes..."

"You almost make me want to try it!"

Alexander gave me a troubled look. "You have tried it. It was absinthe you drank that night at Dorian's party, and I suspect it is to thank for your nightmare."

I was too surprised to answer. Finally Alexander resumed his story:

"So, we were drinking a bottle Antoine claimed to have brought from France. Now, Russians are well acquainted with strong liquor, but whatever was in that bottle was something beyond my experience. Let that be my qualifier for what came next."

He didn't look at me now, but at the portrait of the twins. "It has often struck me as odd, since I was so very drunk at the time, that this is the only one of my conversations with Antoine that I remember with any clarity. He was speaking of Anna. I was barely listening until he told me that she was pregnant by him.

"At that I was indignant. Not for my own pride: where Anna was concerned, that was long gone. But I was infuriated that he had taken her when he cared nothing for her. Of course it is not an uncommon situation, but when it was Anna—well, I had never loved her, but I had cared for her, and I was worried. She lived only for Antoine by then; his rejection would crush her.

"So I told him that he must do what was right and marry her. He laughed at me and told me to let go of my outdated moralisms. Perhaps that green fairy really was awakening in me, because as Antoine continued to smile and offer his platitudes, I swung at him.

"I suppose I had expected him to hit me back, or at least to walk out. But instead, before I understood what was happening, he had his arms around me and had kissed me."

He looked at me with penetrating eyes. I knew that he expected me to be shocked, and probably horrified, but somehow I did not find the revelation unexpected. It also explained the affectionate inflection of Dorian's words in the conversation I had overheard, and the coldness of Alexander's.

"Well?" I said, when it seemed Alexander would not continue unprompted.

He shook his head. "His words turned mad. He said that it was me he loved, that it had been so since the first time he heard me play, that it had been his reason for following me. He spoke of his family's wealth, of all that he wanted to see and do, and how he wanted me as his companion in all of it. He asked me to leave Russia with him. And what frightens me still..." He paused, then repeated, "What frightens me still, is that I was nearly seduced by those words.

"It is difficult to explain, even now. I certainly did not love him—not in the way that he meant, nor any other. I knew that it was a devil's deal he offered, that it couldn't come without strings, but he was intoxicating. And so that you retain no delusions about me, Eleanor, I admit that I might very well have been enticed, had it not been for what happened next."

He seemed to expect me to answer him, but I could think of nothing to say. After some minutes he spoke again.

"As we stood there in the parlor of my parents' home, there was a sudden loud rapping on the door. It was one of my old friends, looking very pale and shaken. He told us that Anna's body had just been discovered; she had taken rat's bane. No explanation had been found, but she was several months pregnant.

"Of course they blamed me, and of course I forced Antoine to accept the blame. He did not stay long in St. Petersburg after that. He tried to speak to me several times before he left, but I would not let him near me. The next time I saw him was the day he walked through your music room door."

Alexander set his empty glass on the table. "It was you," he said, "not Anna, of whom we spoke that night—but I trust that you see the parallel. Perhaps now you understand better why I fear for your safety here."

I shook my head. "Even if he could sway my feelings for you, do you honestly think that he could drive me to suicide?"

"I wouldn't have thought it of Anna."

"Well, I assure you, he couldn't."

"Perhaps not. But the fact remains that he is dangerous, and he has chosen you."

"What for?"

"I don't know—and this is what worries me the most."

"You seemed to know that night at the party."

Alexander looked puzzled. "What made you think so?"

"You spoke as if...as if you knew something about me that I didn't."

He scrutinized me for a moment, then said, "Remember that you had drunk a great deal of absinthe. It confuses the senses, and the memory."

"The memory?" I repeated softly.

Alexander shrugged. "I have found it so and heard others

say the same."

"If you don't know, then, why do you think Dorian is here?"

He sighed. "I could believe that he followed me, or, equally, that his claim to Joyous Garde is legitimate and the rest eventuality. But I suppose that deep down, I believe there is something else that he wants, and that he came here to find it.

"I do know two things for certain. First, Dorian is nothing he claims to be, and second, he is somehow linked to those two." He indicated the painting of the twins.

Alexander's look softened as he turned back to me. He took my glass and set it down, then twined his fingers with mine. "That's enough of this. Come to bed now, love—if you'll still have me."

"Of course I will," I said, kissing his cheek.

He smiled briefly, then said, "I meant to tell you earlier, Eleanor: I must go to Baton Rouge tomorrow. I'm meeting with an agent about some engagements for the autumn. But I'll be back by evening. Will you be all right? Do you want to come with me?"

I shook my head. "I should use the time with no distractions. I've been letting my work slide terribly these last weeks."

He raised his eyebrows. "Oh? And what might be the cause of that, Miss Rose?"

"I blush to say it, Mr. Trevozhov," I answered with a laugh.

"Well, do come upstairs and explain it to me, Miss Rose," he said, kissing me.

"Only if you promise..." I looked at him, suddenly anxious. "Come back safely, Alexander."

His eyebrows drew together for a moment before he smiled. "Don't worry, Elenka. What could possibly happen in a few hours?"

2

Alexander left under an ominous sky. "Colette says that it'll storm tonight," I told him as he got into the car I had lent him for the day. "Promise me you'll stay in town if it looks bad."

Alexander laughed at my worry. "You're beginning to sound like Mary."

"I'll take care of him, mademoiselle," Jean-Pierre said to me.

"Thank you," I told him, then kissed Alexander good-bye.

I spent the morning at the piano. The first drops of rain spattered the windows as Tasha, Mary and I sat around the lunch table. We all ran to the window to watch the storm descend, still in awe of the violence of Louisiana weather.

It was not long before we needed lamps to see through the storm's murky twilight. We sat in the music room most of that long afternoon, Mary reading, I practicing, Tasha playing quietly on the floor with her dolls. Gloomy afternoon faded listlessly into evening, with barely a sentence passed between the three of us.

Mary had just stood up to turn on more lights when Tasha started, and looked toward the front windows. A moment later Mary and I heard the rumble of the car motor, the crunch of its wheels on the drive.

"It's early for Alexander to be back," Mary commented, looking at her watch.

However, the sodden figure at the door was not Alexander but Dorian. He lifted his dripping hat from his head, pushed the wet hair away from his face, and smiled brilliantly.

"I'm sorry to disturb you," he said, "but the road is washed out just past Eden. I can walk it as soon as the rain lets up."

"Nonsense!" Mary cried, helping him off with his coat. "It's wild out there, and almost dark. You'll stay here until the road is passable again."

Tasha slipped a cold little hand into mine. "Do you think that Dyadya's all right?" she whispered to me, her eyes swarming with anxiety.

"He's fine, sweetheart," I told her with more confidence than I felt.

"Is something amiss with Mr. Trevozhov?" Dorian asked.

I was wary of letting Dorian know that we were alone, but before I could concoct a lie, Mary was saying, "He's gone to Baton Rouge."

"Well, then," Dorian said, "he won't be back tonight."

His words chilled me, but I tried not to let him see it.

"It will be an adventure," Mary said. I stared at her incredulously. "Like snowstorms in Boston. We'll make a fire, and popcorn."

"I'm afraid," Tasha said, her eyebrows drawing together and her lips pushing outward, as a child's do when she is close to tears. "I want my Dyadya."

"He'll be fine," I soothed, hugging her. "He's safer there than here just now." As soon as I spoke the words, I wondered why I had chosen them; they had an ominous sound, though I'd meant them innocently enough.

Dorian fixed me with quizzical eyes, then said, "Mary's right—as long as we're stranded here, why not make the most of it?"

"Indeed!" Mary said, obviously pleased. "Colette will be putting supper together; would you care for a brandy first?"

"Not now, thank you," he said. "Perhaps afterward."

"Of course. And perhaps you can play for us."

"Oh, I have no particular talent for the piano," he said offhandedly. "I had rather hoped I might hear Miss Rose play."

Looking at him, I could only think of the hardened inertia of his face in the nightmare, and the way it had seemed to crack and pile like river ice into sheets of menace when he spoke of Eve's unnamed "sin." I shuddered inwardly but refused to lose my composure.

"Perhaps," I said. "Now, do please join us for supper."

"Thank you," he said and followed us into the dining room.

We sat down to the stew and rice Colette had set out for us. Usually I loved her cooking, but that night I could barely swallow the food; my throat seemed blocked with trepidation. Tasha also seemed to have lost her appetite. She sat watching Dorian with wide, unblinking eyes.

"Eat your dinner, love," Mary said to her absently. "You know you need the strength."

Tasha obediently picked up her fork, dipped it into the rice, and then appeared to forget about it again. Her eyes traveled back to Dorian's face and stopped there, her forehead creased as if in puzzlement. His own attention, however, was focused on me.

"Did Mary tell you about our idea of throwing a party in the house on the hill? Many of the Baton Rouge faction are beginning to wonder when you'll make another appearance."

"I hadn't thought they'd notice," I replied.

He laughed. "Indeed? You all made quite an impression the other night, with Alexander's tremendous performance and your hasty retreat. The mystery about you and Eden has only grown."

"There's nothing mysterious about us!" Mary laughed.

"Why Eden?" I asked carefully.

He seemed surprised by the question. "Why, because no one has been invited to this house since your grandmother died! It was one thing when it was closed up, but you've lived here half a year now. Why shouldn't they be suspicious?"

"Suspicious? Of what?"

There was a slight falter before Dorian smiled. "Sorry. I meant to say 'curious'."

"But why would I invite people I don't know?" I cried, annoyed by his indirect reprimand.

Dorian shrugged. "Most young people like to vary their company."

I was opening my mouth to retort when Mary interrupted me. "I think he's right, Eleanor. You yourself were talking about entertaining only a month ago."

I bit back my anger, and answered, "Things have changed since then."

Dorian smiled deliberately, leaning back in his chair. "That is quite clear." I glared at him. "But devotion to one does not necessarily exclude the company of others. Well, it shouldn't."

I looked into his eyes, like two round scraps of sky. I knew that I was cornered. "All right," I said. "We'll have a party, if it's so very important. But doesn't it defeat the purpose if we don't have it here?"

"There's time for that," he said, with authority I considered dubious.

"Well then, I'll leave it to you and Mary to work out the details."

"We'll have a costume ball!" Mary cried. "Just like the ones your grandmother had."

My heart sank at the prospect, but before I could say anything, Dorian had answered:

"A brilliant idea! Everyone will love it!"

"Will she come?" Tasha asked abruptly. Her eyes were wide and troubled.

"Who?" Dorian asked, before I could.

"The lady," Tasha answered, looking intently at me. "The lady painted twice in the picture."

Dorian looked at Mary and me with perfect incredulity.

"Do you mean the painting over the piano?" I asked.

"Yes," she repeated, with weary patience. "The lady painted twice, who looks like you."

Dorian was looking at me intently. "She's talking about a portrait of the Fairfax twins," I told Dorian, whose look betrayed nothing. I turned to Tasha. "I suppose no one's ever explained it to you. That painting isn't of one lady, but of two who look alike. They're sisters, and when sisters or brothers are born together, looking alike, they're called twins. One of them was my mother. But I'm afraid they won't be at the party, because they both died a long time ago."

"Yes," Tasha said, sighing softly. It sounded more like agreement with something she already knew, than acceptance of a new fact.

"I didn't know that you had a painting of the twins," Dorian said.

"Oh, yes," Mary answered. "It's what started Eleanor's

intrigue with them. We didn't know there were twins before we found the painting."

"Your mother never told you?" Dorian asked me.

"I barely remember my mother," I answered coldly, "never mind what she said to me."

I could see that Mary was irritated, but I never guessed that she would betray me as she did when she spoke next. "It's all been quite a shock to Eleanor. Really, it's no wonder she has nightmares."

"Indeed not," Dorian said after a barely perceptible hesitation. His face remained impassive, his eyes fixed on the wine glass hanging like a jewel in the loose setting of his fingers.

I was furious beyond words but as it turned out I didn't need them, because Tasha said in her quiet, unassuming way, "I dream of her, too."

I looked at the child's earnest blue eyes and could not think how to answer her. By that time, though, Mary had realized her transgression, and she grasped at the first change of subject she thought of:

"Come, Tasha," she said, "let's get you ready for bed. The sooner you go to sleep, the sooner you will see Alexander."

"But I'll miss Eleanor's playing!" she implored.

"If I play," I answered, "I promise to open the door so that you can listen."

Placated by this assurance, she slipped off her chair and out of the room, with Mary at her heels. I heard her staccato footfalls moving up the stairs, and then, more faintly, over our heads.

I attempted a bright smile and stood up. "Now, Mr. Ducoeur, when Mary returns, I think that you should play for us."

He shook his head. "I've told you, I would much rather hear you."

The arched windows were open to the breeze the rain brought with it. I thought of what Alexander's fingers could do with that hush. Under his hands, the mute whisper of the rain would catch and spin the voices of the ghosts trapped out on this miserable night, weaving them into the cry of the growing things that took the rainwater and converted it to wild lifeblood. I was struck with a pang of missing him, craved the solace of his presence. This was what the poets suffer over, I thought. In that light, the ballade I had always scorned began to make sense.

"He will come back to you," Dorian said softly, "and there is no disloyalty to him in playing for me."

I was surprised to see pain on his face, real and recent. "Why do you say that?" I asked.

He shrugged, covering his distress with one of his unimpeachable smiles. "It is not difficult to read the stamp of love, particularly when it is written on a face so expressive as yours."

I was unable to think of a response that would be quite caustic enough, and I wasn't certain that I wanted to.

"Come on, then," I said. I didn't turn to see whether he followed.

The air in the music room was hot and sluggish; nobody had opened the windows. Now I opened them all, and when I came to the last, I saw that the screen had a jagged tear down the centre. Peering into the dim patch of light on the lawn beneath, I saw that a branch had fallen from a nearby tree, tearing the screen as it fell.

"This is a savage land still," Dorian said at my shoulder. I whirled around to find him behind me, looking, as I had looked, out into the inky blackness.

"Do you choose to emphasize your entrances by frightening people half to death," I demanded, "or can't you help it?"

"You were absorbed in whatever you were looking at," he suggested, "and you didn't hear me for the rain."

He touched my arm lightly. His fingers were warm, and my skin tingled at the contact. I drew away, both from the familiarity and from the realization that something significant had passed between us with that touch. I moved back into the light, toward the piano, just as Mary came back into the room. Dorian immediately turned his attention to her.

I picked the first volume of music that came under my hand: Bach's partitas for keyboard. I couldn't have chosen better if I had tried. I opened the book to the fourth piece and began to play, concentrating on the precise mathematical intricacies of the first movement. I told myself that I could not stop until I had made it through the entire suite, that I would be calmer then. As much as I tried to ignore it, though, I felt Dorian's presence, just as I felt the threads of rain angling down around us, sewing the house to the soft earth.

But when the last notes of the minuet died in the close atmosphere of the room, I found I had lost the desire to play any more. Dorian's eyes rested on me; his chin rested on one hand, his fingers covering his lips.

"Seldom does one hear Bach executed with such feeling," he finally said.

I shrugged listlessly, sad for no reason but the ultimate fragility of that perfect music, the way it seemed to come to nothing in this place. Rather than calming me, the music had drained me, leaving my worries stark as shipwrecks.

"Bach always seemed to me to go with rain," I said, then turned to choose another book.

Eve's presence seemed very near me then; perhaps it was she who inspired my next choice, Ravel's "Pavane for a Dead Princess." I only half-listened to the music, my mind more on the soft rush of rain beyond the window.

When I had finished, Dorian said, “Such sad music you choose tonight. Is it only for want of your love?”

“It seems to suit tonight,” I answered curtly.

“Well,” Mary said appeasingly, “I thought they were both lovely, but now I must excuse myself. I have a bit of a headache.” Her face was pale. I promised myself once again that I would find her a doctor.

“Eleanor, will you show Dorian to one of the guest rooms when he’s ready?”

“Of course,” I answered, though I wanted nothing less.

Colette stood up with Mary. “It was lovely, mademoiselle, thank you,” she said to me, and then, to Dorian, “monsieur,” with a decided coldness in her look. It made me all the more uneasy to be left alone with him.

The silence that followed in the wake of the women’s leaving was augmented by the sound of the rain.

“If you like, I’ll show you upstairs now,” I said to Dorian, standing with my fingertips still on the piano keys, carefully avoiding his eyes.

“Actually,” he said, his voice warm and enveloping, “I’d be obliged for the chance to speak with you alone. It seems to me that our relationship suffers from a lack of understanding, which might perhaps be mended, given time to talk unimpeded by others.”

I looked up at him. “I wasn’t aware that we had a relationship.”

“I get the distinct impression that you don’t care for me,” he said, “though I can’t think what I’ve done to cause this.”

“Can’t you?” I slid the cover over the piano keys more forcefully than I’d meant to; dissonant harmonics wavered from its innards.

"No...unless someone has been speaking ill of me to you."

His expression was ingenuous, but I was tired and out of patience. "You knew that I was listening to your conversation with Alexander that night at the party, didn't you."

"So that's the cause of your antipathy," he said, settling back into his chair. "You heard me speaking to Alexander, and he must have told you some story about the nature of our acquaintance."

"He told me the truth about you!" I said, anger finally overriding caution. "I know that you're not who you say you are, Dorian Ducoeur. Or is it Antoine Fontainebleau? I might as well turn you out of my house, storm or not, for what I know about you!"

"And what, exactly, do you know about me?" he asked in an untroubled voice.

"This is my house. I am under no obligation to explain myself to you."

He sighed. "Lend me half an hour to explain, then."

"You have five minutes."

Resignation flashed across his countenance before he spoke again. It was only for a moment, but it was enough to show me that he could not be as young as I had originally thought. Without the supercilious grin, the skin around his eyes and forehead collapsed into a web of fine lines.

"All right then," he said. "Five minutes, and if you don't want to hear the rest of the story, I'll go without complaint." He paused. "You'll appreciate that this is difficult. Perhaps we could have a drink?"

The truth was, I felt more than a passing need of a drink myself. So I poured two glasses of port from the decanter in the corner and handed him one of them. He sipped from his glass; I took a deep swallow.

“Five minutes,” I reiterated.

He sighed. “Then you leave me no choice but to say this brutally. Your Alexander has lied to you about everything he is, beginning with his name. He is indeed the son of a Russian nobleman, but he was disinherited long ago for his Communist sympathies, and not long afterward his family were shot as imperialists. One wonders how they were discovered.”

I stared at him, shocked beyond words.

“This is not the first time Alexander has left Russia,” he continued, “though his previous travels were government errands whose nature I wouldn’t like to consider.”

“This is unspeakable!” I cried when I recovered my voice. “Leave my house this instant!”

“I’ll leave if you like, Eleanor,” Dorian said calmly, “but you know that if I do, you’ll wonder about the rest. You won’t sleep tonight for wondering, and by morning it will begin to drive you mad.” He smiled and leaned toward me confidentially. “You know there is a piece of Alexander that he has kept hidden from you—perhaps quite a substantial piece. In your secret heart you have always suspected that one day you might hear something like this.”

I was true that I hated him; yet something in me wavered despite it, and for that I hated myself.

“Why would you tell me these things?” I asked softly.

He shrugged. “I merely mean to clear my name, since Alexander has obviously been slandering it.”

“And why do you care what I think of you?”

He paused. “Let’s change the subject for a moment. I’ve been wondering what the child meant tonight when she asked if the woman in the painting would come to the ball.”

His voice seemed oddly distant, and I was beginning to feel dizzy. “I’m sure that Tasha meant exactly what she said,”

I answered without thinking, not wanting him to see my discomfiture.

"It seemed to interest you."

"It was a peculiar thing to say."

"It was indeed peculiar. Particularly her confession that she dreams about the twins...just like you do. It made me wonder whether someone could have been talking to her. Or to you, for that matter."

"Talking to her? What do you mean?"

He reached into his pocket for a cigarette, lit it, and dropped the spent match into his empty glass.

"Surely you must know about your grandmother's dreams."

I didn't answer. My vision was beginning to blur.

"You do know of her illness, though?"

"Of course I do."

"She was a deeply spiritual woman—not religious, but something deeper, more personal. After your mother ran away, your grandmother was said to have been consumed by particularly vivid dreams of her lost daughter."

"How do you know all of this?" I demanded, trying desperately to control the tremor in my voice. "I thought you were here only as a child."

"Oh, I had letters over the years, and you can imagine the effect of a scandal such as your mother's disappearance on a community as small as this—particularly coupled with her own mother's illness." He paused, waiting for a response, but I kept silent. "Apparently Claudine came to connect her missing daughter with the story of the Garden of Eden, and it was all played out in her dreams."

Dorian looked closely at me. When I still didn't answer, he reached forward and touched the diamond at my throat.

"Pretty," he said. "Was it your mother's?"

"Enough!" I cried, leaping up. It was only then that I became aware of the extent to which the alcohol had affected me. I put my hands to my swimming head. "Whatever you think I'm hiding from you, it doesn't exist! I don't care about you. I didn't even know you existed until you wrote me that letter!"

He regarded me calmly. "I didn't mean to upset you, Eleanor. Nor—despite what you may think—do I have any wish to end what has begun between you and Alexander."

"How generous of you," I wavered.

"In fact, from what I know of him he is a fine man, if a bit...vehement...in some of his beliefs. After Anna's death, he took care of their child devotedly—"

It was too much. I didn't consider the reasons he might have to lie about this; I couldn't bear to be in the room with him a moment longer. I stumbled in what I thought was the direction of the door, but found myself instead by the window with the torn screen. I clutched the sill, dizzy and sobbing and impotent.

I don't know how long I stood like that; it seemed at most a few seconds. When I turned around, though, Dorian was gone.

The next moment, something crashed against the screen behind me. I cried out, doubling back and covering my face with my arms, and then I stumbled to my knees. Finally I righted myself, and plunged blindly toward the door—straight into Alexander's arms. He looked down at me anxiously through tendrils of sodden hair.

"Eleanor, what is it?" he asked.

Still unable to answer him, I turned back to the room, gesturing toward the coffee table where we had left our wineglasses; but they were gone. Looking around, I saw all six glasses neatly tipped upside down by the port decanter, and no sign that Dorian Ducoeur had ever been there.

3

Alexander led me to the sofa where Dorian had sat, and handed me a handkerchief. My mind was still foggy with alcohol; I couldn't catch my breath or control my shaking limbs. The room felt too hot.

"Was it another nightmare?" he asked.

I looked at him in confusion.

"That frightened you," he explained. "That made you run into the hallway."

Slowly I shook my head. "It was Dorian. And...and something else."

Alexander's face tightened. "He was here?"

"He said that the road was washed out beyond Eden, and he couldn't get the car through to Joyous Garde."

Alexander was looking at the window with the torn screen. "How long ago did he leave?"

"I—I don't know. Not more than a few minutes ago."

Alexander looked at me closely, as though expecting to find more information in my face. Finally he said, "There's no other door out of this room. You would think I would have run into him."

"There are windows."

"And there was no car in the drive when we arrived. We

certainly didn't pass one on the road."

"Don't you believe me?" I asked.

He didn't answer immediately, and this was a blow as painful as Dorian's accusations had been.

"Eleanor," he said soothingly after that slight pause, putting an arm around me, "of course I believe you."

Of course. I would have been happier without those words. We fell into silence, both lost in our own troubled thoughts. I knew that I couldn't keep mine to myself much longer, yet I didn't know how to begin. In the end Alexander solved the dilemma for me.

"So," he asked bitterly, "how did he try to turn you against me?"

A part of me knew those words were nothing more than logical. Yet they were also a very real and threatening indication that Alexander had something to fear from Dorian. Looking at him, I was even more certain that I saw doubt and fear looking back at me.

"Why do you think that?" I asked.

Alexander sighed. "Eleanor, I've told you, Dorian and I were opposed to each other before any of us came to Eden. I've also told you why he might wish to turn you against me."

I shook my head. "Why do you think that I would listen to him?"

Alexander looked at me a moment longer, then he embraced me, smoothing my hair as if I were a child. "You're right. I'm sorry."

We sat again in silence. It was only then that I realized the rain had stopped. The grandfather clock in the hallway chimed two o'clock.

"Alexander, I'll tell you all of it tomorrow. But right now, I need to go to bed."

"You must be exhausted," he agreed. We both stood up. "Do you want me to come with you? Or would you rather be alone?"

The questioning of what before had been an unspoken agreement opened the crack in our fortress a little wider, but I didn't have the energy to confront it then.

"I don't want to be alone," I said.

Alexander was asleep within minutes, but I lay awake, my mind turning over all that Dorian had said. Finally, unable to stand my own unyielding thoughts any longer, I got up, rummaged around on the dressing table, and located the bottle of chloral hydrate. I mixed up a strong dose and drank all of it off, then lay down to an uneasy sleep.

I awakened early. I lay for a long time, leaden with the aftereffects of the drug, watching the breeze move the curtains out into the room and then draw them back against the screens. Through their gauzy lens I could see that the sky was clear blue, with high, billowy clouds. It was not unlike the sky of a Boston summer day: the first like it I had seen in Eden since the winter. For the first time since I had moved away from the city, I felt a pang of homesickness.

I could tell by his breathing that Alexander was awake. "Maybe you're right," I said. "Maybe we should go back north this autumn."

He propped his head up on his elbow and looked down at me, his face more animated than it had been in a long time. "Really?"

"Really."

"Why the change of heart?"

"I suppose it's as you've been saying. Eden is too secluded. I certainly won't further my career staying here. Nor will you, and if you go...well, I can't imagine staying here without you."

"So...you have not changed your mind about me?"

For the first time, this expression struck me as odd—entirely inadequate for the situations in which it is so often used. "It's my heart that matters," I said. "And that will never change."

Something that had hardened in his face the night before finally relaxed. "In that case..." he said, then pulled his jacket from the chair by the bed and rummaged in the pocket. "I did lie to you, Eleanor." When he brought his hand out, there was something closed within it. My heart was suddenly beating hard. "I didn't go to Baton Rouge to meet an agent yesterday. I went for this."

He handed me a small, velvet-covered box. The room seemed suddenly bereft of air. Perhaps it was naïve, but I had never seen this coming. Suddenly all of the past night's anger and hesitation made sense.

I opened the box. Inside was a ring of white gold, set with a rose-cut diamond.

"It's been in my family for a long time," he said. "It was one of the things we managed to save. Will you wear it, Eleanor? Will you marry me?"

Before I could reply, Mary's voice called up the stairs. "Eleanor! Are you up yet?" There was a hint of irritation in her tone.

The room was spinning, but Alexander's eyes were still. "Yes," I heard myself say, then, "yes," again, more definitively. Alexander paused, as if he couldn't quite believe it; then he smiled, and slipped the ring onto my finger, and gathered me into his arms.

"Eleanor!" Mary called again.

"Her timing has always been terrible," I said. I got out of bed and opened the door a crack. "I'll be downstairs in a few minutes, Mary," I called.

She didn't answer, but I heard her speaking to someone down the corridor. I opened my door wider and leaned out into the hallway. They were too far away to distinguish their words, but I knew the other voice was definitely Dorian's. I shut the door.

"It's him," I said.

"Could you hear what they were saying?"

"No." I sat down on the bed, suddenly tired and heavy again.

"You must stay away from him, Eleanor."

"It might not be possible," I answered, averting my face from his penetrating eyes.

"What do you mean?"

"Whatever else he might be, he's the only person here who knew the twins."

He smiled bitterly. "And what's to stop him lying to you about what he knew?"

Looking at the diamond on my finger, I wondered how much of Alexander's aversion to my contact with Dorian was a product of his own pride and jealousy.

"It's all I have," I said without thinking.

Anger flashed across his face. "Is that man destined always to come between me and—" he began. Seeing the look on my face, he stopped himself. I wanted to cry for the rift we were widening with every word.

"Eleanor," he said softly, taking me in his arms. "Elenka. I'm sorry. Again."

"And you're right, again," I said. "He means to drive us apart, and it seems he works on us even in his absence."

"It is his way," Alexander agreed. "He speaks in riddles, confuses common sense, makes one imagine the most terrible things...."

"Then we must hold on to the truth," I said. "Let me tell you what he has been saying—"

Alexander was shaking his head. "It was my pride which asked you that. You are not beholden to me. I trust your heart, Eleanor."

I looked at him for a long moment, and the devotion I saw made me despise myself for having allowed Dorian to speak his terrible words the night before. I vowed not to be so caught by him again.

"I'll need to stay out the summer here," I said, brushing the hair out of his face, "and then we can leave him and all of this behind."

Alexander took my hand and kissed it. "Don't think that I underestimate the importance of Eden to you. Just remember that I love you, and I can never accept that it is worth sacrificing any part of yourself."

I nodded. He stood up then and began to get dressed. When he was finished, I said, "Will you have breakfast with us? Mary will want to congratulate us both."

"Let me go home and see to a few things; I'll come before lunch. All right?" I nodded again, and he kissed me.

I stood in the doorway until he disappeared around the curve of the stairs, then went to the front window to watch him on his way home. It was some time before he emerged from the front door, and when he did, Dorian was with him. They faced each other like unfamiliar cats: warily, with thinly covered hostility charging the space between them. They exchanged a few words, then Alexander stiffened, turned, and walked quickly toward his house. Dorian watched him go, and though he was too far away for me to be certain, I could have sworn that he was smiling. Sighing, I began to get dressed.

The day was cooler than most that summer had been, but

the residual effects of the chloral made me as listless as the most stifling heat. When I came down to the dining room and found Mary waiting for me with a chastising look, it was all I could do not to turn around and go back to bed.

I sat down across from her, sipped the coffee she poured for me, and then pushed it aside.

"Have you stopped eating, Eleanor?" Her look was oddly guarded; if I hadn't known better, I would have gone as far as to say it was wary.

"I'm not hungry," I answered.

"Dorian's just left."

I sighed. "I know."

Her eyebrows drew together. "And you didn't come down to ask after his trip home last night? Honestly, Eleanor—to think you'd let him leave in that kind of weather."

"I was with Alexander."

Mary's look changed to one of disbelief. "Alexander?"

"He came back late last night."

"Well, that's love, I suppose."

The mention of Alexander had dissolved Mary's acrimony. At least, I thought, he had charmed her as effectively as Dorian had. I knew that I should tell her about our engagement, but her sharp words had made the moment seem wrong.

So instead, I asked, "What did Dorian want?"

Mary handed me a piece of paper that had been lying beside her breakfast plate. "Only to give you this. The guest list for the party."

"So he really means to go through with it."

"What do you mean by that?" The annoyance had returned. "Honestly, Eleanor, you agreed to this party."

"I'm sorry, Mary, I'm exhausted this morning. Please don't take anything I say to heart."

She looked carefully at me, straining against her weak eyes for a clue to my ailment. Now I was certain that there was distrust in her look, and that she was trying to hide it. "Haven't you been sleeping well?"

"It's the heat," I answered.

"Have you had more nightmares?" She put this question to me carefully, as though she had been thinking about it but did not want me to know that she had.

"No," I answered, "I haven't had any more nightmares."

"What about your medicine?"

"It makes me feel worse than not sleeping."

"Eleanor," she said, her tone suddenly gentler. By the blood rising in her face, I knew what she was thinking.

To save her the embarrassment of asking me outright, I said, "I'm not...in that condition, if that's what you're wondering."

She looked up quickly, the blush deepening. "I didn't mean to pry, but after all—"

"You're within your rights to wonder," I said.

She was silent for a moment, then finally said, "Eleanor, I've been meaning to speak to you about Alexander. About your...relations with him."

I felt my defenses rising, and reminded myself that this conversation was to be expected, was indeed long overdue. Yet any desire I'd had in the past to discuss it with her was gone.

Mary smiled uncomfortably and looked down at her hands. "Eleanor, you know that I'm not old-fashioned in my views, and I suppose I know the...the extent of your relations with him."

"Mary –" I began, but she plunged on.

"Alexander doesn't seem the type to abandon you in

unpleasant circumstances, and so I see nothing wrong with the affair myself."

My cheeks burned. "Mary, please—"

"But you can be certain that there will be other people who will see it differently—who won't take it lightly. In Boston, for instance—"

"Mary, we're engaged." I lifted my hand from beneath the table; the diamond glinted in the morning sunlight.

I had imagined many reactions to this announcement, but not the horror that froze her face. I went cold.

"Eleanor," she stammered finally, "I had no idea…I would never have gone on so…"

"It's all right," I said, but she still looked panic-stricken. "Although, I had rather thought you would be happy for me."

She tried to smile. "I am happy for you, Eleanor…"

"But?"

"Well…you're so young, and he's so much older."

"Is that so unheard of?"

"No, but…are you quite certain of him, Eleanor?"

I couldn't quite find it in myself to be angry with her when she seemed so very concerned for me, despite its apparent senselessness. "As certain as I've ever been of anything," I told her. "Don't worry about me."

She nodded. "I suppose you can announce your engagement at the ball."

Though this idea was hardly appealing, I smiled. "That's a fine idea."

"At any rate," she said hurriedly, as though trying to push the conversation behind her as quickly as possible, "you'd best see a doctor about your sleeping problems. You can't plan a wedding if you're exhausted." She smiled with a touch of pity and that new, strange anxiety. "We worry about you, Eleanor."

The "we" sent a shiver down my spine, but again I made myself smile. She reached across the table and took back the list I had not yet looked at.

"Don't worry about these," she said. "Colette and I will write the invitations. All you'll have to think about is a suitable speech, and a costume."

"Costume?"

She sighed. "Remember, Eleanor, it's a costume ball."

"Where will I find a costume, here?"

Mary's eyes narrowed with an idea. "Perhaps one of those gowns from the attic will fit you. You can go as one of your own ancestors!"

To me this idea was repugnant, but she was immediately caught up in it. Before I knew quite what had happened, I found myself holding a candle in the attic while Mary rummaged in the old trunk.

On close inspection, we found that many of the garments had borne the attacks of mice and moths, and others were the wrong size. However, buried beneath the yellowed wedding dress, where I would have sworn that there had been nothing but a layer of brittle tissue paper, lay two dresses I knew would fit me only too well. One was made of crimson silk shot through with gold, the other of a fluttery white fabric. I suppose I ought to have been shocked to see them there, but like so many recent oddities, I felt almost that I had expected it.

"Do you think they could really be…?" Mary said as she picked up the red one.

"They certainly look like the dresses from the painting," I answered.

Apparently oblivious to my grimness, she held the dress up

to my shoulders. "You'd look lovely in this, Eleanor."

I reached into the trunk, picked up the white gown, and shook out the wrinkles. It looked as though it had never been worn. "I think it would be more fitting if I wore my mother's," I said, the words falling flat on the heavy, dusty air.

As I said it, part of me wondered what difference it made; the rest knew that it didn't matter. My choice was driven by the same intractable purpose that drove me in search of a truth that could deliver only pain. Whatever was happening to me would continue to happen whether or not I understood why.

"Of course," Mary said, then added, "perhaps we ought to bring the wedding dress down, too. You might want to have it re-cut."

I looked at the yellowed silk, desiccate as book pages, and wondered how Mary could even suggest it. Willing away the feeling of foreboding, I said, "I don't think it will be that kind of wedding."

"Ah, well," she sighed as she bent to put the red dress back into the trunk, "you know where it is if you change your mind."

We went back downstairs. As I turned toward the music room, Mary called back to me, "Letter for you." She picked up the envelope that lay by my untouched breakfast plate. "From Paris; I wonder what that could be?"

She didn't wait to find out, but bustled off about her tasks, leaving me staring at the return address. When she was gone, I tore open the envelope. The letter inside was written in English.

Mlle Rose,

With regard to your enquiry into the death of Elizabeth Ducoeur: I regret to inform you that I have been through all of the records of 1905 and find no account of a woman by that name being admitted to our hospital, for typhus fever or any other ailment. Moreover, I have contacted the authorities with whom such a death would have been registered, and they have no record of it, either. I am sorry not to be of more help, but I do wish you luck in finding the information you are seeking.

Yours sincerely,

Etc.

My first thought was to run to Alexander with this information. However, it was no different from what he had expected, and after our talk that morning, I had no wish to delve again into unpleasant topics. In the end I folded the letter back up, put it in my writing desk, and forgot about it.

4

Over the next few days, no conversation about Dorian or the twins interrupted the harmony that had existed between Alexander and me since we had become engaged. Yet though our days resumed something of their old pattern, a subtle tension imbued everything we did, no matter how routine. Moreover, my sleep, though still dreamless, was as troubled as it had been since the night of Dorian's party; not even my medicine helped any longer. The combination of nervous energy and insomnia exhausted me mentally and physically. Practice at the piano was a labor, and my daily sessions in the music room grew continually shorter and less productive.

The prospect of the costume ball had thrown a further pall over everything. I felt out of my depth in the local society, and I dreaded Dorian's reaction to the announcement of our engagement. However, I dared not speak this fear to Alexander; I couldn't face another argument.

Two days before the event, he and I sat reading in the shade of one of the rose arbors. I was staring into space, my book facedown in my lap, trying to ignore the noise of Mary and Colette's bustling preparations, when Alexander said:

"Tell me what's troubling you."

"How did you know?"

He smiled. "You will need to do some work if you mean to keep your feelings from me."

I sighed.

"It's the party, isn't it."

"You know me too well!"

"Is it the thought of entertaining that worries you?"

"No. It's only that...I haven't seen Dorian since that night—"

He took my hand. "I don't think that even Dorian could find a way to harm you in the presence of so many others."

"I suppose not."

"Besides, I would kill him before I let him hurt you again."

I couldn't answer, only kissed his hands and wished once again that I had never given Dorian the credit of listening to his lies.

Saturday was overcast, the air as close and damp as that of a hothouse. I deliberated for most of the afternoon about whether I really wanted to wear the old-fashioned dress, with its tight bodice and layers of fabric. In the end Mary insisted.

"You don't have another costume," she said, tugging at the laces of the corset she had unearthed to go with the dress. "You can't be the only one without one at your own costume ball!"

I groaned as the bone caging tightened around my waist and ribs. "Thank God I was born too late to have to wear one of these!"

"As well you might," Mary agreed. "I wore one from the time I was thirteen, and burned it when the fashion world finally came to its senses." She pursed her lips. "It's a hot night for it, especially when you're not used to wearing one. But the dress will never fit without it. There." She fastened the back of the dress. "Have a look."

Obediently I looked in the mirror, knowing already what I

would see. But for the fair hair, I could have been my mother in the painting. I sighed.

"What's the matter?"

"Nothing. It's a lovely dress."

She put one bird's-wing arm around my shoulders and pulled me close, as she had when I was a little girl. "Cheer up, Eleanor. I'm certain that the party will be a success."

I noted that she said nothing of Alexander's and my planned announcement. She had hardly said a word about it, in fact, since the morning I told her. This would have worried me, if so many other things hadn't.

When Mary finally left I sank onto the bed, resting my aching forehead against my palms. I had sat like that for some time, the shadows deepening around me, when there was a soft tapping at the door. I roused myself, smoothed my hair, and then went to open it. Alexander was standing there in a suit of approximately the same era as my own gown. He looked me up and down, then smiled wryly.

"Coming out of the darkness like that, you looked like a ghost."

"My mother's ghost, or Eve's?" I asked dismally.

"Come, Eleanor, cheer up. Remember that we're celebrating our engagement."

I tried to smile. "I think I would have preferred a bottle of wine and an early night."

He put a reassuring arm around me and kissed my forehead. "There will be plenty of those. For now, we are where we are. Shall we go?"

Hand-in-hand we walked downstairs and out to the car, where Mary was already waiting, wrapped in a peony-pink kimono.

The first guests were pulling up to the house on the hill

when we arrived. I had kept clear of the preparations, so the house's appearance was as much a surprise to me as to my guests. The windows had been washed, the worst of the broken stonework repaired, and the closer gardens re-planted. Inside, the transformation was even more profound. Though the house was wired for electricity, Mary had chosen candlelight. Everywhere I looked were vases of flowers. There were tables laid with hors d'oeuvres, and maids stood ready with trays of drinks.

In no time at all the room was full of people, many of whom I remembered from the last gathering. They seemed to revel in the decrepit state of the house and furniture; several of them congratulated me on the ingenuity of the idea of having a costume ball in such an atmospheric setting. I thanked them and deferred the compliments to Dorian.

I wasn't aware of his arrival, but about an hour into the party I noticed him standing at the opposite side of the crowded front hall, in a magician's dark cape. He caught my eye and raised his glass to me, his own eyes lingering for a moment on my dress. I turned away, but I knew that I had not been quick enough for him to miss my anger, and I was uncomfortably aware that this was precisely the response he had sought to generate.

Alexander touched my elbow. "You must not let him intimidate you," he said softly, so that the people around us would not hear. I nodded. "The musicians are here and ready to play. Perhaps you should call everyone into the ballroom?"

"Let's just tell them to start playing. People will come when they hear the music."

I took the arm Alexander offered, and we walked into the ballroom. At my signal, the string quartet struck up a Brahms waltz. We began to dance, and soon the rest of the guests were pouring into the room to join us. The illustrations on the ceiling came alive in the candlelight, seeming to leap and waver across the blue expanse. The open doors to the garden let in the hard white light of the gibbous moon, and the heady smell of night-blooming flowers.

As we danced, I caught sight of Dorian again, this time speaking with Mary by the spiral stair. Both of their faces were serious, and from time to time I caught Mary stealing glances at us. No doubt she had told him our news; I wondered whether he was attempting to poison her mind toward Alexander as he had tried to poison mine.

Or perhaps, I thought, he had already begun. All at once, Mary's reaction to my engagement began to make sense. As I thought of the morning after the rainstorm, and the conversation between Dorian and Mary that I hadn't quite been able to hear, my heart sank.

Alexander caught my look and its source, and said again, "He can't harm you here."

"No," I answered, "but I think he may have gotten to Mary."

Before Alexander could answer, an elderly lawyer from Baton Rouge cut in on us. Next I danced with his son, who had recently bought a tobacco plantation, then a young man who had just moved from Savannah, whose occupation I never learned. After I had thanked this last partner, I made my way toward a clutch of chairs. Halfway there, though, a hand caught my elbow. I knew immediately that it was Dorian's; no one else would have dared. I whirled around.

"Mary told me your news," he said in his smoke-smooth voice, half-smile firmly in place. "Let me be the first to offer my congratulations."

"Many thanks," I replied coldly, attempting to disengage my arm.

"Still angry with me? Well, I suppose it can be difficult to hear the truth."

"The truth?" I hissed. "No doubt you'll understand if I credit the word of my fiancé over yours."

"So Alexander denied it all, did he? I'd taken him for more of a man than that."

Despite my anger, I couldn't meet his eyes.

"Or was it you I misjudged?" I tried again to pull away, and Dorian laughed softly. "You never told him, did you. You must be going absolutely mad, wondering."

I battled a sudden urge to cry. "Lord, if you knew how I hate you!"

"It really isn't worth the effort," he said benignly. "Listen—a waltz. Dance with me, Eleanor." He had already taken me firmly in his arms.

At first my fury was such that I couldn't look at him. Yet as I felt his eyes unrelentingly fixed on me, I soon found that I couldn't look away.

"Why can't you leave me alone?" I demanded.

"You fascinate me."

"How trite."

"I'm being quite frank. You're such an unusual...mix of things." There seemed to be a slight emphasis on the word "mix".

"Can't you answer a question directly?" I asked.

"You don't seem to like it when I do," he returned. Seeing my anger flare, he added, "But if you doubt my directness, why don't you ask me something? I promise to answer you with the utmost honesty."

I had intended a sharp retort, but something occurred to me then. "All right," I said. "Whatever became of Elizabeth Ducoeur?"

For a moment he appeared taken aback. By the time he answered, though, the half-smile was back. "What an odd question."

"Why odd? I never knew my aunt. You did." I watched carefully for any indication that he knew about the switch, but his face remained impassive as he answered:

"Only as a child. I recall receiving an invitation to her wedding. I also remember hearing that the marriage didn't last. No doubt there's more, but it's not for lack of honesty that I don't tell you." He paused. "And now perhaps you can tell me something."

"What could I possibly know that would be of any interest to you?"

We were close to the French doors now. In the cold light of the moon, Dorian's smile became a leer. "What became of Elizabeth Ducoeur?"

For a moment I could only stare at him. Then I whispered, "What are you doing?"

He shrugged. "Looking for information—like you."

"It ought to be clear to you that I know nothing about her."

"And yet, you dream of her."

I tried to remember whether I had ever actually said this to him, but my mind was numb. I looked for Alexander, but he was engaged in conversation with the tobacco planter, his back to us.

"You'd do better to rely on yourself," Dorian said, following my glance. Then, before I could reply, he asked, "Do you remember what I told you about your grandmother's illness?"

"I doubt you meant me to forget it."

"I've wondered since then whether her dreams were not madness at all, but some kind of divine insight."

I couldn't help the pause before I answered, "It would be folly to give so much credit to dreams."

"Ah—I see that I've touched upon something. Miss Rose is suddenly quite pale."

"You're mistaken—about all of it."

He clutched me tightly then, pinning my arms to my sides. "You don't lie any better than he does," he said through clenched teeth.

"I don't know what you're talking about," I said, real fear beginning to take hold.

"I know what you think you've discovered!"

His face was inches from mine, his eyes narrow and menacing, but behind the anger I saw stark fear. I didn't have much time to consider its meaning, however. At that moment, Alexander's face loomed behind Dorian's shoulder, dark with rage.

"What is the meaning of this?" he demanded.

Abruptly, Dorian let me go and turned. "Miss Rose and I were simply clearing up some differences," he said, his face unruffled again.

"You had no right to touch her!"

Dorian's face was contemptuous, Alexander's contorted by hatred. I put a hand on Alexander's arm, to try to draw him away from this confrontation, but he paid me no heed.

"I've warned you before to leave her alone," he said to Dorian. "If you can't do so, then I think it's best you go."

"Leave my own party?" Dorian asked incredulously. "Why do you so fear my contact with her?"

"I have already witnessed enough of your contact with her to make me long to see you dead!"

By now, some of the guests had noticed the commotion and turned unabashedly to watch.

“Those are strong words, Mr. Trevozhov,” Dorian said. “Are you certain that you mean them?”

“Alexander, please, let it go,” I said, gripping his arm.

He shook his head. “I’ve let it go long enough. I don’t know what this man is after, but it is clear that he means to use you to get to it.”

“On the contrary, Mr. Trevozhov. You know very well what I’m after.”

I looked at Alexander. His arm came around my waist, but his eyes remained fixed on Dorian.

“And if you are still under the illusion that your Alexander is innocent,” Dorian said to me, “then I suggest you consult the proof to the contrary. Either that, or embrace your grandmother’s fate.” He turned, and the crowd parted to let him through.

“Wait!” I heard myself call, before I even realized that I meant to do it. Alexander’s arm jerked convulsively against my back, and then, slowly, dropped back to his side. When Dorian turned, there was a look of triumph on his face that nearly made me shrink from my purpose.

“What proof?” I managed to ask, though my voice shook, and I was suddenly light-headed.

Dorian’s smile was like a crack on a winter pond, his eyes full of the moon’s piercing light. “You’ll see,” he said. After a moment’s consideration, he added, “It may seem that time keeps its secrets, but given long enough it always unravels them again. Wait a little longer, Eleanor. You’ll find I’m right.”

He turned, laughing softly to himself, and in a moment he was lost in the silent crowd. They stared at Alexander and me for what seemed an eternity, and then Alexander called, “Musicians!”

The quartet took up their instruments again and people turned away, the gradual crescendo of their resumed conversations obliterating the echo of Dorian's words. I turned to look at Alexander. He was looking back at me in disbelief.

"What?" I flared.

"If I didn't know better," he said tightly, "I might think you believed whatever he has been saying about me."

Though I had anticipated a reprimand, the starkness of his anger was like a physical blow. "Alexander, he thinks that we know something we shouldn't. I had to ask him what he meant."

His fine face twisted so at that, it was almost ugly. "And what, exactly, have you learned from his answer?"

I couldn't answer.

"Precisely—nothing! It is always the same with him, always shadow and trickery." He looked at the door's dark glass. "It would have been better for both of us never to have known him, or any of this."

"How can you say that to me?" I cried. "Do you wish that I had never known the truth about my family?"

"You know that I was not referring to your family," he said wearily.

"To me, it's one and the same."

Alexander took me by the shoulders. His eyes were dark and heavy as storm clouds. I wondered then how I had failed to see his exhaustion before.

"Have you ever considered that Dorian's interest in you might have nothing to do with your family at all?"

"What do you mean?"

"Eleanor, I have told you of my history with that man. Have you never thought that he might see you as an easy way to get at me? And what better way to gain control of you than to dangle the twins as bait?"

"Why would he be so intent on hurting you? Unless there's something you haven't told me."

Alexander looked away. We stood in silence for a few moments: long enough for the anger to drain out of me and leave a heavy pessimism in its place.

"I want to go home," I said.

I thought he would argue with me, but he only said, "All right. I'll take you."

I was angry at his acquiescence in the same way I used to be angry with my grandfather when I'd storm out of a room and he wouldn't follow me. But I'd left myself no choice other than to push toward the door, trying my best to ignore the curious stares that followed me.

Mary was just outside the ballroom with a group of people who were complimenting her on the decorations. She smiled when she saw me. "Oh, Eleanor, everyone's been asking about you. You must come and meet some people—"

"I'm not feeling well," I said. "Alexander's going to take me home."

Mary's smile faded. "Not again!"

I smiled wanly. "I'm afraid so."

"Oh, I knew the corset wouldn't work out. It's just too hot, when you aren't used to it."

"That must be it," I agreed.

"And your announcement—"

"It can't be helped," I interrupted. "Now, we really must go."

"Will Alexander be coming back? I just saw Dorian leave, and I could use the help."

Alexander and I looked at each other in confusion. He said, "If Eleanor doesn't mind."

I did mind, of course, but I didn't want Mary to guess how unsettled I was. So I answered, "It's all right. Colette and Tasha are there."

"Well, then," Alexander said, "we had better be going." He took my arm and, with a feeling of foreboding, I allowed him to lead me away.

5

A pensive silence hung between us all the way back to Eden. I knew that Alexander was still angry, and though a part of me wanted to apologize for my contribution to this, my pride was stronger.

Yet when we arrived back at the house and Jean-Pierre opened the door for me, Alexander held out his hand with his old, gentle smile. "Truce?" he asked.

I threw my arms around his neck. "I'm sorry," I said.

"So am I," he answered.

All of the maids had been requisitioned for the party, so the house was dark and quiet when we entered. Alexander followed me upstairs and, after we'd looked in on Tasha, helped me get out of the constrictive costume and into bed.

"Is there anything you'd like? Some books, or a drink?"

"Some tea would be nice."

"I'll be right back."

In a short while he returned with a steaming mug. I took a sip. The liquid was sweet and fruity; Alexander laughed at my surprise. "That is how we make tea in Russia. With jam instead of sugar."

I smiled. "It's good."

"I thought you'd like it. Sleep well, Eleanor."

"Will you come back?"

He paused. "I know how tired you've been. You don't need me waking you up again. I'll come in the morning."

I didn't like this, but I didn't have the will left to argue. "All right," I said. "Alexander—take care."

He smiled, leaned down and kissed me, then shut the door softly behind him. For the first time in months I felt utterly alone. I had to fight the urge to run after him, to beg him not to leave.

In an effort to distract myself, I picked up Eve's journal, which had lain with my mother's on the table beside my bed since Mary and I first found them. I reread the passage describing the onset of their mother's illness, but there wasn't any reference to dreams, let alone the nightmares Dorian had spoken of.

Still, I could not help feeling that there must be something in the journals I was missing, the piece of the puzzle that would link the others. I fanned through the pages, letting the book fall open at random. The entry was the one in which Eve described Louis's planned murals:

He intends to paint the story of the Fall in four panels. But he says that he does not want them to look like church frescoes, so he will make them modern in their setting, using our own gardens, and Lizzie and me as models...imagine!

Imagine, I thought grimly. It was all I could do.

I closed the book, and drained the last of Alexander's tea. It had indeed calmed my nerves; in fact, for the first time in days I was overwhelmingly sleepy. I put the book and the empty cup on the bedside table and shut off the reading light. Darkness settled over me like a mantle, and I lay for a time listening to the faint whir of insects beyond the screens and the deep, hypnotic tick of the grandfather clock in the corridor below. Then the sounds receded, and sleep closed its fist around me.

I looked up through clouded eyes into the face of a stone figure. At first I thought that it was the gargoyle from Joyous Garde, but gradually the haziness cleared, and I realized that it was not a monster at all, but the stone angel from the Boston Public Garden.

When I turned, however, I found that I was not in the Public Garden, but the rose garden beside the ballroom of the house on the hill. It was evening, overcast and chill. From beyond the closed French doors came the sounds of a string quartet playing a waltz I didn't recognize: melancholy, yet imminently compelling. Opening the nearest door, I stepped into the ballroom.

The great chandelier was filled with lit candles, which had melted and dripped such that it no longer looked like a chandelier at all, but the ponderous, glowing hive of some colony of bright-bodied insects. In this dubious light, couples in late-nineteenth century clothing danced to the thin, plaintive strains of the string players. Something about the people was wrong, but enveloped as I was by the woolly confusion particular to dreams—which is never quite thick enough to block the conviction that things are not as they should be, nor transparent enough to discern what is amiss—I couldn't tell what.

Then I chanced to look up. Where the fantastically painted ceiling should have been, there was instead a limitless void, dark as a night without stars or moon. Taut golden threads emanated from the darkness. Following them downward with my eyes, I saw that each thread joined with one of the dancing figures, disappearing mutely beneath the costumes of their owners.

Summoning my courage, I touched the arm of a man near me. He let go of his partner, who drifted away in a trail of white, and turned to me. The man was Alexander, his face fixed in an expression of latent fear.

"We must not stop the dance," he said in a low, excitable voice.

"Only tell me what they're for," I answered, indicating the filament that ran from his coat to the lightless sky.

He turned to me and opened his jacket. In the centre of his chest a red, living heart was exposed, beating in time to the music, the golden filament wound around it like scaffolding. I took a step back in horror. He saw the revulsion in my face, and his own took on a look of condescending pity, not unlike what I had seen of late in Mary's.

"I'm sorry," he said, looking into the blank darkness above, "but we are all bound, and the dance does not stop for anyone—"

Suddenly Alexander's face contorted with terror and pain. The other dancers seemed oblivious, even as he staggered and let out a terrible cry, clutching his exposed heart. Then, like a discarded marionette, he fell lifeless on the checkered floor, the frayed end of the snapped cord swinging lazily above him.

I flung myself on him, but he was still and cold. As I wept over him, something soft and white brushed my cheek, the same gauzy white of his partner's skirt. Looking up, I saw that she was one of the twins, but I could not tell which. Though her gown was white, as Elizabeth's always seemed to be, the jewel glinting at her throat was a ruby.

She looked at me, her eyes sympathetic but her face circumspect. "He lost his step," she said. "You couldn't have saved him." Then she turned away again and disappeared into the crowd.

"Wait!" I cried, pushing against the people who had closed

around the woman, trying to reach her retreating figure. When I finally caught up to her, she was face-to-face with Dorian.

"So, you have come for a partner," he said to her.

"Not him," said another voice, before she could answer. It was the other twin, dressed in red with a diamond necklace. All three of them had the same golden lines running from their breasts to the boundless reaches above, and I sickened at the thought of the livid hearts hidden by their clothing.

"You must choose," Dorian said.

"Your will is your own," the woman in red retorted.

The woman in white looked from one to the other. Then, with a melancholy smile, she stepped toward her sister. With a cry of rage and pain, Dorian ran at them. Reaching up, he took hold of both their filaments and snapped them. They crumpled without a sound, but as they hit the floor their forms thinned and vanished, leaving only a pale-pink rose. Dorian looked at the flower for a moment, and then crushed it beneath his heel.

Before I could make sense of the violent action, the ballroom disappeared. I stood in the garden with the statue of the boy flautist. The tree's branches were bare against the overcast sky. Dry leaves tumbled across the yellow grass, catching in the sunken hollow that had been a pool.

With a feeling of dread I knelt and cleared the drift of desiccated leaves from the depression, revealing a pane of ice. It covered the still, white face of one of the twins. Her hands, crossed over her shrouded breast, were bound with a length of frayed golden cord. There was a dark gash across her cheek.

I couldn't look at that face and its terrible implications. I tried to cover it with leaves again, but the wind cleared them as quickly as I set them there. As I struggled with mounting frustration, the incongruous sound of a clock's chiming filled my head. The chimes grew louder and louder, until I thought I could not bear another second of the sound; then, with a final, ear-splitting toll of the bell, the dream shattered.

I jerked awake in a sweat as the last bell of four o'clock rang through the quiet hallways of Eden. As it died away, Dorian's parting words from the party echoed in my mind, intertwined with the images from the dream, and that random passage I had read from Eve's journal; together, they formed an idea that on any other night I would have called madness.

I bolted from my bed, and then clutched at one of its posts as the room swam and melted around me. For a moment I couldn't think what was wrong; but the sensation was not unfamiliar, and then I knew that the tea had been drugged, probably with my own chloral hydrate—a good deal of it. Though I knew that he had meant to help, it was an effort to push aside my anger at Alexander and focus again on the matter at hand.

When I felt steady enough, I fumbled the door open and stepped out into the hallway. A night-light burned at one end, but it was nothing more than a reassurance; I could see only a short distance in front of me. My breath came in short, sharp gasps as I crept down the stairs, which slid and jumped as the drug wreaked havoc on my vision. I turned right into the corridor at the bottom, where the grandfather clock measured seconds like a ponderous metronome. I slid my thumbnail under a peeling corner of the red paper that lined the wall behind it. It came away easily, and I didn't know whether to be sickened or elated when I found not bare plaster underneath but a painted spray of flowers.

I needed more light but didn't want to risk waking anyone.

After a moment's consideration I opened the door to the library and turned on the lamp on my grandfather's desk. Enough of its light filtered out into the hall to allow me to see what I was doing.

I tore the wallpaper off in wide swaths, barely noticing when it cut my fingers, aware only of the growing picture of the garden beneath. Then I uncovered a face: the face of a woman, white and heart-shaped, with black Byzantine eyes.

"Eleanor!" a voice cried, shocking me from my numbness. I turned and met Mary's bemused face. "What in God's name are you doing?"

I pointed with a trembling finger at the twin's face, looking down at us from the middle of the wall. Mary looked at it, then at me. She reached out tentatively and touched my cheek; at the coolness of her fingers, I realized how hot I was.

"I—I had a dream," I said, hoping to quell the anxiety that was tightening her face. "A nightmare. Alexander was dead, and Dorian killed the twins...and then I knew that it was here." I gestured to the mural.

Mary grasped my arm. "Eleanor, you're ill. Let me take you back to bed."

I pulled away and tore two more ribbons of paper from the wall, uncovering another image of the woman's face, her eyes downcast and sad.

"Don't you see?" I cried. "They're Louis' paintings!"

"Come away now, Eleanor," she said. "Please."

Something was wrong; she seemed afraid. "Mary? Are you all right?"

"Of course I am," she said with false brightness. "Everything's going to be all right."

She wouldn't meet my eyes. All at once, the pieces began to fall into place.

"It's not what you think," I said, because, finally, I did know what she thought. I also realized that I had no idea how to disabuse her of it. Dorian had been working on her for weeks, after all, as he had been working on us all, but unlike Alexander and me, she had had no confidante to check his influence.

"It's the medicine," I pleaded. "Alexander gave me too much medicine!"

Mary looked at me, frightened and uncomprehending. When I considered how I must look to her—soaked with sweat, hollow-eyed, weak and shaking—I almost didn't blame her for the conclusion she had drawn. Now, too, the clarity of mind I had awakened with was dissipating back into drugged fog. As Mary led me back to my bed, I wondered sluggishly whether my grandmother had ever actually been ill at all.

After what seemed an eternity, we reached my room. Mary urged me gently back into bed, then turned on a light. I heard her shifting bottles on my dressing table. She returned with the bottle of chloral hydrate. I didn't have the strength left to fight her when she poured some into the glass of water by my bed and made me swallow it.

Promising that she would be back soon to check on me, she shut off the light and closed the door. Before her footsteps moved away, I heard the soft, insidious click of the lock sliding into place.

I dreamed of Eve again directly before waking. Or perhaps it was my mother: even in sleep, my mind was too muddled by the drug to be certain. She came to me out of the darkness, her face white and pinched, her eyes flickering fear.

"Eleanor!" she cried, moving toward me, arms outstretched.

"I'm here," I answered, stretching my own arms to meet hers.

She took them gently, entreatingly, and said, "You must listen to him."

"Who?" I asked.

She didn't answer, or perhaps she couldn't. She simply said, "You are in grave danger."

The feeling of her fingers on my arms was fading, her black eyes and white face growing dim. "Wait!" I cried, panicked at the thought of her leaving me alone.

She only repeated, "Listen to him." Then she was gone. For a few moments I was alone in the dark silence with the gutted feeling of abandonment, before the dream faded into the gray light of morning.

6

I awakened to dull light. It was some time before I could focus my eyes, still longer before I could turn my leaden body so that I lay on my back. My tongue was thick and dry in my mouth, and the feeling seemed to translate directly to my other senses: there was a cottony grayness in the peripheral vision, and sounds seemed to come to me from behind a thick pane of glass. My head pounded, not with pain but with a density that seemed both to be inside trying to get out and outside trying to get in.

I only realized I was not alone when my companion shifted position in the chair next to my bed and coughed politely. I turned my head slowly, expecting to see Alexander, and instead met Dorian's direct stare.

Despite my foggy head and heavy limbs I sat up, clutching the sheets to my neck as though this would lessen the feeling of violation. "What are you doing here?" I asked, my voice shaky and querulous.

Dorian laughed, the sound rolling deep in his throat. "I came to offer my apologies for last night. And when I heard that you were ill...well, you can imagine my concern." His words were distant, tinny, secondary to the discord of his presence.

"How did you get in here?" I heard myself ask.

"Mary let me in. She seemed to think that seeing me might be beneficial to you."

"Get out," I told him flatly.

He raised his eyebrows in professed surprise. "Miss Rose, I know that we've had our disagreements—"

"Mary!" I cried, knowing that she could not be far away. In a moment she appeared in the doorway, the expression on her face that of a scolded dog who cannot decide whether to ask its master's forgiveness or run away and cower.

"Please, make him leave," I said.

She looked from one of us to the other, wringing her hands. I began to raise myself with the intention of standing, but Dorian got up first.

"Don't trouble yourself," he said. "I'll come later, when you're feeling more yourself." He leaned toward me, as if to kiss my cheek, but instead he whispered, "I've seen the pictures. Not quite the reaction I was hoping for. You're a clever one, Eleanor Rose...but you can't outsmart me."

Shutting my eyes and mustering my strength, I cried, "Mary!"

She fluttered in the doorway a moment longer, her stricken eyes on me. Then she said, "I'm so sorry, Mr. Ducoeur—"

Dorian smiled placatingly at her. "You needn't worry, Mrs. Bishop. I imagine it's to be expected of someone in her condition." His eyes flickered over mine again, apparently to make certain that I had registered the remark. "I'm sorry to trouble you. Oh, and do let me know if you'd like help restoring those fabulous murals. I've had some experience in that kind of work, you know." He smiled again, then exited.

Mary came to the bedside and looked down at me. Now both anger and helplessness were on her face, along with the fear. "Eleanor, I know that you're ill, but I can't abide your treating him so badly."

Again I tried to think of a way to make her aware of how he was using her, and again I realized that my mind in its present state was not equal to the task.

"I don't want him here," was all I could say.

"You might have chosen a more ladylike way of telling him so."

As Mary continued to lecture, my gummed mind replayed Dorian's parting words. It was clear that he was afraid of me, but without knowing why, I couldn't imagine what he might do next. What I did know was that in this state I could never defend myself against him.

"Mary," I interrupted, "I need to see Alexander."

"Eleanor, I really don't know whether—"

"Please, Mary!"

She looked at me for a long moment, then said, "All right, I'll get him. But I'm calling the doctor as well."

"If you think it's best," I said, settling back against the pillows, already exhausted again. "Please hurry."

I must have dozed, because it seemed only a moment had passed before Alexander entered. He shut the door softly behind him and sat down in the chair that Dorian had vacated.

I struggled upright and clutched his hand. "Why did you give me the medicine, Alexander?

"I only meant to help you," he said miserably.

"And instead, I've played right into Dorian's hands."

His eyebrows drew together. "What do you mean?"

"Apparently, he's been suggesting to Mary that I'm going mad," I said. "And after last night, she believes it."

"That's preposterous! Mary knows you better than that!"

"Not anymore."

"Eleanor, honestly—"

"Go and ask her."

He looked at me skeptically for a moment, then said, "All right."

He went out the door, and I shut my eyes again. It seemed that many minutes went by before he returned.

"Well?" I asked as he sat down again.

"She said...that she is afraid you are showing the first signs of your grandmother's illness. And she showed me two letters she said you'd hidden from her—one from a local doctor, the other from that hospital in Paris. I tried to explain it to her, but she didn't listen."

The room spun. I closed my eyes. Thinking of Dorian, my mind wandered back to the night I'd sat up with Tasha and she'd spoken his name. Against the backdrop of his unknown menace, she was like a white moth fluttering too near the web of a particularly cunning spider. A fragile white moth with the sun on its wings...a luminous angel...the sun in blond hair...a fragile white dress. Eve's overexposed photograph of her mother materialized behind my eyes and then dissolved again into the image of the moth, which in turn changed to a pale rose, tumbling through the dark.

I opened my eyes to find Alexander leaning over me, his brows furrowed. "Eleanor? What is it?"

"The roses," I said, closing my eyes against the light from the windows, which stung them like wind-driven rain.

Alexander put a hand on either side of my face, gentle but firm. "What are you talking about?"

I wanted to drift away from the voice, to melt into the soft, beckoning haze. Yet my mind clung to the images and refused to let go: a little girl in white, with her face buried in a bunch of roses far too sophisticated for her, and a fragile woman in white, her eyes turgid with fear.

"Tasha's illness," I said. "It was like my grandmother's. It had no apparent cause."

"Eleanor?"

I gripped his hand, forcing my mind to encompass the whole of what I was thinking.

"The day Dorian first came here," I said, "he gave Tasha roses. When did you put them by her bed?"

"I didn't," Alexander said softly, his eyes still resting on my face but seeing something else entirely. "Mary brought them to her when she first became ill."

"And suddenly she was more ill," I continued, as understanding began to creep across his face. "My grandmother was ill too, for years, with a disease that no one could diagnose. That last night with Tasha, when you were asleep, I threw the roses away. The next morning she was better."

Alexander was shaking his head. "Why would Dorian wish to harm Tasha?"

"I believe the roses were meant for me. But perhaps, when he saw her, he saw a different kind of opportunity."

Alexander sighed deeply. "All right. But I still don't see what this could have to do with your grandmother."

I shook my head, then regretted it as yellow spangles flurried in front of my eyes and the shapes of the room swam. I cursed all of them for reducing me to this state.

"If only I could think...."

"No, Eleanor; that is exactly what you must not do. You must allow yourself to recover."

"I won't recover," I said flatly. "Not as long as it's useful to him to keep me this way."

"Remember that this particular misfortune is my fault." He was silent for a moment, his jaw working. Then he said, "Give this first dose of medicine time to wear off, then perhaps Mary will see sense. In the meantime, I will think of something."

Before I could answer, there was a businesslike rapping on the door, and Mary entered, followed by a tall man with thinning grey hair and a long, drooping moustache.

"Eleanor, this is the doctor to see you. Alexander, if you wouldn't mind..."

"Yes, of course—" he began, but I didn't like the look of this doctor.

"Alexander can stay," I said.

Mary frowned, but it was the doctor who said, "I understand your concern, but I prefer to speak to Miss Rose first without distractions. I will be happy to meet with Mr.—"

"Trevozhov," Alexander said.

"—afterward, if he so wishes."

I began to protest again, but Alexander silenced me with a look in Mary's direction. I didn't like it, but I knew he was right; better to submit to her doctor's examination if I wanted to convince her that she was mistaken.

Alexander stood up to go, but I stopped him. I took Eve's journal from the top of the pile on my bedside table and held it out to him.

"You asked for this a long time ago," I said. "It's what led me to the murals. Maybe you'll see something else in it."

Alexander pocketed the book, then bent down to kiss me goodbye. "Don't worry, my love," he said softly, "I won't go far."

I thought that his assurance would give me the willpower to face Mary and the doctor with poise, but even this was about to shatter.

"Eleanor," Mary said, "this is Dr. Dunham. I called him in specially, as he treated your grandmother."

I blinked at her in disbelief, as a chill spread across me. The doctor smiled, but the smile seemed pasted on and his grey eyes remained aloof. I looked at Mary in appeal, but she was already backing away.

"I'll come back up with your lunch when the doctor's finished," she said, forcing another smile into the clenched muscles of her face.

When she had gone, the doctor's smile faded, leaving the rest of his face as calculating as his eyes. He proceeded to examine me physically from head to toe, then he asked me a series of questions that I imagined were designed to probe my mental state. At the end of the examination, he stepped out into the hallway and began consulting in low tones with Mary. He hadn't shut the door entirely, and thanks to the uneven floors of the old house it inched open as they talked, allowing me to hear a portion of their conversation.

"...state brought on by the changed climate, isolation, and lack of healthy occupation."

"Then you don't think it has anything to do with...the grandmother?" Mary asked tentatively.

There was a long pause before the doctor answered. "I looked over my old records, and it appears that Mrs. Fairfax's delusions manifested in a similar way to Miss Rose's—namely, through her dreams. Such delusions are often symptomatic of mental illness; but they are not necessarily diagnostic. We must remember that Mrs. Fairfax was ill for many years before the dementia manifested itself, and Miss Rose has only recently fallen ill. The patient knows her grandmother's history, and this in itself could be producing anxiety-based delusions, particularly when combined with the unusual factors of her environment.

"I will conduct more tests if she isn't better within a few days. For now, try to distract her from her obsession with the past. I am going to leave you with a small supply of sedative tablets, to be administered at the onset of a hysterical episode such as you witnessed last night. I must make it clear that these should not be used until her current sedation has worn off. You must be careful not to exceed the recommended dosage, either; she was given far too much medication last night."

"Yes, I'm afraid that was my fault. I didn't know that she'd already had some."

"Of course, it's understandable in the circumstances. Nonetheless, I need to be certain that you can take responsibility for all of this; otherwise, I'll send a nurse."

"No, I'll take care of it."

"Good. Now, several last things. She must be watched carefully at all times. Do not under any circumstances allow her to go off on her own, even if she seems perfectly recovered. It's typical of a manic or hysterical state—"

Before I could hear the end of the sentence, one or the other of them realized that the door was ajar and shut it again, then moved further off down the hallway, so that their voices were lost. The heavy sickness was too much to combat any longer. I drifted back into a half sleep, while a tiny, still-clear part of my mind chimed its warning.

7

The rest of that day was a hell of dazed consciousness. Fractured images from the last few days mingled with scraps of dreams, so that even my conscious moments were dislocated, and I couldn't separate my memories of dream and reality. In the convolutions of my mind I searched by a river for something lost and unnamed; a moment later I stood in the midst of a fire, looking up at a hard, dark sky. I sewed a quilt from squares of snow, stitching them together with gold thread and icicle needles, and laid it over Alexander's prostrate form. I stood by a piano encased in a cube of glass and cried as I battered at its smooth, intractable sides, knowing that I would never penetrate them. At one point I was certain that I saw a dark-haired woman standing by the window with her back to me; when I looked again, it was only Mary, her worried eyes fixed on my face. I could hear Tasha playing outside, singing songs to herself, or perhaps to an obliging adult, in Russian. More than once I thought that I felt my hand in someone else's, and I did not know whether to be comforted or frightened.

Toward evening the effects of the drug finally began to abate. When I could stand without the dizzy spangles cluttering my vision, I walked to the French door and out onto the gallery. It looked down onto a sheltered corner of lawn at the left side of the house, bordered by live oaks. Wildflowers and long grass swayed in the evening breeze. The tops of the trees glowed dusty gold in the last light of the setting sun. For a moment I felt at peace; I could almost believe that the last few days had been nothing more than a fever dream. Then Mary opened the bedroom door, a bowl of soup in her hands and that drawn, restive look on her face, and all of it was real again.

"Eleanor," she said, the relief evident in her voice. "I thought you'd never wake up."

I managed a wan smile. "I was beginning to think so, too."

"Oh, Eleanor," she said, and I was surprised by the tears that filled her eyes. "I'm so sorry. I didn't know that you'd already had so much medicine, or I never would have—"

"I know."

For a moment, I saw the old Mary. She opened her mouth, as if there was something else that she wanted to say; then she seemed to recall herself, and her sympathy retreated behind its new casing of fear. She set the soup bowl on my bedside table.

"I brought this," she said. "You haven't eaten in over a day. You must be hungry."

The thought of food made my stomach churn, but I knew that the most important thing now was to convince her that I was recovered. "Yes, thank you." Drawing a breath, I said, "I'm still quite tired," hoping that she would take this as a polite request to be alone.

Instead she answered, "I'll just sit with you while you eat, then I'll leave you to rest."

I forced another smile and allowed myself to be led back to bed. I choked down the soup, spoonful by spoonful, while Mary made small talk about the servants, the gardens, the weather. The care she took not to mention Dorian or the party, our calamitous meeting by the painting the night before, or the doctor's visit that morning weighed on me until it was almost more than I could bear. Then, just as I was reaching the end of my endurance, she said something that grabbed my attention again. She tossed it into the conversation almost perfunctorily, but I knew that she was watching carefully for my reaction:

"Oh, and we uncovered the rest of those paintings this afternoon."

I made myself take another spoonful of soup before I replied, "Did you?" wondering who constituted the "we".

"Perhaps if you're feeling more rested later, you'd like to come see them?"

I let the spoon settle back into the bowl and looked at her. There was nothing in her face to tell me what had prompted the suggestion.

"All right," I answered, then added after another moment's thought, "Why don't we look at them now?"

Still watching me with neutral eyes, she said, "If you feel up to it."

I climbed carefully out of bed, and donned my red silk wrapper. My heart was beating fast when we rounded the bottom of the staircase and started down the corridor. I was acutely aware of the sound of my own breathing, of every step I took. Mary went ahead of me to turn on the floodlight that somebody had brought in, so the murals were brightly lit when I turned to face them.

There were four in all, just as Eve's journal had suggested. They filled the spaces inside square borders of plaster molding, which stretched almost from floor to ceiling, so the figures in the paintings were life size. Louis had adopted the design of illuminated manuscript pages, bordering each painting with stylized vines and gilded scrollwork that reminded me of the books in the library in the house on the hill.

The first painting depicted morning in a garden with a flowering apple tree, ringed by water. One of the twins knelt in front of the tree, in what looked very like the wedding gown from the attic. He lap was full of pale-pink roses. She smiled out of the picture with radiant happiness. It was the first time I made the correlation among the dream garden, the real one with its burnt stump, and the Fontaine family's crest.

The same tree stood at the centre of the second painting, covered with golden apples and bright noontime light. One twin stood beneath the tree in a rose-colored dress, her hair full of petals. Her eyes were cast down, her face partly averted from the man who leaned from the branches of the tree, extending an apple to her with one long-fingered hand. Despite his expression of supercilious cunning, he bore more than a passing resemblance to Alexander.

The third painting was set in the same garden, but now the woman's gown was blue, the tree's leaves yellow. She sat beneath the tree, long branch-shadows crossing her like bars. She looked down with a beatific half-smile at the baby sleeping in her arms; a baby who already had a wealth of golden curls. I wrapped my arms around myself and moved on to the last image.

The sky was dark and full of stars, the tree's branches bare. The moon above was a waning crescent, reflected in the ring of water. Something about the reflection looked wrong. I stepped closer to get a better look; what I saw sent my heart racing. The white crescent was not the moon at all, but a woman's face turned in profile with a swath of dark hair curving across it. Her eyes were closed. A line from a play I had read at school came back to me then: Cover her face; mine eyes dazzle; she died young.

I was unaware of having spoken the words aloud until Mary said tentatively, "Eleanor?"

I shook my head. "I'm sorry. This picture reminded me of something I read once." I turned back to it, and found the signature in the bottom right corner: L. Ducoeur, 1902–4.

"Has Alexander seen them?" I asked.

"Yes," she said. There was an equivocation in her tone that I didn't like.

"Where is he now?"

"I don't know, he didn't say much—he only asked to borrow the car to go to the village. He left in a hurry. It was a bit odd."

The expectant look was still on her face, but I had no idea what she wanted to hear, and no desire to feed her fears about my state of mind by saying the wrong thing. I suppose she saw my hesitation, and perhaps guessed its source, because she hastened to say, "I hope I haven't done anything to upset you, Eleanor."

"What upset me yesterday has nothing to do with you."

"But Dorian, and the party—"

"I should have told you how I felt about him before it came to all of this."

Relief flooded across her face, but like a river around rocks, it only made the doubts Dr. Dunham had fed her that morning more obvious. She must be watched carefully at all times…even if she seems perfectly recovered. I wondered whether Dorian had bought the doctor, or if it had all been a convenient coincidence.

"I don't suppose you found out why they were papered over?"

Mary shook her head. "Although now that you mention it, Dorian did say something…"

"Well?"

"He said you might have thought better of tearing that wallpaper down, because it was a limited edition William Morris. He said he's only seen it once before, in London."

I was trying to remember when William Morris had begun designing wallpaper, when Mary voiced the question that must have been troubling her since the previous night. "Eleanor...how did you know they were here?"

"Intuition," I answered after a moment's consideration. "Besides, valuable or not, that wallpaper has never seemed to belong." Then I said, "I know how I must have seemed last night, Mary. But you can imagine what a shock it was, finding these here."

She answered without a hint of the retraction I had hoped for. "Of course; particularly when you weren't well."

I waited, but she said nothing else. Her unwillingness to see what was so clearly in front of her was hard to take, but I knew that I must take it, or dig my own grave deeper. So, pleading tiredness again, I escaped to my room.

In actuality, the drug's dissipation had left me feeling a peculiar, lucid emptiness, as though the hazy confusion it had caused on entering my body reversed itself on leaving it. I was restless, but I didn't want Mary to hear me pacing. Instead, I picked up the second of my mother's journals and began leafing through it, hoping to find some reference to the murals I had missed in my prior examinations.

What I found reduced the fragile stability I had rebuilt over the last few hours to rubble. The photograph slipped from the book like an ugly secret from a thoughtless tongue. It had the poor, grainy quality of the pictures Eve had taken of Eden, but this one had been taken in Boston. Snow covered the ground, the trees, the ice on the pond in the Public Garden. The two central figures sat on one of the benches, clearly oblivious to the cold. They looked at each other as only young lovers can look: the girl's face, one of the twins', bright and expectant beneath her fur-lined hood, Alexander's half-averted, as if he was shy of the camera.

With shaking fingers, I turned the picture over. On the back, in Eve's sloppy, scrawling hand, was an inscription: Elizabeth Fairfax and Alexander Rose, January 1898.

Alexander Rose: the father who had abandoned my mother with a child, whose name I'd never known. I looked at the photograph once more before my shaking hand closed around it. I could not comfort myself with even a glimmer of doubt that the boy in the photograph bore a mere likeness to my lover; I knew the smile and penetrating eyes better than my own.

Overcome with a wave of nausea, I ran to the gallery. Once there, though, the catharsis of sickness eluded me. I stared into the darkness, my mind as full of the obvious, preposterous truth as my blocked throat was of bile. I began to sob uncontrollably, and pitched gracelessly to the floor. I kept trying to tell myself that I must somehow be mistaken, that somewhere, somehow there must be a reasonable explanation for what I saw in that picture. But Dorian's final warning kept playing in my mind, dragging with it the monstrous image of my mother smiling at the man who by all logic must be my father.

I was crying too violently to hear Mary calling. By the time her hands came down on my shoulders, she was shaking almost as badly as I was. I heard her speaking to me, demanding that I calm down and tell her what was wrong, her voice a perplexity of solicitude and panic. I can only imagine what I must have looked like: a fury wailing gibberish into the night.

I pity her now. A part of me can even understand what she

did later, in light of what I must have seemed to be then. But at that moment I was too wounded even to be able to feel sorry for myself, let alone appease Mary with the rational, if preposterous, explanation for my outburst which might have saved us all so much grief.

After a time she went away, and I began to calm down; at any rate, I seemed to have exhausted my tears. Still, I didn't move from my place by the gallery railing, nor relinquish the hem of my wrapper, which I had pressed against my eyes as a kind of security blanket against the truth I could not face. After some minutes I heard Mary's footsteps climbing the stairs again with the inevitable others. At the thought of seeing Alexander hysteria consumed me again, so that by the time he and Mary entered the room I must have appeared to be in much the same state she had left me in earlier.

"I don't know what to do," I heard her say. Her voice echoed in my ears with the protracted dissonance of nightmare. "I can't possibly give her more medication yet. I don't know what started it. She won't tell me; she doesn't even seem to hear me."

"Eleanor," I heard Alexander say, from somewhere quite near by.

I screamed when he touched my hands, but he dragged them away from my face anyway. I kept them clenched as stubbornly shut as my eyes, but it was too late to hide my discovery. Alexander pried my fingers apart and exhumed the crumpled picture from its temporary tomb. My eyes opened too, as though some deeper part of me needed to see what his reaction would be. His face whitened, and the horror on it mirrored my own.

"What is it?" Mary asked, moving toward him. "I can't see."

Alexander closed his own fingers over the picture, turned

to her, and said with tremulous authority, “Mary, please leave us alone.”

“But—” she began.

“Please,” he repeated. “It will be all right, but I need to speak with Eleanor alone.”

I don’t think she believed him any more than I did, but something in his face or tone apparently convinced her to obey him. Reluctantly she turned and left, closing the door behind her with what sounded to me too much like finality.

8

"Eleanor, it isn't what you think," Alexander said as soon as she was gone. He passed a hand over his eyes, and if possible, his face was whiter when he looked at me again than it had been before. "I assure you that I am not your father."

Though these were the words I had hoped to hear, their realization was oddly hollow, and bereft of comfort. I didn't know what I would say, or even whether I could say anything, until I heard my own voice grating in my ears:

"Am I enough like her? Or do you still think of her when you sleep with me?"

I had intended to hurt him, believing all my feeling for him to be dead. Yet I found that some remaining shred of sentiment made me flinch as the words hit their target. I turned away from his ravaged face, pressing my own against the gallery's wooden balusters. My tears were spent, and now I could only ache for us both.

"Eleanor," Alexander finally said, his voice still gentle, but now also indisputably authoritative. "Elenka, turn around."

Hating myself for still being compelled by him, I turned. He stood in the arched doorway, silhouetted against the tarnished lamplight of the room, clutching either side of it as if for support. As he stood there a finger of breeze lifted the curtains behind him, turning them to wings. The rising moon shed enough light to show me his face. I had expected it to wear guilt, embarrassment, and anger—and all of them were there—but not the love that was there too, entangled with the rest.

"Where did you find it?" he asked.

"It...it was in my mother's journal."

In one stride he was kneeling in front of me, taking my limp hands in his. The photograph fluttered for a moment in his slipstream, then settled to the floor.

"Eleanor, forgive me," he said, his own voice full of tears.

"Let me go!" I insisted, trying to pull away from him, but he held my hands fast.

"Just hear what I have to say," he pleaded. Though I didn't want to hear anything more, I also knew that Dorian had been right—right again—when he said that the truth would find me. So, face averted, I listened as Alexander began to speak.

"Do you remember the conversation we had the night of Dorian's party, after you heard the two of us talking?" he asked. "Do you remember how I told you to forget what you had heard and believe only what you saw? Well, I was wrong." The words surprised me into meeting his eyes. Like touchstones, they betrayed the volatility his face had so long hidden.

"It is true that once I loved Elizabeth Fairfax, and that a lifetime ago the woman you knew as your mother was my wife." He paused again, then said, "But if you believe nothing else that I have said, please believe this: I love you as I have never loved anyone else. It is for that reason and no other that I kept this secret from you. I thought, or perhaps convinced myself, that the past made no difference. By the time I realized how much my knowledge would mean to you, I loved you too much to deliberately destroy your feeling for me. I couldn't bear for you to think of me as your mother's lover or, worse, the man who abandoned you."

The sting of the spoken words was sharp, but as it subsided I found that I could think more clearly. Still, I couldn't bring myself to look at Alexander; instead I looked slightly to the side of him, at the blurred forms of the bedroom beyond. Unspoken questions crowded my mind, so plentiful that I could barely think through one before another surfaced and obliterated it. I wanted to demand answers to all of them at once, but at the same time I knew that he was desperate for an overture even as tenuous as that, and I still wanted to hurt him.

Finally, though, curiosity won over stubborn spite.

"If you aren't my father," I demanded, "then who is?"

Alexander looked at me with a raw mixture of pity, pain, and dread. "Are you certain you want to know?"

"How can you ask me that?" I spat back.

He drew a breath and let it out with quiet finality. "To begin with, then, you must understand that you are no more Elizabeth's daughter than you are mine."

I flushed and then chilled. Alexander reached toward me, but I jerked away from him, pressing myself back against the railing until it bruised my back. I saw that this hurt him more than anything I had yet said or done, but I couldn't bring myself to pity him, couldn't bear for him to touch me.

"All right," he said wearily. "Eleanor...your real mother was Eve. She gave you to her sister to raise as her own, under circumstances that left her little choice."

His face receded as shock darkened my vision once again. I swallowed hard, fighting the returning urge to be sick. "You knew this all along, and you didn't tell me?"

"How could I?"

"How couldn't you?" I wailed.

"Wait, Eleanor. Before you judge any of us, try to imagine what it was like."

Only Alexander's eyes remained steady; everything else around me swam with the outrageous surreality of his words. I wanted to scream again, to kick and flail and refuse him even the cold comfort of justifying himself to me, but my newfound capacity for hysteria seemed to have been as temporary a catharsis as tears. Meanwhile, he pressed on relentlessly with his confession, which only half made sense to me.

"Eve and Elizabeth had imprisoned themselves in their own deception. Eve didn't see it until later, but Elizabeth...she tortured herself from the day she ran away, no doubt until the day she died. The deception was bad enough: in her mind, it negated everything she was and believed in. But the worst of it was that by virtue of it, she'd exiled herself from her family at the time when she knew her sister would need her the most, because Elizabeth saw the cruel side of Louis Ducoeur as Eve could not. When Eve finally realized the mistake she had made, it was too late to save herself, but she could not bear to see you suffer the consequences of her transgressions. So she gave you to us."

With every word he spoke, with their very credibility, I felt his past deception widen the schism between us. "That explains a lot," I said coldly, folding my arms over my chest. "Now get out."

"Eleanor, you must—"

"Must what? Everyone has lied to me, and you worst of all. That's all I need to know."

He sighed, closed his eyes for a moment, and then opened them again. "I'm afraid there's a good deal more that you need to know."

"To soothe your guilty conscience?"

"To save your life."

I looked at him for a moment, then said, "You can't be serious."

"I am all too serious."

I moved past him, back into the bedroom. I heard him follow me. "I'm listening," I said, when it was clear that he wouldn't continue without such an assurance.

Still he paused, apparently trying to gather and sort his thoughts. Finally he said, "Louis Ducoeur was a jealous man. Like all jealous men, he couldn't be happy with what he had—or, to be fair, what he seemed to have. Of course, I can't imagine how I would react if a woman who had shown me only coldness for years suddenly overflowed with passionate devotion. But he took it to an extreme. Eve wrote that he suspected she had a secret lover, even that the child she was carrying wasn't his own. And the twins' own deception justified him in suspecting her, because he knew that there had been a rival for Elizabeth's affections."

He paused again, then said, "Elizabeth believed that Eve's life was in danger, and perhaps yours, too. I didn't believe that a man would kill his wife out of purely speculative jealousy. But I hadn't yet met Louis Ducoeur. Or rather, I didn't know that I had met him."

"This is madness," I said, though a part of me knew that it wasn't. "We know that Eve died in Paris, under Elizabeth's name, a few months after I was born."

I don't know why I said this. I certainly remembered the letter I'd had from Paris negating everything that certificate had said. I suppose a part of me already knew what was coming, and wanted to deflect it however I could.

Alexander's eyes were deep with sympathy. I turned away, hating him for maintaining his composure as my world disintegrated. Yet this time when he reached for my arms I let him catch them.

"You asked for the truth, Eleanor, and this is the truth as I have been able to discern it: Eve Fairfax, your mother, known in 1905 as Elizabeth Ducoeur, was never in Paris. That death certificate we found was Louis's flimsy attempt to cover up the fact that he murdered her out of blind jealousy."

He was looking at me as though he expected me to register some sort of epiphany. "If you want me to believe my life is in danger," I said, "you're going to have to provide better evidence than a speculative theory that a phantom father killed a mother I never knew, when I was too young to realize what was happening."

He looked at me askance, as though still wondering whether my incomprehension was merely affected. "It's only speculative insofar as no one ever found her body...and I would have thought you'd have realized by now that your father is a very tangible danger to both of us."

"You speak as if you know him," I said, balking at the foreboding in my own voice.

Alexander sighed patiently. "I do know him, Eleanor. So do you. I don't honestly believe I need to tell you how, but if you will demand proof, here it is."

He reached into his pocket and took out Eve's journal, opened it to the page where she had pasted the fragment of Louis's letter to Elizabeth, and handed it to me. He had marked the page with a bit of heavy, pale blue paper. It was Dorian's invitation to the costume ball. The handwriting on the invitation was the same as that on the burned fragment.

I blinked at the two pieces of paper for a moment, and then

I dropped them. Alexander caught me as my legs buckled, and led me gently to the bed.

"How...how long have you known?" I asked.

He sighed. "I suspected it all along. I was almost certain when I matched up the handwriting, so I went to the village today and looked up the newspaper clippings of their wedding photographs."

"And those things Dorian told me about you—were they true?"

"They are as true as anything he's told you, which is to say that they are as much his interpretation of facts as they are facts in and of themselves."

"One could say the same of that answer."

Alexander shook his head. "I lied to you, Eleanor, but I did it as much to protect you as myself."

I scrutinized his haggard face. "Why did you leave my mother?"

Alexander sighed once more. "There's no easy answer, Eleanor...unless you believe that we were never meant to be together. And perhaps we weren't, any more than Louis and Eve. The twins belonged to each other before anyone else; in the end, no love was greater than their love for each other."

He paused, his eyes on the dark sky beyond the open balcony door. Then he said, "I told you that Elizabeth never forgave herself for her part in the deception, but it was no simple guilt. It was fundamental, and it changed her. I resented the change, and she resented me for not understanding it. And then you came, and she had nothing left for me." He paused, then let out a long breath. "There is nothing so ugly or so painful as a marriage in which the love has become bitterness. So we separated, by mutual agreement. I went back to Russia, and you know the rest."

Among all of the weighty ones, a trivial thought had repeatedly occurred to me over the last few minutes. "What about your name?"

"My family name was Rostov. The first time I came to America, the immigration officer couldn't spell it, and changed it to Rose. The second time, I changed it myself. I didn't want anyone to trace me."

We were both silent for some minutes, contemplating our separate miseries. Finally Alexander began speaking again:

"What you don't know, and can never know, is how you haunted me. It was as if you had become my conscience. I dreamed of you, and in those dreams you grew into a beautiful woman, like Elizabeth but stronger, all your own. My life became more and more hollow. I replayed the past, always wondering whether I ought to have chosen differently. And then that night at the concert in Boston you stepped back into my life, and I could not help but see it as fate offering me a second chance."

The reticence of his tone and the way he stumbled over words his fluency had previously mastered told me that these were thoughts that had lived in his secret heart for a long time. Though half of me was still appalled at his duplicity, something deeper was moved by his sudden vulnerability. Insidious or beatific—even now I can't decide which—that inner voice was telling me that I had no right to judge him. His love might be a thicket of duplicity and remorse, but it was still the basis of all he had done, not calculation or cruelty. And so, despite everything, in my own heart I began to forgive him.

"I knew that it was you from that first moment," he was saying when I was again aware of his words. "After that night you seemed to disappear, but I devoted myself to finding you. When Martha Kelly came to me with your offer of a house,

I was even further convinced that we had been reunited for some purpose. When we finally met, of course, I knew what it was. And when Louis arrived, I saw that there was a second reason for my finding you. To save you from him," he said, before I could speak the question. "As I failed to do the first time. Do you see?"

What in fact I saw was the image of my grandmother's fearful, accusatory eyes as they had looked in Eve's overexposed photograph.

The penny finally dropped. Claudine Fairfax would never have looked at her daughter the way she was looking at that photographer. All along I had assumed that she had simply accepted my grand-father's decision that Elizabeth would marry Louis, but perhaps she hadn't. If she hadn't, and if she had exerted any kind of control over her husband's decisions, then she would have had to have been silenced before that marriage could have taken place. Cover her face, my mind whispered, mine eyes dazzle...

"There is a connection between Tasha's illness and my grand-mother's," I cried, "and now mine as well."

"Eleanor—"

"No, listen. All of us have shared similar symptoms: fevers, and nightmares. Louis—Dorian—killed her. He drove her mad and then poisoned her!" I thought about this, then added, "But it still doesn't explain why he thinks I'm a threat."

There was speculation in Alexander's look now, and also a shade of relief. "Unless he never found out about the switch," he said slowly. "In that case, he would have attributed all he knew of Elizabeth's history to his wife, Eve. He must have assumed he had a rival. Given that, and Elizabeth's sudden willingness to marry him, the arrival of a child so soon afterward might have made a better man suspicious."

“So he thinks that I’m yours. That’s the secret he’s been holding over me all this time.” I had thought that I had nothing left to fear; now I saw that I was wrong. “He wants revenge on us for what he thinks you and my mother did to him. And yet, that doesn’t explain his fear…”

“Unless he believes we know what he did to Eve.”

“What am I going to do?” I murmured.

I didn’t listen to his answer. Instead my spent mind turned a single memory over and over again, snapping it against my battered heart like the loose end of a film in an abandoned projector. The first time I had awakened with Alexander beside me, I had looked past the curve of his shoulder at the sunlight filtering through a small flowering tree in the garden below. I had never noticed the tree before, but suddenly it was the most beautiful thing I had ever seen, an intricate lantern hissing with light.

I hadn’t watched the light fade. I don’t know whether I would have taken heed if I had. Either way, the metaphor was apt: I had guarded my love so carefully, but as Dorian had said, nothing could guard it from time.

Yet I realized something else as I sat looking into the dark garden. The light might have faded, the blossoms withered, but the roots of my love for Alexander ran as deep as those of any tree. As long as I dug and as much as I made him hurt me, I would never entirely stop loving him.

I curled up on the bed then, my back to Alexander, too exhausted even to think of an answer when he asked me whether I wanted him to stay with me or not. After a moment of hesitation he turned off the bedside lamp and lay down beside me; after another I felt him begin to stroke my hair, gingerly, as though he were afraid I might break. And though I knew that it should not, this comforted me.

9

After the first few hours of fatigued unconsciousness, I slept little that night. I didn't dwell on the disturbing facts that had come to light that evening; instead, I was thinking about what to do next. For I had realized two things in the course of that night: first, that I wasn't yet ready to relinquish my love for Alexander, and second, that if there was any hope of salvaging it, we had to get away from Eden. By the time the first light dissolved the darkness of the sky, I had decided that if it were in my power to arrange it, we would leave that day.

Of all my memories of Eden, this is the one I most often return to: lying in the moth-colored light, listening to the muted rhythm of Alexander's breathing, believing myself finally free of the past. I used to think that its potency was a result of what happened afterward, but now I'm not so certain. Until that moment, I had always allowed someone or something else to steer me, whether it was to my own good or not. I believed that the decision to leave Eden was my first adult one. I couldn't see it for what it was: a desperate attempt to transplant my love for Alexander into a more concrete world, where the drama and uncertainty and deception that had characterized it at Eden couldn't threaten it.

I was twenty-one. Alexander was my first experience of love,

Eden of adult life. Both were products of a wildly distorted reality. I don't know whether our love could have survived a more mundane kind of existence, whether there was even any true love left between us. That morning, though, I believed both.

I lived my last day with Alexander with more enthusiasm than I had most that summer. We seemed to have come to an unspoken truce. I didn't have the energy left to speak of the past night's trauma, and he, no doubt, lacked the desire. This is one of the things that has made me wonder whether even then, he suspected what lay ahead.

However, that confrontation was still hours away, and we filled the ones between with the simple pleasures we had previously neglected. In the morning we played with Tasha in the shallows of the lake, then lay on the warm spit of sand in the lacy shadows of a black cypress as the sun centered itself in the sky. That afternoon we picked peaches from the orchard by the stables, then tucked Tasha, sticky and sweet, into her bed for a nap. While she slept Alexander played the piano for me. He played his own music, and I knew that every note was an appeal for forgiveness. I didn't yet know whether I could accept it, but I felt something in me ease.

I didn't tell him about the tickets to Boston. I didn't want anything to mar the brittle beauty of that day. Instead, the reminder of our recent troubles came from Mary. Though she hadn't seemed worried when we went out in the morning, her look was dubious when the three of us came back to the house that evening. She was quiet throughout dinner, and when I got up to leave with Alexander afterward, she said, "Eleanor, I wish you would stay here tonight."

"What? Why?"

"You must be tired." Her words sounded forced, as if they were not her own.

I looked at Alexander. His mouth had turned down into a tight frown. "Eleanor is perfectly recovered," he said.

"Yes, she seems to be. I don't want anything to threaten that."

The two of them looked at each other, their eyes in silent conflict. It was Alexander who backed down.

"You'd better listen to Mary," he said.

"But—"

"It's only one night." He smiled reassuringly. "I'll come in the morning. Sleep well, Eleanor," Alexander said, kissing both my cheeks. He smiled tautly at Mary and then left.

When I was sure that he was beyond hearing, I demanded, "Don't you trust him, either?"

Her face had collapsed into a mesh of fine lines. "Of course I do. It's just that the doctor said—"

"I heard what the doctor said! I can't believe that you listened."

"It's…it's not that I don't think you're well, Eleanor—"

"I'm not mad like my grandmother. In fact, I'm beginning to think that she wasn't mad, either."

"Meaning?"

"Maybe she was tormented by something she knew—something no one else would believe." Mary looked up at me, but she didn't answer. So I asked, "Who referred you to Dr. Dunham?"

"What?" There was fear in her tone now.

"It was Dorian, wasn't it?"

"I know what you think of him, but he only meant to help."

"It doesn't matter anymore, Mary. I've reserved our tickets home. Are you coming?"

“I thought…” she began, and then trailed off. She wouldn’t meet my eyes.

“Everything has changed. I don’t want to stay here anymore. If that doctor tries to stop me, I imagine there are plenty of others who can be bought.” I didn’t wait for a reply, but turned and went upstairs.

The breeze from the open door touched my face, quelling my anger. The full moon was just rising over the tops of the live oaks. Its pale face saddened me inexplicably; despite the close warmth of the night, I shivered. I moved away from the window, took off my dress, and wrapped myself in my red dressing gown, buttoning it right up to the neck. Its touch was like human skin, familiar and comforting.

Despite my previous sleepless night, I wasn’t at all tired. I paced the room for several minutes, then sat down at the dressing table, rummaged in one of the bottom drawers, and located the packet of tobacco and rolling papers I had hidden there months before. Smoking was a habit I had never really embraced and had completely given up when I moved to Eden, as Mary wouldn’t abide it. Now, though, I longed for the tobacco’s rush of optimism. I lit the cigarette and inhaled deeply.

Soon enough I was pacing again, my former unease growing. It was only when I heard Mary calling to Colette along the corridor below that I realized she might well be listening to my anxious footsteps. I dragged the armchair out onto the gallery and rolled another cigarette by the light of the climbing moon.

I missed Alexander with an uneasiness that threatened to flower into panic. I knew that I would never sleep that night without his reassuring presence. My anger at Mary began to surface again: after all, Eden was my house, she had no right to hold me prisoner. After a moment I gathered my resolve, stubbed out my third cigarette, and opened the door.

Mary sat in a chair on the stair landing, knitting. It was a moment before I regained enough composure to ask her, "What are you doing?"

"I thought you might try to leave," she answered with a touch of smugness.

"I'm not a child, Mary. I can decide for myself when to come and go."

"I can't let you leave, Eleanor."

"For God's sake! It's my mind, and I promise you that there's nothing wrong with it!"

"Of course not," she said quickly. "But you had such a day yesterday—you must give yourself time to recover."

"Keeping me from Alexander isn't going to help."

"He could have stayed here if it meant that much to him."

The insinuation in her words was quite clear. I began to push past her, but she caught my wrist in a surprisingly strong grasp.

"I can't let you leave," she repeated, no longer meeting my eyes. I knew that she would wrestle me back to my room if she had to, and that she was quite likely capable, given the little sleep and food I'd had lately.

Keeping my eyes on her face, I pulled my arm free. I turned to go back to my room, but she followed me. "You don't need to watch me," I said bitterly, damning the day I'd asked her to come to Eden.

Her eyes flickered over to the open door, the chair on the gallery. "Perhaps you ought to take some medicine," she said.

"Hasn't that done enough damage?"

"I only meant a little bit. To help you sleep."

Without waiting for me to answer, she took a bottle from

her pocket. It wasn't my own chloral, but a bottle of pills. She shook two of them onto her palm and proffered them to me. I knew she wouldn't leave until I swallowed them. I put the bitter pills on my tongue, took the water glass from the bedside table, and swallowed a mouthful.

When I had set the glass back on the table, she embraced me and kissed my cheek.

"Everything's going to be all right, Eleanor," she said.

I smiled half-heartedly. She turned toward the door. Before shutting it she said, "I'll be right outside if you need anything." I forced another smile, and finally she left me alone.

I waited until I heard her settle in her chair, then spat the pills out again. They had largely disintegrated, but there was little else to be done. I went back to the bed and lay down, feeling sick and desolate. The sheets were still twisted and rippled with the patterns of the past night. I pressed my face into the pillow where Alexander had lain. It had kept a trace of his smell; I turned over on my side, hugging it to my body as if it could dilute my fears, or lessen the ache of my unresolved feelings for him.

My sleepless night and active day must have caught up with me then, or perhaps some of Mary's medicine had been absorbed into my system, for after a time I drifted into a fitful doze.

Alexander and I knelt on the floor of the ballroom. Cold, grey light filtered onto us. Alexander wore the dark suit that he had worn to the costume ball; I wore Eve's wedding dress. We looked at each other for a time without speaking, and then I leaned over, kissed his cheek, stood up, and said, "Good-bye."

I left the ballroom through another open door and, without

looking back, stepped into black nothingness. There was a sensation of rapid movement, and then I found myself in the garden with the boy flautist. I stood above the ice pane set into the ground, looking at the gashed white face beneath it. It seemed I stood there a long time, without thought or emotion, just looking.

In the moments before I awakened, the face changed. It grew younger and younger, until it was the face of a child. For a moment I thought it was mine; then I saw the auburn hair, the wasted look of one who has barely survived a deadly illness.

10

I awakened with Tasha's name on my lips, and I knew there was no time to lose. I didn't dare risk Mary's still being awake; instead, I slipped on a pair of sandals and went out onto the gallery.

Leaning over the balustrade, I made out the gnarled fingers of a wisteria vine twined around the pillar below. I swung over the railing and felt around with one foot for the vine. There was a giddy moment when I could not find a foothold, but once I located one, it wasn't difficult to ease myself downward. Then I ran around the house and down the path through the topiary garden to the lake's edge.

The light from Alexander's study window shone through the trees. When I reached it, though, I found that the room was empty. I ran around to the front door and flung it open, calling his name and Tasha's. There was no answer. My perfunctory search confirmed what I already knew: Tasha's bed was rumpled but vacant, Alexander's untouched. There was no clue as to where either of them had gone, but I suppose in my heart I had known all along where I would find them.

My compulsion was to make a straight line for the house on the hill, but I retained enough composure to realize that this was folly. I would never find my way in time to help them, if I found it at all. Fighting panic, I hurried back to Eden, then around the house to the driveway. The car was parked in the shadows of the magnolia. I knew that Jean-Paul left the key in the ignition; I only hoped that I could start it on the first try. Hardly breathing, I put the car in gear, turned the key and pressed the switch. I almost didn't believe it when the engine coughed into life. As I pulled forward, I could see shadows moving behind the house's lit windows in the rear-view mirror; and then the light was gone.

I had only a rudimentary grasp of driving, but by the time I reached the turn-off for the house on the hill, I had managed to shift gears and speed up. Moonlight flickered still between the trees, but the weather had begun to change. Earlier, when I had fallen asleep, the sky had been clear. Now tattered clouds skittered across it like dry leaves.

Lightning flickered on the horizon as I pulled up in front of the dark house. After a moment a rumble of thunder answered it. Despite the wind gathering in the trees, the air was close and stale. The leaves of the oaks by the side of the house fretted like anxious hands, their silvery undersides flashing in the intermittent patches of moonlight. My grandfather had told me once that a storm is coming when the leaves show their backs.

I stood in the long, dew-wet grass, trying to gather the courage to face the dark rooms alone. As if answering this thought, the stormy cowl shifted from the face of the moon. It shone clearly for a long moment, dragging me from my torpor.

Drawing a deep breath of the stagnant air, I moved toward the doorway. As I pushed through the long, damp grass, the strap of one sandal snagged on something and broke. I took both shoes off, then stood staring at my bare feet. In the dark, the jacquard of the dressing gown took on a greater contrast, its vines and tendrils black against the dusky red. With a sinking heart, I crossed the last few feet to the front door, and took a few tentative steps into the room beyond.

Somebody had closed the curtains and shutters after the party. I moved carefully, trailing a hand along the wall to my left, my eyes straining into the insufficient light. Gradually the furniture became lighter patches, the doorways darker. I didn't allow myself to look at anything more than a few feet away. I knew that if I did, my mind would begin to make things of the shadows that I didn't want to see.

In this way I crept to the antechamber of the ballroom. I put my hand on the doorknob and let it rest there for a moment. I suppose a part of me had expected to hear music, but the house retained its recalcitrant silence. With great effort I broke through the spell of inertia that had settled on me for the second time, and turned the knob.

The little light left in the sky shone softly through the glass doors, illuminating the marble floor. One of them was ajar. The piano hulked against its muted light, and I kept as far from it as I could.

The rose garden lay bleak and mute under the cloud-covered sky. The only movement was the rippling of the long grass in the spasmodic gusts of wind, the only sound its rasp against the broken stone of the bench and fountain. I walked past these, toward the ivy-covered door in the wall. This door, too, was open.

I pushed through the ivy into the round garden beyond. But for the stone flautist, it was empty. By the entrance to the maze I stopped, trying to remember the pattern that Alexander had explained to me. That sunny afternoon seemed years rather than weeks in the past. I knew that if something happened, it could be days before anyone thought to search here. I also knew that looking for Tasha and Alexander here was little better than a whim. In the end, though, my fear for their safety won over my trepidation.

Before entering the maze, I filled my pockets with the limp petals of overblown roses; I dropped them every few steps. A pervading sense of claustrophobia descended as I made the first turn among the high hedges. I kept my eyes on the path ahead and concentrated on my rose-petal trail. I made my way slowly, counting turns, and finally came to the place where I thought the first statue ought to be. Rounding the corner, I came up against a solid wall of branches.

For a moment I could only stare at it. Then I turned to follow the rose-petal path back the way I had come, just in time to see the last pale snips twirling away on a gust of wind. It was too much. I ran blindly after the wayward petals, as if catching them could save me. I followed them down a narrow corridor, half-aware of the folly but too afraid to care, and by luck or fate I stumbled up against Diana's stone legs.

For a few minutes I clung to the statue and sobbed, oblivious to the rising wind, the thunder rolling ever closer, or the pinkish flickers of lightning behind the recumbent clouds. Finally, awareness of my predicament broke through the primitive fear. I pulled myself together as best I could and forced myself to think of what Alexander had said about the pattern. The last part of his explanation, at least, was solid in my mind: at the clearings, I had to return to the beginning of the sequence.

I looked up at Diana's face; her stone composure helped me to compose myself. More of the pattern came back to me, then. It began with two right turns and one left, and I was fairly certain that this was meant to be repeated, then reversed. I couldn't remember whether I had followed the reversal once or twice on my first attempt. Realizing that there was no way to tell except to try it, I made my way out of Diana's clearing and into the first part of the sequence. I decided to try the reversal twice, and almost burst into tears again from pure relief when I found myself in another clearing with a statue.

Returning confidence cleared my head faster than any amount of willpower. With only two more wrong turns I had established the pattern, and soon I was twisting my way through the narrow evergreen alleys at a fair pace. Nevertheless, it seemed that hours had passed before the path finally opened out into the oblong clearing with its dead tree.

Beside the tree was a darker shadow. I moved toward it cautiously, until I could see that it was not Dorian but Alexander. I ran toward him then, but when I saw what he was holding I stopped short. In his arms, Tasha lay still and pale. He was rocking her gently, blank-faced, looking at nothing.

I put a hand on Alexander's shoulder. He did not start or pull away, but covered it with one of his own, as cold as the fear balling in my stomach. He turned to me, and there was no surprise on his face, only implacable acceptance.

"I hoped that you wouldn't come," he said.

"But you knew that I would." I moved his arms gently aside and bent down to put an ear to the child's chest. Her heart was still beating, and though her breathing was rapid and shallow, it was regular. I sat back and looked at Alexander.

"Do you know how she came to be here?"

He shrugged. "I can imagine."

"She's your daughter, isn't she, Alexander?"

He turned his face from me.

"For Christ's sake, how many times do I have to ask for the truth?"

Slowly he turned back, and looked at me across the turgid darkness. Finally he said, "The truth is, I don't know."

"But she's Anna's child. All of that was true."

He nodded.

"So if she isn't yours, she's his." He said nothing. I shook my head. "Why did you lie about this, of all things?"

"For the same reason Elizabeth lied to you. So that she would never think herself unwanted."

I couldn't bear to ask whether there was more. Perhaps a part of me already knew that it no longer mattered. I turned away, hiding the pain of the confession beneath brusque efficiency.

"Come on," I said. "We have to get her out of here."

"He's worked so hard to bring us here, I hardly think he'll let us leave so easily."

"We can try," I snapped, "unless you'd prefer to wait here for him to find you." I began to walk back the way I had come. In a moment, I heard him follow.

All the while we made our way through the maze, my intuition of impending disaster deepened. Therefore, I wasn't much surprised to see the faint glow in the window of the tower room when we arrived back in the rose garden. We hurried through the ballroom into the room with the deer's head, but when I tried to open the door that would take us to the entrance hall, it was locked.

"How can it be locked?" I cried.

Alexander tried it as well, but it wouldn't give. Trying the shutters on the nearby windows, we found that they had been latched from the outside.

"Can we get out through the gardens?" he asked.

"Maybe," I said, "if we can find a way over the wall. But there might be a better way. Come on."

Without waiting to see whether he followed, I rushed off through the door that led toward the tower. The doors I tried along the way were all locked. When we reached the hallway that led to the tower, it seemed too dark. I groped along the wall to my left. There were no inner shutters, but there were outer ones, and they'd been closed and no doubt locked over the iron-latticed panes.

With deepening foreboding, I made my way down the corridor and pushed open the door to the tower stair. I didn't have much hope that Dorian would have overlooked this last means of escape, so I wasn't really disappointed when I found the door under the stairs tightly locked as well.

I couldn't see Alexander; I reached out, and our hands met and linked. "This has gone on long enough," I said. "Let's go up and have this over with."

"I'll go up," Alexander said with a touch of vehemence that suggested his spirit wasn't entirely broken. He handed Tasha to me. "You take her and find a way out of here—there must be one, somewhere."

"And I could break both our necks looking."

"This is my fight, Eleanor."

"No, Alexander, it's ours."

"At least stay down here."

"And what if he's not up there at all? What if he's hoping that you'll leave me alone, just like this?"

He sighed. "Come, then, but stay behind me."

We weren't half way up the stairs before my arms were aching with Tasha's weight, my head thick with dizziness brought on by lack of food and sleep and the array of substances my body had absorbed over the past few days. When we finally reached the top, Alexander stopped short in the doorway, but I pushed past him.

Dorian turned from the French door and regarded us for a moment. Then his smile widened and slid into the nightmare leer. Inadvertently I stumbled backward. Alexander's arms closed around me, and we stood like that in the doorway, staring at Dorian as he crossed his arms over his chest and said with polite coolness, "Won't you come in?"

11

Alexander was the first to break the deadlocked silence. "What have you done to Natalya?"

Dorian smiled. "You don't really think it would be to my advantage to tell you that yet?" I noticed that the British clip was gone from his voice; a faint French accent had replaced it.

"Damn you! What could possibly be worth a child's life?"

"Or a wife's," I said.

Dorian's smile slackened to a frown. "That's a dangerous speculation."

I met his eyes squarely. "It's no speculation. It's all there in the painting."

"Eleanor," Alexander warned.

Dorian took a step toward us, and then seemed to think better of whatever impulsive menace he had intended. Instead, he began to pace the margins of the room.

"A painting doesn't prove anything," he said. "Nor can you."

"If you believed that, you wouldn't have tricked Mary into thinking I was mad."

He laughed tonelessly. "Mary came to her own conclusions."

"With assistance, no doubt," I retorted. "Just as my grandmother was assisted into madness."

Dorian approached us again, but stopped a few feet away. "Let's suppose for a moment that you're right, and I did kill my wife. Do you think that I would resort to such extreme measures without just cause?" He didn't allow time for an answer. "Let me tell you a story."

"I've had enough of your stories," I retorted.

"Oh, you'll be interested in this one." His eyes lighted on Alexander briefly, and when they returned to me, there was a flicker of amusement in them. "It's about your aunt and mother. It begins years ago, when they were just sixteen years old. I was twenty, and I'd had my share of affairs, but nothing could have prepared me for Elizabeth Fairfax. I knew the first time I set eyes on her that if I lived till Judgment Day, I would never meet a lovelier woman, or a finer."

Dorian paused, studying his smooth hands, then said, "I suppose she wasn't the obvious choice. Eve was the one men lost their hearts to. She was passionate, dashing, and she made no secret of her admiration for me. But something about Elizabeth's quiet shyness touched me."

He looked up at us, his eyes oddly bright. "Everyone thinks that his own love is the greatest, the purest, the strongest that has ever been or will be." He didn't bother to hide the condescension in his tone or in the look that he cast our way. "But I knew it. Every aspect of her character met and matched a corresponding part of mine, like a balm meets an ache. For years I had been tormented by the boundless desire to know and achieve. By the time I met her, I was ragged from searching for a fulfillment I could neither define nor reject. Yet in her presence, I forgot it all. I could rest." He looked at us again, and there was a plea for understanding in his eyes that almost made me pity him, despite all that he had done.

"I had come to doubt a woman's ability to live up to the ideals of virtue and goodness set for her by men. Elizabeth both embodied and eradicated them. Her spiritual wealth was never more obvious than when she played the piano. I think she knew it, too, and that was why she played so rarely.

"I knew that I could love a woman like her infinitely; I also knew that she did not love me. But I convinced myself that she would come to. I could not conceive, then, that such a love as mine could go unrequited. So I asked her parents for her hand.

"Mrs. Fairfax had hesitations. Elizabeth was her favorite, and she knew that her daughter was opposed to the idea. But Mr. Fairfax was only too keen. Perhaps he suspected that his daughter meant to attach herself to someone less seemly." Again Dorian's eyes settled for a moment on Alexander, then quickly moved on.

"My one worry was Eve. I knew that hers was but a childish fancy for me; such a volatile girl couldn't love with the depth and constancy of someone like Elizabeth. Still, the sisters were close, and I doubted that Elizabeth would warm to me if she felt that her twin had been slighted. But I supposed Eve would find someone to console herself with soon enough. Which, of course, she did."

He directed this last remark at me. I stiffened with anger, but Alexander checked me silently again.

"I see that you are becoming impatient," Dorian said. "There isn't much more to tell. Elizabeth was a dutiful daughter. She bowed to her father's wishes, wrote to me at regular intervals through my remaining years in Europe, and submitted to her situation gracefully when I returned to Louisiana. I could see that her feelings for me had not changed. Once again, I convinced myself that time would bring her around, but she was so cold and silent in the weeks preceding our wedding that even I began to have misgivings.

"So you can imagine my joy when for the first time, on our wedding day, I saw my love reciprocated in Elizabeth's eyes. I was surprised by the sudden change, more so by the passion with which she met me that night."

He paused for a moment, his eyes restlessly wandering the bare walls. When he continued, his tone had thinned and taken on the hard, sardonic edge that was more familiar.

"I should have suspected her then, but love blinded me. We moved into the house we'd built between the plantations—this house. I lived in blissful ignorance of the fact that I had married a whore, until she came to me several weeks later with the news that she was expecting a child. It was then that I began to doubt the virtue I had praised so highly. When the child was born at eight months, I knew that I had been played for a fool. Yet I didn't have proof, and without it I couldn't send her back to her parents."

He paused, looking at me, and the alien coldness in his eyes made me shudder. When he resumed his narrative, his tone had hardened such that the falseness of its forced disinterest was clear.

"It was only a matter of time. Before it was a year old, Elizabeth sent the child away. She claimed to have been unwell since its birth and unable to take care of it properly. She told me she sent the child to Eve, who had run away herself by then. She also claimed not to know where Eve was living; a convenient, if unlikely, omission.

"Of course I realized that the wretched child was with its father, and that my wife meant to join them as soon as she could rid herself of me. I didn't give her the opportunity. As soon as I knew what she had done, I locked her up in this tower. I turned visitors away, and explained to the servants that my wife was unwell and wished to be left alone.

"I attempted without success to have her sister and the child traced. Time passed; Elizabeth maintained her innocence. She challenged me to find proof of her betrayal, knowing that I couldn't act without it. Hard as I tried, I could not. I even began to wonder if I had been mistaken…and then she made her great mistake."

Dorian turned to face us. He reached into the inner pocket of his jacket, withdrew a tattered piece of paper, and held it toward me. I handed Tasha to Alexander and took the paper from Dorian. It was blotting paper, covered in faint scrawls and ink spots, but on one side it showed the reverse images of several lines of writing:

…tell you I am coming to you, just as soon as I can find a way out. Louis suspects treachery, and will no doubt harm me if he should discover our secret. If something should happen to me, please keep Eleanor safe, and when she's old enough, tell her about us. Give her this necklace to remember me by.

"She'd already sent the letter through one of the servants," he said. "But she'd forgotten to destroy all of the evidence."

I looked up at him, my mind full of the image of Eve's gashed face beneath the icy window in the ground. "You bastard," I said.

His smile tightened. The candle guttered in a breath of wind, and thunder rolled again, this time much closer. "It's you, my dear, who are the bastard—and that's the least of it." He looked contemptuously from my face to Alexander's. "If that photograph didn't prove it to you, then this paper should, just as it proves that your mother was a whore."

"You're wrong!" I cried.

Alexander reached for my arm, as if to pull me back. "Eleanor, don't."

Shaking him off, I said, "She was writing to her sister! She loved you more than you deserved, even if she did lie to you."

Dorian's look fluctuated between interest and uncertainty. "How would you know that?"

"Eleanor!" Alexander cried, but it was too late. Every moment since I had met Dorian Ducoeur had been building toward this confrontation, and there was no way to stop it now.

"You fool!" I said. "You could see that she'd changed on your wedding day, but not why. Elizabeth never loved you, and she never could have pretended to."

"Don't toy with me, Eleanor," he said through clenched teeth.

"This is no game! Elizabeth wasn't my mother, Alexander isn't my father." He continued to stare at me, uncomprehending. "You are!" I cried. "You married Eve!"

For a terrible moment we all stood paralyzed by the words. Then Dorian reached out and struck me across the face. Through the tears that sprang to my eyes, I caught my reflection in the cracked mirror. There was a long red scratch along one cheek. The next second I leaped at Dorian and tore at his face with my fingernails until he managed to pin my wrists together.

"That's enough," he said.

I seethed with fury, beginning to comprehend the magnitude of what he had taken from me. "You killed her!" I screamed. "You killed my mother!"

Alexander laid Tasha down, stepped forward, and pried Dorian's fingers from my wrists. He pushed me toward the doorway, putting himself between Dorian and me.

"You won't kill another innocent woman," he said.

"Perhaps not," Dorian answered, smiling faintly. "One way or another, though, you two will pay."

"For what?" Alexander cried. "Eve Fairfax was innocent. The only crime committed here was yours!"

"And you are the only two people who know it," Dorian said, advancing on us with clenched fists.

For a moment, sound and movement were suspended; even the candle flame ceased its restless flickering. The next, everything collapsed into noise and confusion. The wind blew the French doors open with a clash, shattering most of the panes, and the candle went out. A roll of thunder crashed, followed by a flash of lightning. Dorian lunged toward me, but Alexander interceded, smashing a fist into his perpetual half-smile. As Dorian reeled back, Alexander turned to me, clutching my arms so hard that they showed the marks of his fingers for days afterward.

"Take Tasha and get out of here however you can."

"No!" I cried, panic finally obliterating logic. "I won't leave you!"

"Please, Eleanor! Think of Tasha!" Alexander's eyes were wild, his chin in the stubborn set I knew so well. I closed my eyes; he took it as agreement. "Don't stop until you're back at Eden. I'll find you..."

He kissed me, then turned to face the dark shape that was advancing again. Clutching Tasha, I ran down to the next landing, wrenched the door open, and entered the labyrinthine corridors.

Slowly my eyes adjusted to the dark again, and I finally found a hallway that looked familiar. By the time I reached the main staircase it seemed that hours had passed.

On the first-floor landing, I caught the smell of smoke. By

the time I reached the bottom we were enveloped in an acrid haze, which seemed to come from the direction of the tower. I laid Tasha on a sofa and grabbed a candelabrum from a table, then began to hammer at the lock of one of the shutters. After what seemed an interminable effort, it broke. An unnatural brightness showed through the cracks of the outer one. I smashed the window, and easily broke the rotten wood of the outer shutter. Then, lifting Tasha, I climbed through.

Lightning had split one of the oaks by the tower, and half of it had fallen against the side of the house. It must have been this that started the fire that was spreading now in leaps and bounds, devouring the dry wood of the house's interior. I sank to my knees in the grass, powerless to do anything but watch and weep.

As if echoing this sentiment, the rain that had threatened all night finally came. It was not the usual heavy, pelting rain, but a soft one, warm as blood, without the strength to thwart the fire. I knelt there and watched as Tasha came to her senses enough to wrap her arms around my neck and bury her face against my breast. I knelt there as the last window filled with fire. I knelt until Colette's strong brown hands came under my elbows, forcing me to my feet, and Mary prized Tasha from my shivering grasp. They took one look at the house and turned away. They accepted what I would not accept for months: they had arrived too late.

12

It was years before Mary admitted to me how close I came to dying in the next two weeks. Mercifully, I don't remember much about them. My first memory following the fire is of a sky so blue it seemed to be a mistake, enclosed by a utilitarian white window frame. Shifting my eyes downward, I saw that I lay in a similarly white bed in a white room with a strong, sterile smell, which could not quite cover the insidious smell of sickness. I was unmoved by the sight of the tubes snaking into my arms from lunglike bags above me, nor by the pity in the eyes of the young nurse who sat by my side, adjusting the flow of liquid through those tubes. Each breath I took was a massive effort to shift the weight of my rib cage. My chest ached and my throat was raw, but I managed to whisper:

"Where am I?"

The nurse smiled at me. "You're at St. Anastase Hospital, in New Orleans."

"Where is Mary?" I asked.

"Mrs. Bishop is with the child, Tasha." The nurse's voice was like a lullaby. I wondered whether the voice was a result of her calling or vice-versa. "You can't see her yet, but I'll tell her that you've asked for her. She'll be glad. She's been terribly worried."

These words took a moment to sink in. When they did, I asked, "What's wrong with me?"

"You have double pneumonia. You've come through the worst of it, but you had us all worried for a while."

I put a hand to my throat. It was only when I touched bare skin that I recognized the unconscious impetus, and that the diamond was gone.

"Where is my necklace?" I asked.

The nurse gave me a puzzled look. "You had no jewelry on when they brought you in, except the ring."

I found that I could not face the thought of either. "I must have been mistaken," I told the nurse as she gently laid my intubated arm back on the white sheet. Then I slipped back into a merciful semi-sleep.

When I opened my eyes again, it wasn't quite such an effort to breathe. Outside the window the sky was dusky, but I had no idea whether it was evening or morning, or how far I had come from the blue afternoon with the gentle nurse. I turned my head. Mary sat beside me, her face more creased than I remembered it, squinting down at her knitting as though trying to determine what it was. When she heard me shift position, she dropped her needles and looked up. The relief I saw when she met my eyes almost made me forgive her.

"Eleanor," she said, as if she was about to tell me a hundred things. Then she stopped, apparently at a loss. Finally she said, "I'm so glad to have you back."

There were tears in her eyes, and none of the fear that had haunted them before. I held a shaking hand toward her, and she took it, squeezing it gently.

"How is Tasha?" I asked.

"She's had a bad cold, but nothing more serious came of it. She'll be glad to see you."

"How long have I been here?"

"A week. You were in Baton Rouge before that, but...well, you needed to be here."

I looked at her for another moment, bracing myself, then asked, "Alexander?"

The tears that had filled her eyes spilled over onto her crepe-paper cheeks. She squeezed my hand again, but this time the movement was convulsive. "He...they didn't find any trace of him or...the other. But the house burned to the ground. He's presumed dead."

I repeated the words in my head, waiting for the ensuing pain, but it never came. In fact, it would be many weeks before the numbness of shock would wear thin enough for me to feel anything at all. Even then, the worst of it would only come out in nightmares from which I would wake screaming and crying, and which I seldom remembered afterward.

I looked at Mary, who was still crying silently, and asked, "When can I leave?"

"They want to keep you here for another week."

"I want to go as soon as possible."

"I've already bought the tickets."

"And Tasha?"

She shook her head. "No relatives could be located."

"She'll stay with us, then."

Mary nodded silently. "What about the house?"

I cringed. "Sell it. Give it away if you like. I never want to see it again."

She ran her fingers over the knitting in her lap, as if she couldn't find a place for them to settle. "I'll go tomorrow to gather our things."

I shook my head. "I don't want anything from there. Take what you want, and give the rest to the staff."

Mary nodded. Eyes still on her knitting, she asked, "What about Alexander's things?"

I thought for a long time, trying to force myself to picture him and the things that had been close to him, but the images were as slippery as river rocks. I couldn't even conjure a steady picture of his face.

"Give them away as well," I told her in the end, "except for what Tasha might want someday."

"Don't you want anything for yourself?"

She asked this gently, but as I looked at her teary face, I was suddenly filled with anger. She was already grieving for him, while my attempts to think of him hit a grey deadness which I knew would only prolong the pain when it came.

Finally, I said, "If he kept portfolios of his own music, I'd like to have them."

The thought of looking at that heartbroken music again, let alone trying to play any of it, left me sick. But I suspected that the time would come when I would be glad that I had preserved them: my only link to a past so strange that I sometimes doubted that it had happened at all.

We were silent again for a long while. Then something else occurred to me. "Is it only pneumonia?" I asked. "Is there anything else wrong with me?"

Mary reddened, then paled again. "It's not what you think...what I thought." She paused, clearly having difficulty controlling her emotions. "The doctors couldn't awaken you at first. They asked me if you'd taken anything unusual, so I brought them your medicine from Boston and—and the other one. They had them tested, and found that both had been mixed with belladonna. The tablets were nearly pure extract, with a little chloral mixed in." She looked ready to break down again, but managed to finish. "They told me that it can cause fevers, delusions, hallucinations, nightmares, and in high doses…" She broke down again and covered her face with her hands.

"Never mind," I said. "I understand."

And finally I did understand: the bizarre, story-like nightmares, the scrambled senses, the shaking and fevers and shortness of breath, even that terrible night with Dorian when I had seemed to lose a chunk of time. No doubt my grandmother's and Tasha's illnesses had been caused by something similar.

When Mary had regained her composure, she continued, "Both you and Tasha had taken it that night. Tasha also had a good deal of chloral hydrate in her system. She's lucky to be alive. So no, Eleanor. There was never anything wrong with you, mentally or physically, other than the effects of the drug."

The words of Eve's glowing journal entry came back to me: a precocious student, a Renaissance man with degrees in art and science by the time he was twenty. To Dorian, using substances to control me—and, perhaps, others before me—must have been as simple as his parlor tricks.

I sighed. "Don't cry, Mary."

"I can't help it. Tasha told me what happened that night, as well as she could; you yourself told us the rest, in your delirium. These last days and nights it's been all I could think of. I should never have doubted you, or trusted him."

"None of us acted any more wisely."

"Thank you for saying so, Eleanor," she said, but I knew the words had been little comfort.

We boarded the train to Boston under a sky the faded blue of autumn. Tasha sat quietly on Mary's lap, her eyes fixed on the passing landscape. She had spoken little during the few days we had been reunited, and not at all of Alexander. At the time I thought that it was the shock of losing him, and that she would regain her buoyancy as his memory faded. However, the inward look on her face that day would never quite leave it again. It was a premonition for us all.

With the hindsight of more than half a century, I would venture to guess that Tasha knew that day that in leaving Louisiana, she was leaving behind what remained of her childhood. If she regretted it, she never showed it then or later; she was a docile, dutiful child who grew into an intelligent, quiet woman. Through her girlhood she applied herself diligently to her studies; she graduated from Harvard Medical School the year Hitler shot himself in his bunker under Berlin. She seldom spoke of Alexander, and when she did, it was as someone might speak of a relative she has heard of but never met.

Like Tasha, Mary lived silently with her regret, but I know that she never stopped feeling it, nor the guilt she had shouldered when she learned how near I had come to dying, if inadvertently, by her hand. She lost her taste for society, preferring instead to help Tasha with her studies. Her eyesight continued to deteriorate over the next few years, but it was only when she was almost fully blind that she allowed me to take her to a specialist. He told us what Mary must have feared for a long time: that her sight loss and headaches were caused by a malignant tumor. She died quietly at home a few months before her sixtieth birthday.

The year after Alexander died was a trial I would never wish on anybody. I ran from grief, never sparing a thought for the ways loving and losing him had changed me. I should have, for they were often both obvious and destructive. I gave up music and took up writing. I married twice, but never had a child of my own. I was, for a time, both quite famous and intensely lonely. It was an empty fame, built on stories I neither liked nor believed in, and an oddly resonant loneliness: the result of having become more than myself through love, and then losing the piece that would make me whole.

Alexander changed me in smaller ways, too, but I only really see them now, when I can look back on my life as a whole, at its patterns and ripples shifting around the jetty of all he was and wasn't. About ten years ago I chanced to overhear an elderly Russian couple speaking in English on a train. They were discussing the death of a friend or family member, I never learned which. The woman was endlessly berating the apparently illicit ways of the deceased, when finally her husband interrupted:

"Yes, but at least he died with music."

With eerie serendipity, a Russian emigrant friend of Tasha's said the same words a few days later. She explained to me that it's a traditional Russian saying, meaning more or less that something has ended in style.

For a time I found this comforting. I began to forgive Alexander for abandoning me a second time, and to appreciate that he died more generously than I have ever lived. Soon afterward I began the slow and difficult process of recording this story.

And yet, finding myself at the end of it, I also find my opinion of what happened in flux once more. One moment I believe that Alexander died consciously, to end a destructive cycle. In the next I wonder if he died involuntarily, for nothing. It is tempting to judge him, and my love for him, and even what I have allowed his memory to make of my life.

In the end, though, it's pointless. Like every struggle, ours culminates in silence.

Epilogue

DECEMBER 1985, BOSTON, MASSACHUSETTS

I thought that I had made my peace with silence when, for the first time in more years than I can count, Eve spoke to me out of it. She appeared in my dreams as she did when I was a girl, and told me that I must finish what I had left incomplete.

This time her meaning was plain to me. In the course of that wretched summer at Eden, Alexander and Dorian paid for their transgressions and, I suppose, finally escaped the past. Eve and Elizabeth, however, remained unabsolved.

Thinking about this, I recalled something Alexander had once said to me: that a haunting is nothing more than an unsettled spirit looking for peace. Yet nor is it anything less. Eve could never find peace as long as I kept the past locked and guarded inside me. How to exhume it, though, was a different matter entirely.

Once again I rifled my memories, opening scars long hardened, unearthing emotional artifacts perhaps better left intact. It only proved Alexander right again. The immaterial cannot satisfy the human heart in its quest for truth.

But where to look for the tangible? I am the last vestige of Eve, her only corporeal legacy. Even her body had disappeared into thin air. It seemed I had nothing left to offer her. I thought about this for a long time; then, all at once, I began to see. Perhaps the tangible was precisely the problem. For there was one, undeniably concrete piece of the past's linked tragedies that I'd clung to all this time, the one I'd most feared and most longed to jettison all along.

Despite Mary's initial gentle urgings, and the not-so-gentle hounding of various property developers later on, I never had sold Eden's Meadow. Whatever I told myself, the reason was simple.

Despite all it had taken from me, knowing that Eden was still there, untouched by time, allowed me to cling to the past and to what I had lost.

Now I realized that this had been selfish as well as self-defeating. The first agent I called bought the whole plantation for more than I could ever have imagined it would be worth. I sent the keys to Louisiana the next day, expecting to feel relief. But though Eve departed from my dreams, my feeling of uneasiness only increased. I could not shake the sensation that selling Eden had not been the whole answer; that something else was still impending.

In the meantime, to distract myself and to ameliorate another stifled part of my conscience, I unearthed Alexander's old folios of music. I copied them and then, for lack of a better idea, sent them to my literary agent in New York. She sold them within a week.

The advance was modest, but it was enough to convince Symphony Hall to put on a benefit performance for Russian orphans. They asked me to introduce it. It would be the first time I had set foot in that hall since my twenty-first birthday, but I could hardly decline to attend. Tasha, for reasons of her own, opted out of the concert, so I went alone.

I was shocked by the change. It was not the physical changes that bothered me—I had expected those—nor that feeling of diminishment upon visiting a once-familiar place after a long absence. Rather, I realized that Symphony Hall, like my memories, had become a hollow shell of a past I had always considered inviolate. The hall was only half full, and most of its patrons were my peers. The carnival air I remembered had evaporated. No one dresses up for the symphony any more.

The performance was lackluster as well. The pianist was a young Asian woman, and though she was technically very good, she didn't understand the music she was playing. I nearly left before she had finished, but in the end I was glad I hadn't. As an encore she played a curious piece by a modern Estonian composer whose name now escapes me. In it I heard aspects of the peculiarly compelling, melancholic passion of Alexander's music, which had been absent from her playing of his own. Near the end of this piece, I looked across the hall, and for a moment Alexander was looking back at me, eyes wide and expectant, cheeks flushed, lips twitching upward into the smile that first caught my heart. I blinked, and the seat was empty.

When I left the hall, the rain that had begun with my recording of this history had finally stopped, and the sky was clearing. I sent my driver home, telling him that I would rather walk. I could see that he wanted to forbid it, but couldn't quite decide how. I left him still trying.

Breathing the air of the autumn night as though it were the first I'd encountered in weeks, I quickened my pace down Newbury Street, glad that rheumatism and obesity had bypassed my old age. I looked into the brightly lit windows of the cafes and restaurants, even stopped for a moment before an odd shop with stained-glass windows and a stone griffin by the open door. A young man with sad, dark eyes not unlike Alexander's looked back at me from the doorway for a moment, then flipped the sign to Closed.

I had begun to feel that I was looking for something, though I didn't know what. When I reached Beacon Street, I glanced up at the lights in my front windows, then turned into the park instead. I knew that this was foolish, that an old woman was an easy target. However, I had had a sudden urge to see my angel, the statue I had watched as a child from my nursery window, and I knew that I would never sleep if I didn't indulge it.

I made my way over the wet grass and slick leaves to the corner where he stood, half hidden now by trees that had been saplings in my childhood. His wings and outstretched fingers dripped with the recent rain; his downcast eyes were dark. I tried to summon the awe that he had once inspired, but it eluded me. Finally I turned and made my way home.

In the end, as we often realize yet never quite anticipate, what I was looking for found me. Tasha was waiting up, as she often did if I went out without her. She had moved away from the Beacon Street house when she married, and raised her children in the suburbs. When her husband died, though, she had come back to live with me. Now she met me at the door. Her eyes were still bright blue, though her auburn hair had long ago faded to grey, and there was a suspicious glint to them, as if she had been crying.

"Something came for you while you were gone," she said, and held out a plain cardboard mailing carton.

"It's far too late for the mail," I said.

"A man brought it. He said to make sure to give it to you, and no one else."

I looked at the box. All that was written on the front was

my name, in mute block letters. I opened it and emptied the contents onto the hall table. Both Natalya and I stood staring at them, at a loss for words.

At the bottom of the pile was a sheaf of staff paper, notated by hand. Resting on this was a small pouch of crimson velvet, a dried, pale-pink tea rose, a lock of blond hair tied with a blue ribbon, and a small, framed photograph of a curly-haired baby. On top of all of it was an envelope inscribed with my name, containing a letter from the real-estate agent in Louisiana. It read:

Ms. Rose,

I can think of no way to prepare you for this information, so I'll come right to the point. While digging a foundation in what was formerly a garden behind the ruins of Louis Ducoeur's house, my workers discovered the body of a young woman.

At first, the forensic team could only determine that she had died around the turn of the century, from a severe head injury. Her identity was a mystery. However, further excavation turned up something else, ironically only feet away from the grave: a metal box containing the items you find with this letter. Among them was a note from one Elizabeth Rose, whom I understand was your mother, addressed to 'Eve.' It said simply that she knew Eve had been murdered, though she couldn't prove it, and that she was burying these items as a memorial in a place she knew Eve had loved.

The authorities have since connected the body and the names on the note with the disappearance of a woman named Elizabeth Ducoeur in 1905, and to her sister Eve Fairfax. Unfortunately, the events surrounding this tragedy will take some time to piece together. The investigators have kept the body and the note from your mother as evidence, but ultimately you will need to decide where to have the body re-interred.

I have complied with your wish to auction any valuable pieces left in the house and dispose of all the rest. However, I felt that the contents of the box buried by your mother would have a personal value to you. Aside from the note, I return them to you intact, with the addition of a necklace which was the only jewelry on the woman's body. Please do not hesitate to contact me if you require further details.

Yours sincerely,

Albert E. Rushworth

"Let me see," Tasha said, gently taking the letter from my shaking hands. As she read it I opened the red pouch and tipped its contents onto the paper beneath. It was a tear-shaped ruby on a chain of yellow gold. Tasha put down the letter and picked up the necklace.

"Didn't you use to wear something like this?" she asked.

I looked at the faded picture, then at the jewel glowing like a quetzal's breast in the light of the table lamp. I couldn't think of anything to say. Instead I took up the sheets of music and began to read through them.

The opening triads sounded in my head, high and sweet and fragile, like frost patterns on glass. The sonorous bass notes joined in a few measures later, pinning the ethereal melody firmly to earth. It was the piece that Alexander had played at Joyous Garde, which I had been certain was meant for a child, and also for me. The manuscript had not been among the others in the folio Mary had salvaged from Eden.

"I lost it ages ago," I finally said.

Tasha looked at me closely, but I was no more able to read what she was thinking than I ever had been. She smiled and said, "I'll help you put it on."

She fastened the chain around my neck, then turned me so that I could see myself in the mirror. I was surprised to find that there were tears in my eyes. She kissed my cheek, then retreated upstairs.

I picked up the rose. The blossom was so well preserved that, without touching it, one might think that it was still living. An undying token of love...

Shuddering, I dropped it back on the table, then picked up the music and moved through the narrow old hallways of the townhouse to the room at the back that I had closed the day I returned from Eden's Meadow, and hadn't opened since. Everything was as it had been then: the furniture from an earlier era, papers scattered on the table, and the grand piano in the corner, holding its breath. I sat down on the stool, still adjusted for my height. I picked up the tarnished ring that lay on the music stand, slipped it on, and spread the closely marked pages in its place. My fingers found their places on the keys as though I had never been away from the instrument.

The piano was out of tune, and I was out of practice, but it didn't matter: I heard the music as I had first heard it through the haze of alcohol and uncertainty in Dorian's music room. Yet that was wrong, I realized now. I had no doubt heard it before that night, a lullaby played by a man who was not my father, yet with whom my life was already inextricably entangled.

My sight blurred as my eyes ran with tears so long avoided, but I played on as if the years of denial had not touched my gift, or my love. I felt him enter the room as I played, knew that he watched me as he had watched in that long-ago dream, and in a past too distant to remember. His presence was so strong that I nearly cried out in disappointment when I turned and saw only the dark, empty room. I sat for a time willing him to appear, but nothing moved in the museum-like hush.

I turned off the lights as I went upstairs, not stopping at my bedroom, but continuing on to the old nursery, long ago remade into my study. I sat down to my sheaf of paper, to pen the end of this story. Yet now I realize, as I should have realized years ago, that it is wrong to think that the end is mine to write, or even that it can be written. There are no words, nor even music, for this absolution. It is the final silence, and I am ready to embrace it. I only have to turn around. He's by my shoulder, waiting.

About the author

Sarah Bryant is originally from Boston, USA, and now lives in the Scottish Borders with her husband and daughter. She has an MLitt in creative writing from St. Andrews, and what free time is left between writing and family goes on horses, printmaking and the celtic harp. Her other novel, *City of the Sun*, is also available from Snowbooks, and a book of poems, *Water Witching*, was published by Cornmill Press in 2004.

A/c settings → Adr